Prodigal Nights

Lisa Buffaloe

Finalist in the 2011 Women of Faith Writing Contest

~ Lisa Buffaloe ~

Prodigal Nights
John 15:11 Publications

Cover photography by Dennis and Lisa Buffaloe.
Cover graphics and design by Scott Buffaloe.

ISBN: 978-0-9859295-1-0
ISBN: 978-0-9859295-2-7 (Electronic)
ASIN: B008RCNAIC (Kindle)

Dedication

To Jesus Christ, my amazing Savior, and His wonderful prodigal-seeking love.

Acknowledgements

My amazing Savior, Jesus Christ, thank You for opening Your loving arms when I returned from my Prodigal ways. Your grace and love make my soul dance for joy.

My sweet husband and son, you are both such wonderful blessings straight from God's hands. Thank you for your continual love, prayers, and encouragement. You guys are the best!

Gwen Smith, thank you so much for giving me the blessing of using your photo for my cover. Wow, what fun! You and the Girlfriends in God are amazing blessings!

Jerry Gramckow, thank you for the proofread edit on the manuscript.

Special hugs and thanks to my wonderful son, Scott Buffaloe, for the cover and graphic design.

My writing friends, thank you for helping me learn and grow. Lena Nelson Dooley, sitting on your couch every Thursday night at critique group was such a fun, incredible blessing. Patricia (Pacjac) Carroll, Jackie Castle, Lena Nelson Dooley, Lynne Gentry, Kellie Gilbert, Janice Olson, Jane Thornton, and so many others were part of those joyous evenings. Thank you!

Frank Ball and the Super Scribes group from the North Texas Writers, thank you for encouraging my early writing. Cec Murphey and DiAnn Mills, thank you for your friendship, mentoring, and prayers.

My prayer and Bible study buddies, thank you for your prayers and encouragement!

Cherie Brown, Barbie Eslin, Janis Filewood, Jo Ann Fore, Julie Garmon, Teena Goble, Hilarey Johnson, Mack and Dottie Kearney, Karen King, and **all** my amazing friends (online and in person), thank you for your edits, prayers, and encouragement. You all such wonderful blessings!

Chapter 1

Disfrusied. Maybe not a word, but that summed up her week—disappointed, frustrated, and worried. Bethany Davis checked her speedometer and eased up on the accelerator. Getting a ticket wouldn't help.

Three years ago, she swore she'd never come back for more than a quick visit. The phone call from her oldest brother changed everything. Dad was in the hospital, and only family made it worth facing Southburg, Virginia, again.

Bethany turned into the hospital parking lot and snatched the last available space. Leaning over her steering wheel, she scanned the visitor's lot. Good. No media vans or pesky reporters. Her father's executive-level involvement in the defense industry drew constant attention. The last thing she wanted to do was bring her dad additional stress.

The coast clear, she stepped out of her car. Hot air stuck in her lungs. Thunderclouds hung low in the distance, threatening the May sky. She willed her feet forward. Part of her wanted to run to her dad's side. The other part wanted to run away. She probably shouldn't have promised to move back home for three weeks. But when her brother mentioned her parents wanted her home, she'd jumped at the opportunity for reconciliation.

Quick trips during holidays at neutral resorts had never been enough to clear the tension hanging in the air since her divorce. She couldn't risk something happening to her dad without setting things right.

Straightening her shoulders, she hurried her step. Her insides whimpered, but a good Davis didn't show emotion. Dad would be okay. He had to. Besides, nothing stopped him. Not being shot while serving in the military. Not cancer. Not even nosy newsmen.

Plaza Hospital's lobby bustled with activity. Families huddled in groups. Two children squealed and giggled as they played chase with a pink *Congratulations* balloon. A dark-haired man sat in the corner reading a newspaper. Antiseptic smells mingled with the scent of popcorn served from a vendor cart.

Bethany hesitated at the gift shop entrance. Should she take something to her father? Flowers were out of the question. She'd learned that lesson when she was six. He had accepted her hand-picked flowers, chastised her for picking them, and then thrown them in the garbage. How could she have known the plant she'd chosen to wrap her bouquet in was poison ivy?

She walked inside the small shop brimming with flowers and gifts and went straight for the cards. Most were mushy and sentimental. Some were funny. One with a sunset shot of the ocean caught her eye—nothing too sappy, just a few simple statements wishing the person a speedy recovery. Oh, how she hoped he would fully recover.

At the counter, a guy paid for a candy bar then turned to face her. A smile lit his handsome face. Tall and muscular with a slender frame, he stood in her way, staring at her.

Bethany met his gaze. Did she know him? "Excuse me. Can I pay for my card?"

Handsome guy blinked as though clearing his vision. "Sorry." He still didn't move.

She leaned to the right and made eye contact with the

young man who stood at the cash register. "How much for the card?"

The cashier tapped the guy on the shoulder. "Dude, could you move so she can pay?"

Clueless, handsome guy flinched and moved to the left, but his eyes never left her face.

Not sure if she should elbow him or give him a big smile, Bethany stepped forward and paid for her purchase.

When she finished, the guy was already walking away. Shame she couldn't get her past to vanish that easily.

She stepped back into the lobby, sat in a chair, and pulled out the card. What should she write? A zillion thoughts zinged through her head, and all of them made her feel like a lost little girl. Ugh, she was a grown woman. Okay, at twenty-five maybe a semi-grown woman who still wanted her daddy. She signed the card, "I've missed you and love you, Bethany."

Only two weeks ago they had been together for her college graduation. Elena and Charles Davis, Bethany's always perfectly coifed, perfectly in charge, perfectly perfect parents, had congratulated her, taken her to dinner, and wished her the best. Quick hugs, quick release, not much discussed.

Just like when Bethany left Southburg. The lies and gossip about her divorce were never discussed, and unfortunately never addressed by her parents. No one stood up or fought for her, and she left her marriage in a cloud of false accusations.

Bethany stood, walked to the elevator, and waited next to a man in green scrubs. The shiny stainless doors reflected his image. Good looking with brown hair and a shadow of a goatee. Seemingly oblivious to her presence, he flipped through a patient's chart.

The elevator doors opened, and he followed her inside.

Bethany pressed the seventh-floor button. He punched the eighth and moved next to her, invading her space with his seductive cologne. Cute or not, Bethany took a step away from him. She had enough regrets.

Bethany exited the elevator into the small, empty waiting area. Craning her neck, she checked the area. Clear. She turned to the stairs and jogged down two flights just like her overly cautious dad had taught her.

Being careful back in her hometown came naturally. Shame she hadn't used more caution the last three years while away at college.

Maybe now, back home for a few weeks, she could sort things through and get a clean start. Repair any damage left in her wake with her family and move on far away from the memories of Southburg.

Two of her father's bodyguards nodded their recognition and opened the door of room 473. In the oversized, private room, machines silently monitored her father's progress. Even asleep, Charles Davis looked in control. Military straight, he lay on his back, eyes closed.

Her mother, wearing classic black pants and white silk shirt, rose to her feet. Normally nothing about her mother would be out of place—not a hair, and definitely nothing ever wrinkled. Today, one side of her salt and pepper hair lay tight against her head, the rest perfect as always. Her clothes hung loose and wrinkled.

Mom seemed to waver, her eyes taking in every ounce of Bethany as though they hadn't seen one another in ages. Without a word, Elena rushed to Bethany and clung to her. "I'm so glad you're here." Her mom's voice caught. Obviously fighting for self-control, she took a step back. Tears rimming her eyes and bottom lip quivering, she motioned for Bethany to sit next to her by her dad's bed.

"He's been sleeping for the last hour." Dark circles framed her mom's eyes. She patted Bethany's hand and squeezed.

The thought of losing her dad left a ten-pound brick lodged in her stomach. He'd always been the strong one—the planner who drove the family and his business to success.

"Did you get any rest last night?" Bethany kept hold of her mother's soft grip, wishing she could transport back to childhood days when life was innocent, and Mom's touch could remove any hurt.

"As much as I could." Her mother responded with a weak smile as her tiny frame seemed to shrink under the weight of worry.

A folded blanket sat on the reclining chair in the corner. Mom's designer purse drooped against the arm. However, no sign of her older brother. Her brother's frantic phone call had given her the willies. Chase never showed emotion, and yet he had broken down on the phone. She thought for sure Dad had died.

"Where's Chase?"

"He went back this morning after we got the latest test results."

"He didn't stay?"

"With the defense contract going through Senate hearings, your father made him go back. When Chase said you had promised to stay for three months ...." Her mom broke down, tears streaming down her cheeks. "Oh Bethany, that is just the sweetest thing you have ever done." She dabbed her eyes with a tissue, her gentle expression drinking in Bethany as though she had been gone forever. "Your father and I are thrilled. And since your father's test results show he only had a minor stroke, we should have plenty of time to spend together."

Bethany choked, coughed, gasped for air. Three *months?*

"Bethany?" The deep, slightly slurred voice came from the bed.

"Dad." His normally tanned face held a chalky pallor. Bethany tentatively took her father's big hand. For once, he didn't pull away. "How are you feeling?" The little girl in her wanted to curl up in his arms, hear him say everything would be fine and that he loved her. But that wouldn't happen—never had happened—feelings were never shown. Not in their military household.

His gaze locked with hers, and moisture gathered in his dark eyes. He gripped her hand. "I'm glad you're home." His voice rattled. He coughed clearing his throat. "This will be a good summer."

She nodded, all words trapped in her tight throat.

He swallowed hard, emotions flickering across his face. Emotions she hadn't seen except at his mother's funeral. His jaw tightened. Releasing her hand, he struggled to sit.

Her mom rubbed his arm. "Please don't push yourself."

"Too much going on with the company. Can't jeopardize the contract. Has there been anything in the news?"

"Nothing in detail." Elena's rubbing turned to nervous patting. "Only that you've been hospitalized."

He swore and pointed at Bethany. "Keep those news bloodhounds off my tail. If word gets out that I'm not fit to work, everything will be in jeopardy. " He took a deep breath, turned his focus to her mother. "Tell the doctors to run tests for a yearly physical. I don't want the word stroke mentioned by *anyone*, especially a reporter."

Bethany stared at the linoleum floor. She'd horsewhip

Chase. She had offered three weeks, not three months. No way he misunderstood. He set her up. Probably so he wouldn't have to come back home and most definitely to torture her. He hated her. Hated the minute she was born and did everything in his power to drive her crazy. She could see the headlines: *Big brother finally sends little sister over the edge of sanity.*

She looked over at her mom who was studying her.

Mom smiled, tender and sweet, and mouthed, "I love you."

Jason Ross paced in the lobby. Why couldn't he have said something intelligent instead of standing there like an idiot in the gift shop?

What was he thinking? God would never reward or trust him with someone like her. Not with his past wild years. He believed in God's grace and knew he was forgiven, but surely for someone that amazing, he'd have to do ten years penance in some obscure country ministering to headhunters.

He turned toward the emergency room to check on his co-worker—a human accident waiting to happen. Warren Carver's latest fiasco involved cutting through the power cord with hedge-clippers. Thanks to a surge protector, he wasn't electrocuted. But from there, how on earth could someone with a genius IQ get mauled by a weed-whacker?

Anita, the white-haired nurse at the ER front desk smiled at Jason. "Doc just gave our loveable walking disaster a couple of stitches on his face and arm. At least his singed hair looks better than last week." She pointed to the back.

"Except for the missing eyebrow, he just about looks normal." Jason chuckled to himself. Warren and hibachi grills

7

were not a good combination. His guardian angel should get hazard pay.

Jason walked through the two large doors to the treatment rooms. Warren sat cross-legged on the first bed on the right. Several leaves and a small twig clung to his dark hair. His shirt, stained with blood and grass, looked like something out of a laundry detergent commercial.

He cocked his remaining eyebrow at Jason. "Thanks for coming."

"I stopped by your house and cleaned up the mess on your front lawn. Your hedges look terminal. Want to explain what happened?"

"After the clippers died, I thought I'd improvise. I guess weed-eaters are best left to lawn care ... not shrubbery."

"I think you should pay someone to do your yard work."

"But I enjoy working outside." Warren rubbed his chin smearing a streak of dirt still clinging to his stubble. "I probably just need more powerful equipment."

Jason choked back a laugh. "Well, at least your attempts keep you and the medical staff in stitches."

Chapter 2

Jason parked his car and grabbed his ball cap. Warren was now stitched up and safe at home, and all yard items stowed and out of reach. The guy needed a full time medic. Thankfully, there weren't too many places he could get into trouble at work—other than the unfortunate event with the electric stapler.

Jason hurried to the ball field. Parents, grandparents, and friends cheered in the stands. Spotting his sister, Kelly, he climbed the home team's bleachers, and weaved his way through the crowd until he reached the top. "Has Daniel batted yet?"

"You missed it." Kelly put down her video camera. "He just hit a home run."

Jason groaned. "Did you get it on tape?"

"Of course." She nudged him. "You can watch it when you make a copy."

Jason inwardly kicked himself. He couldn't believe he missed his nephew's first home run. "How far did the ball go?"

"It rolled off the tee. The catcher just stood there, so the pitcher ran to get the ball, but had to fight off the first baseman and several outfielders. The third baseman got it and threw it to the remaining outfielder who chased Daniel from first base to third base. But I guess he got tired because he stopped, so

Daniel talked to him a few minutes. The coach finally yelled loud enough for Daniel to pay attention. He finished his run with half the other team following him even though the third baseman sat in the dirt, rolling the ball back and forth."

"Man, I love t-ball. Can't wait to see the video. Where's Elizabeth?"

"She's playing with some friends by the concession stand. The girls are helping Jill sell popcorn."

He searched until he saw his niece's blonde ponytail. "They're growing up fast."

"I can't believe she'll be eight next month."

"Will Matt be home for her birthday party?"

"I don't know." Kelly's shoulders slumped. "There's a chance, but the Army won't give guarantees." Tears rimmed her eyes. "Thank you for being here for us."

He swallowed hard and tried to concentrate on the game. "I wouldn't miss it for the world."

"You know you could have a life." She playfully jabbed him. "Are you dating anyone?"

"No." He couldn't take any chances. He'd live the life of a monk if he had to. He owed that much to God for not annihilating him during his heathen years.

"Want me to set you up again?" Feistiness showed in Kelly's grin. "I heard the singles' group at church has a pool party next weekend. No guts. No glory."

"Please don't do me any more favors."

"I worry about you. The pickings are slim when all you do is hang around us."

"Don't worry. I'm fine." He put his arm around her shoulder. "Besides, you're not getting rid of your little brother that easy. You couldn't beat me away with a stick. I love those kids."

Bethany exited the elevator on the first floor. Her mom had eaten dinner, and her dad sat in bed flipping through news channels and growling at any nurse who dared to enter. Hopefully Dad would be okay. He'd be released tomorrow afternoon, and home health would take over his care—if they could find someone who could put up with his temperament.

Different scenarios ran through her mind on how to deal with her brother, most of which would get her a lifetime behind bars. She dialed Chase's cell. The call immediately went to voice mail. Anything she had to say to him was better left off a recording. Maybe she could talk her dad's defense company into testing some weapon on her brother.

Oh man, she needed a distraction.

Her peripheral vision caught movement. Before she could react, she bumped into some guy backing up from the water fountain.

He whirled around and faced her. "I'm sorry. I should've paid attention."

"No problem." She sidestepped around him. What was it these days with the male population of Southburg? Did they all need vision correction?

"Can I make it up to you somehow?" He had caught up with her and hovered next to her left shoulder. "Maybe buy you a cup of coffee?"

"That's not necessary."

"The coffee shop across the street has the best Café Mocha in town. You look like the chocolate and whipped cream type."

Bethany stopped. "Excuse me?" She recognized him as the guy in green scrubs on the elevator this morning. Now in

11

jeans and a polo shirt, he appeared younger than she initially thought. She'd smack him if he wasn't so cute.

"That wasn't meant to be offensive. I'm Tom Chambers." His grin looked a touch mischievous. "What do you say about that coffee?"

A distraction offering coffee. Anything to divert her thoughts from her older brother. "Café Mocha sounds nice." Bethany glanced at the man beside her as they walked across the street. Thanks to kickboxing classes, if he gave her any trouble, she could take him.

Tom held the coffee shop door open for her. "Were you visiting a friend in the hospital?"

"You could say that."

Fresh-brewed coffee and pastries smelled wonderful. A tiny, elderly woman wearing a purple jogging suit and red sneakers questioned the clerk about every drink. While waiting their turn, Bethany glanced around the shop. A couple sat in the corner, a group of young women surrounded a table and spoke in animated tones, and a bearded man typed away on his laptop.

Tom drew her attention with a slight touch on her shoulder. "So tell me about yourself. What do you do?"

"I'm not sure."

"Are you looking for a job?"

Bethany shrugged. "Maybe." Everything hinged on how fast her dad recovered and if she heard back from a firm in Chicago. Her dream job, great work, and far away from Virginia.

"I can probably help."

He seemed so sure of himself, she couldn't resist. "Do you know of any openings for an applications engineer embedded computer systems analyst?"

His eyebrows rose to his hairline. "What?"

"Never mind." Not that she knew what it meant either, but the title sounded great from a job board she'd searched. Thank goodness her field was architecture. "What do you do?"

The woman in front of them finally received her order.

Tom stepped to the counter and looked at Bethany. "Do you know what you want?"

"I thought you already knew."

"Right. We'll have two tall Café Mochas." He took out his wallet and fumbled for money.

Bethany glimpsed a press pass for the local paper. *Interesting.* At least her evening could be entertaining. She waited until he paid. "You didn't answer my question about your occupation."

He coughed into his fist. "Um, I work at the hospital. I'm kind of a gopher."

"Medical gopher." She kept her expression serious. "Must be an exciting field."

"It pays the bills." Drinks in hand, he led her to a round, wooden table in the back. After setting down the cups, he pulled out a chair for her. "Do you have family?" He sat next to her.

She backed her chair away from his. *Let the games begin.* "Don't most people?"

"I meant, does your family live here?"

"Here?" Bethany glanced around the room. "No."

Tom's forehead creased while he sipped his drink.

She gave him a moment to stew in his confusion. "How about you? Do you live here?"

"Yeah." He wiped off his whipped cream mustache. "I have an apartment."

Bethany tried to look innocent. *This would be so easy.*

"How long have you been out of school?" She blew on her coffee and watched the steam rise and swirl.

"Just graduated in December from N.C. State." His voice carried a level of pride.

"Raleigh is a nice place."

He nodded. "Lots of good times."

"Good sports to watch, great degree programs." She leaned toward him. "Not too far from the beach."

"Yeah, it was great."

"The mountains close by for hiking."

His eyes glazed in seeming pleasure. "Boone and Blowing Rock are the best."

"Friends, parties, fun."

"Yeah." He got that blissful, far-away look.

She had him. "In school, did you take professional or creative writing?"

"Professional." After a pause, the color drained from his face.

"You'll learn." She picked up her cup. "Thanks for the coffee, but there'll be no story today."

Bethany left Tom sitting at the table with a dazed expression. A good mental sparring match always put her in a better mood. She slid back into her car and started the long trip back to her parents' estate.

Night's darkness kept her vision limited to the swath revealed by her headlights. If she focused on getting Dad healthy and helping around the house, maybe being back in the area wouldn't be so hard. Maybe she could even make three months.

The thought filled her stomach with acid. Three months? She gripped the wheel until her knuckles went white. She could do this. A little downtime after college could be okay, catch up on some non-school related reading, work on her tan, and avoid old enemies like the plague. Getting to spend time with her grandfather would be a highlight. He was the one person who understood her.

Security stopped her at the gate, and a flashlight flickered over her face. "Welcome home, Bethany. I know your parents are grateful you're here."

The unknown guard waved her through. She had come by the house earlier to drop off her bag and her pup, but did everyone know she was coming? Dad probably kept micromanaging everyone's life, even from a hospital bed. Bethany wheeled down the long drive, jumped out of the car, and slipped into the empty house.

Her Shi-Tzu, Jedi, greeted her with his tail wagging. Thankfully she had left lights on when she left this morning. Jedi hated the dark, and being alone in the Davis mansion would have been tough on him, and her.

Carrying her furry baby, she stopped at her old bedroom. The room tastefully redecorated by Mom, was now used for guests. Not that her family needed another guest room, the other three should've been plenty.

Bethany moved the plush bed covers and placed the small dog in the middle. His whole body wagged as she rubbed his soft, black and white fur. Jedi, the perfect male, loved her unconditionally, always loyal, and would do anything for a belly rub. Unfortunately there were no good men left—no one faithful and trustworthy like her grandfather.

Plopping next to Jedi, she relaxed into the silky smooth cotton sheets, and turned off the light.

She woke with a start and blinked in the darkness. Had she heard something? Where was she? She rolled over and glanced at the clock on the nightstand—11:43. The ringing phone shrilled through her brain.

Who would be calling this late? Mom stayed at the hospital. Had something happened to Dad?

Bethany grabbed for the phone. "Hello?"

Silence.

"Hello?"

The line disconnected.

Caller-ID didn't help. No number registered.

Blowing out a breath, she tried to think rationally. At least the call didn't come from the hospital. Probably a wrong number or some kids playing a prank.

Bethany hugged a pillow to her chest and stared into the darkness. She hated sleeping alone. The tears no longer flowed—they'd been used up long ago. Crying didn't take away the emptiness.

Nothing did.

###

The next afternoon, Bethany's father sat erect in the wheelchair as a nurse's assistant wheeled him through the hospital lobby. The determined, *don't mess with me*, look in his eyes kept a wide berth around their entourage. Bodyguards stayed close.

Bethany kept watch for clueless handsome guys and reporters. For Tom Chambers' efforts, she just might send him a stuffed gopher wearing medical scrubs with a little notepad in its furry hand.

When they returned home, she helped Dad get settled. He visited with her, keeping the subjects light and cheery, something totally out of character for him.

He paused, and his eyes misted. "We're thankful you're

home."

Dad didn't usually show emotion, and his comment and tone surprised her. Bethany busied herself arranging the items on his table. "I'm glad I can help."

He cleared his throat, reached for a magazine, and leaned back in his recliner. "I'll be fine if you need to do something else."

Properly dismissed, Bethany stepped outside the door, stopped, and leaned against the wall. She could count on one hand the times her dad had talked at length with her—other than to lecture. His comment about being thankful made her heart hurt, both in positive and negative ways. Did he just say that because the stroke scared him, or did he really care?

Composing herself, she walked to the kitchen. The aroma of cinnamon rolls filled the air. Fortunately, Mom had a tendency to bake when nervous. From the bounty stacked on the counter, the last two days had been a doozy. How could she bake so many things in just a few hours? She could give a small army a sugar coma.

Bethany still couldn't figure out what to do about the time commitment. She did want time with her parents, but the thought of three months made her stomach turn. Chase still hadn't called her or returned her calls. Her brother's life went forward while hers had screeched to a standstill.

Battling the resentment threatening to sour her mood, she stared out the bay window. Azaleas and Dogwoods bloomed in full glory, dotting the wooded lawn with pastel colors. A squirrel scampered past the pool, across the grass, and down the hill toward the river. In the distance, the Chesapeake Bay glistened in the sunlight.

Her mom pulled another baking sheet from the oven, wiped her hands, and poured coffee. She handed the cup to

Bethany. "I'm so glad you are home." Mom glanced toward Dad's briefcase, still standing at attention as if waiting orders. "With Chase in Washington and Brad in Peru, I didn't think I could handle this by myself."

"I'm grateful I could be here for you and Dad."

"Me too, honey." Her mother offered her a cinnamon roll. An offering wrapped in sugar and spice. "You always did love it here. You can use the pool, tennis court, and take the boat anytime you want."

Bethany accepted the roll. Maybe she had forgotten the good things and the beauty of the area.

"Your father seems stronger today." Mom's voice quivered.

"Dad *will* be okay." Bethany gave her a hug. "There's no way a stroke will stop him."

"I'm not worried about that. He'll be home all day. He'll be like caring for a caged, wild animal."

Bethany stifled a laugh. Keeping Dad away from the office would be quite an accomplishment. "Don't worry. His assistant will be here in a few days."

Mom turned off the oven and straightened her back. "Okay, I've got to stop whining and get my act together. If you'll listen for your father, I need to spend some time alone."

Bethany waited for her mom to leave. Hungry, she decided to forget the calories. No matter how much she calculated, planned, and analyzed her life, nothing worked out the way she wanted. She'd never have returned to Southburg for an extended stay without being forced.

Beautiful area or not, being here meant dealing with memories she'd rather forget—including the local back-stabbing gossips with their rumors and lies. Maybe she could face them now. She was stronger. She'd lived a lifetime in the last few years.

Nibbling a roll, she searched the newspaper for apartment listings, noting several complexes to explore. If she couldn't wiggle away before three months, she could at least find her own place.

Based on the doctor's latest assessment, Dad would be back at his office within the month. A small article written by Tom Chambers appeared on the last page of Section D titled, "Davis Firm moves forward on Defense Contract." The piece mentioned Dad's hospitalization, but only for his yearly testing. She'd definitely send Tom the gopher.

She tucked the classified section under her arm and headed toward her bedroom. Pausing outside her mom's study she glanced in. Her mother knelt in front of her Bible, eyes closed, tears streaming down her face.

Bethany swallowed hard and went upstairs.

Jedi yawned and wagged his tail in a lazy salute.

She sat on the edge of the bed and pulled him to her chest. Why would Mom be so upset? Had the doctor told her something else? Maybe that's really why they wanted her home. Maybe that's why dad was emotional. Maybe Chase wasn't being a jerk and really knew something.

Bethany turned and hurried downstairs.

The door to the study stood fully open, her mom gone. Curious, Bethany snuck in and glanced at the Bible. Its well-worn pages lay open to the fifteenth chapter of Luke. Her knees weakened at the sight of her name written in the margin—next to the story of the prodigal son.

Mom had it wrong. Bethany hadn't given up on God.

He'd walked out on her.

Chapter 3

Sunlight spilled through the blinds, pooling warmth across the bed. The aroma of cinnamon rolls, coffee, and bacon filtered into the room. Stomach growling, Bethany yawned, rolled over and found herself face to furry face. Jedi's sleepy eyes opened, and behind him his tail raised in a happy wag. He had adjusted wonderfully to the new environment, mainly because he was spoiled rotten by everyone who lived or worked on the property.

Two weeks had already passed, and she needed to talk to her parents. Dad seemed to be getting along fine and even worked out of his home office. Mom continued to hover over them both. Bethany glanced at Jedi. He didn't move but responded with a hopeful wag. She had to admit she'd wag a little too. Being home these two weeks had been nice—other than of course Dad's stroke, and the fact she was still in Southburg.

She wondered if she'd hear from the architecture firm in Chicago. She had mailed them her portfolio and resume the day before her dad entered the hospital. Chicago would be a great opportunity to start over and make a new life.

Her phone vibrated on the night stand. Bethany fought to get her hands free from under the covers. Finally released from her plush prison, she grabbed her phone.

Chase. The rat himself.

She answered with a snarl. "You are in so much trouble."

"Calm down, you'll thank me one day." His voice, calm, cool, disgustingly collected. She pictured him at his desk, feet up, surveying the Potomac River below.

"Thank you? You told them I was staying for three months. Three months! You know I said three weeks. I have a life, an apartment, and maybe a job waiting in Chicago."

"I never told Mom three months. I said three, and before I could finish, she gasped and said months. Correcting her as she stood watching Dad loaded into an ambulance was not something I would do. You may correct her at any time. Three months isn't that long." Papers shuffled and he let out a sigh. "You owe them."

"I owe them?"

"Do you want me to count the ways? Dad paying for your tuition, apartment, clothes, car, food, parties, etcetera, etcetera, etcetera. By the way, all your belongings from your apartment are being shipped to Southburg and will be kept in a storage unit. And your mail has been forwarded to Mom and Dad's."

"You went through my things, and you're trying to take over my life?" She was so mad she could spit.

"No. I hired a moving company to handle everything. Don't worry, one of dad's security guards supervised."

"Chase, you could have called me. Let me know. Given me an option." Not only were strangers going through her things but a man who reports straight to her dad. Not that she really had much to call her own, mostly garage sale and second-hand-store furniture. But it was still hers.

"Bethany, while Dad has been sidelined, I'm taking care of things. Your apartment had to be dealt with, your lease ends

21

in another week. You now have every option available in the world. It's up to you to do the right thing. Whether you hate me or love me. I love you, and I love Mom and Dad." Click.

She stared at the phone, hit redial. The call went straight to voice mail. She picked up a pillow and muffled a scream.

"I'm trapped in a bad dream." Bethany stood staring at nothing, her eyes filling. "This can't be real."

Jedi laid low, looking up at her. Even his tail stayed down.

She picked him up. "Don't worry. It's not your fault. You're a good boy. Unlike your Uncle Chase who I will someday tear him limb from limb."

Bethany considered beating a pillow to death in place of Chase but decided not to traumatize Jedi.

Homeless. Okay, not homeless but apartmentless. Her things packed away by who knows who. She cringed as she remembered a few things she had squirreled away. Her party girl past was over, but why didn't she remove all trace? Hopefully, whichever bodyguard was chosen for watch duty wouldn't talk.

Maybe she should spend the day in the kitchen with her mom and bake up some delicacy to deliver to the entire security force. Bribery wrapped in sugar, delivered in prim and proper attire with an innocent smile. A smile that says, I've changed, please don't say anything.

Her avenue for escape had been removed. Exiled to Southburg. Rapunzel trapped in the tall tower waiting for her knight in shining armor. If only those kind of guys existed. For now she needed a plan on how to survive three months without driving herself or her parents crazy.

First step, baking.

Second step, find an apartment and a temporary job in

the area. If she was staying three months, it didn't mean she couldn't have some space and a life of her own. And if Chicago called, she'd have a great excuse.

Third step, make the three months and then fly free.

Ten days later, Bethany cranked up the volume on her car radio and settled in for the long commute from her parent's house to her new place of employment. With Dad back at work, she had found a job that seemed tailor-made at an architectural firm.

Design had always been her strong point and something she loved. Thankfully, Smith, Canton, and Associates hired her on the first interview. Her position was temporary, with a possible transition to permanent if she decided to stay in the area or Chicago never called. At least she'd be out of the house and hopefully with people her own age.

For her first day, she chose a fuchsia top to spice up her black pants and jacket. Mom preferred a simple white blouse, but the splash of color kept Bethany's independence and sanity.

The forty-five minute drive left no time for breakfast or even coffee. Not a problem, she'd get by until lunch. She loved driving her grandmother's Lincoln Town Car, a true land-yacht, free of charge, and the perfect place to display her bumper stickers. College friends called it a rolling billboard for ecology groups. More than that, the car represented part of her sweet grandmother. Until she passed on, she believed in Bethany and if she had stood more than five foot two inches, she would have beaten Bethany's ex-husband to death. Bethany loved that woman.

Traffic stayed light on the tree-lined, winding back roads, and force of habit kept her aware of her surroundings. For ten minutes, she'd noticed a silver Lexus in the rearview mirror. Probably a commuter, but with Dad involved in the defense industry, she couldn't take chances. Signaling with her blinker for a left turn, she instead turned right.

The Lexus followed.

Bethany smiled. Evasive driving could be so entertaining. No one had given her a good chase in months. She braced herself for the next move. Cranking the wheel, she turned the big boat in a u-turn. Her tires squealed in protest.

The silver car matched her maneuver, fishtailing to stay on the road. She felt rather proud of herself, a cat-and-mouse game, all without morning caffeine.

She couldn't make out the driver. He could be anyone … a reporter, someone looking for information on Dad's latest project, maybe even a spy. *Now, that would be fun.* With a push of a button on her cell phone, she speed-dialed security and gave her position and the make of the car following.

The freeway entrance loomed ahead. She punched the accelerator and merged into the flow of cars. Swallowed by traffic, she eased into the left-hand lane and waited for an opportunity.

Two cars back, the Lexus trailed.

Bethany breathed deep, keeping her head clear, enjoying the adrenaline pumping through her veins.

The mini-van next to her shifted lanes, and there it was, like the Red Sea parting—just enough space to hit the next exit. She stepped on the gas, swerved behind a sporty blue Mustang, and then crossed two lanes to exit.

The Lexus shot over the white line, weaving through traffic. Horns blared. A black sedan rocketed next to the Lexus, blocking the path.

Help had arrived.

She pitied the driver. Those assigned to her family's security would find out any details. The poor guy didn't have a chance.

Without further incident, Bethany arrived at her new office, parked, and answered her ringing cell phone. One of Dad's bodyguards gave her the news. Her pursuer got away. Yes, she was fine. No, she had no clue who had followed her. Yes, she would call before she left the office. The phone clicked off, and she nodded to the black sedan as it crept past. Dad's shadows would stay nearby.

His call would come next, and now wasn't the time. Knowing how her father would want to handle the situation, she switched off her phone. A gun took too much room in her purse. She wouldn't trade in her car for something more run-of-the-mill, and no bodyguards—unless she got the cute one.

Unfortunately, Dad wouldn't let her have him. With her luck, he'd assign her the bodyguard who never laughed. Reporters and spies she could handle, but someone without a sense of humor was just a crime.

Smith, Canton, & Associates occupied the top two floors of the sprawling five-story office complex overlooking the river. After a stop in Human Resources, Bethany arrived at the fifth-floor office of the man who had hired her only a week before.

George Canton, phone in hand, motioned for her to sit. She chose the leather chair across from his paper-strewn mahogany desk. Models and designs cluttered the table in the corner. He clicked a ball-point pen as he listened intently to the caller. His white dress shirt custom fit his ample belly, the tie expensive. Architectural drawings and framed awards touted the firm's global success.

He hung up the phone and rose to shake her hand. "Bethany, welcome to the firm. Things are a little hectic today. You'll be working with your team leader, Jason Ross."

Feeling confident and comfortable, she followed him

down the hall and onto the elevators. If things didn't work out, she'd be gone in a few months and off to the big city.

Mr. Canton punched the fourth-floor button. "Jason was out of town the day of your interview, but he has your file and portfolio. I'm sure you two will make out fine."

From her original interview with upper-management she expected a pleasant older man like Mr. Canton. But when they entered her team-leader's office, she suppressed a surprised smile.

The guy from the gift shop, clueless handsome guy, stood and shook her hand. "Welcome to the team." His grip sent a tingle up her arm. *A tingle?* What was wrong with her?

Smiling, he studied her for a moment. Recognition flickered in his eyes, and then his face flamed red.

Mr. Canton muttered something about getting back to his office and excused himself.

Jason's smile wavered and faltered, then regained in strength. "I'm glad you're here. I mean, you'll be a great asset." He half-tripped coming around his desk. His face paled, then morphed into stoic business. "Let me introduce you to everyone and show you your office." He led her down the hall and stopped at the first cubicle. "This is yours, and next to you is Valerie. She's our AutoCad whiz."

A young woman with spiky, multi-tinted hair shook her hand. The colors in her long-flowing, cotton skirt and a blouse matched her hair. "Welcome to Sca."

"Sca?" Bethany smiled at her interesting workmate.

"Yeah, it sounds better than Smith, Canton, and Associates. Actually, it sounds worse, which is why I prefer it."

Jason shook his head and steered Bethany to the next cubicle. "This is Rhonda. She's one of our design specialists."

The woman's twinkling brown eyes were surrounded by

her flawless, milk-chocolate complexion. "Nice to meet you, Bethany. Welcome to the team. Stop by if you need anything."

Jason led Bethany farther down the hall. "Nicole Hammond and several others are meeting with a major client. They'll be in later. Alex Thompson is in charge of sales and promotions." He stopped at the closed door with a gold nameplate and knocked.

"Come in." Alex, gorgeous, tan, with dark hair, and deep blue eyes, looked more like a male model than a businessman. "You must be Bethany."

She couldn't believe her luck—two good-looking guys in the same office. Not bad for a first day.

Alex shook her hand, holding onto it as if making a claim. "Good to have you aboard." His gaze skimmed her body and stopped at her chest. "I could use someone with your obvious qualities. Have any sales experience?"

"No." Bethany pulled away and resisted the urge to wipe her hand. She avoided his leer by looking around his office. A dozen pictures covering his glass-and-steel desk showed Alex involved in various sports—scuba diving, skiing, and mountain climbing.

He leaned against his credenza. "Jason, a group is heading to Bermuda for some scuba diving this weekend. Want to join us?" With a mocking grin, Alex didn't wait for a reply. "Oh sorry, I forgot you're usually at soccer games or that mouse pizza place."

"Catch you next time." Though Jason smiled, his eyes narrowed. "Don't forget your Speedos and dress socks."

Bethany hid her laugh with a cough and followed Jason back to her office. He explained her duties, handed her notes on their latest project and then left. She spread out the architectural drawings and schematics and thanked her lucky stars she didn't go into sales. Alex was hot and a jerk—a deadly combination.

Her office overlooked the lush green lawn. At least that's what she decided to tell everyone. Her cubicle sided with an outside wall, and if she stretched on her tiptoes she could glimpse through the window as the grass beyond the parking lot. Not exactly the view she'd hoped for, but at least the job provided her an escape from her parent's watchful eyes.

Rhonda and Valerie checked on her often and answered her questions. Valerie contained enough energy to power a medium-sized town and reminded her of a chipmunk on steroids. Rhonda's easy-going manner seemed to have a calming presence she couldn't quite put her finger on.

At 11:15, Valerie grabbed Bethany and pushed her toward the parking lot. "It's lunchtime. We'll treat you to our favorite deli."

When they reached Valerie's car, Bethany moved aside a beach towel, a pair of sandals, a six-pack of energy drinks, and settled in the backseat of her officemate's bright yellow Volkswagen Beetle.

Valerie rolled down her window and lit a cigarette.

Rhonda's eyes flared wide. "I thought you said you quit."

"I did." Valerie took a long drag and blew out smoke rings. "I didn't have one yesterday or this morning."

"It's going to kill you someday." Rhonda turned on the air conditioning and pointed the vents at her co-worker.

"I'm going to die of something. At least I keep my window down so I can breathe in fresh air."

"*That* will make a big difference."

"Hey, I take my vitamins and drink lots of water." She took a long puff, followed by a mock coughing fit.

During the five-minute ride, Bethany enjoyed their playful banter. For a first day on a new job in a town she'd avoided for years, things were going far better than expected.

The crowded deli reminded Bethany of one she enjoyed at college but without the noisy frat boys. Black and white checked floors, white bead board lining the walls, the tables and booths covered in red vinyl. Rhonda and Bethany ordered the salad bar. Valerie chose pizza and flirted with one of the workers behind the long counter. When they paid, she gave him her phone number.

Valerie covered her pineapple-pepperoni pizza with sunflower seeds and pickles. After swallowing a huge bite, she nudged Bethany. "You just graduated, but you don't have that wild-eyed, new person look."

Bethany shifted to block the tension crawling across her shoulders. "I took some time off after my sophomore year."

Valerie leaned closer. "Did you travel the world?"

"I wish."

"What did you do?"

Not ready to talk, Bethany picked at her salad.

Rhonda punched Valerie. "Girl, you are so nosy."

Valerie took a long drink of her soda, her gaze never leaving Bethany. "I heard you graduated with a 4.0."

"That's a vicious rumor. Don't let it get out." Her party friends back in college would have been amazed she did so well. Book smarts came easy, life just smarted. "What else did you hear?"

"You took a wild variety of courses, interned in the summer months, and made killer grades. You a bookworm?"

Bethany chuckled. "I don't think *anyone* has ever called me that."

"In high school, I received an award for being the most

likely to turn the teacher's hair gray." Valerie picked up her fork, stabbed a black olive that had fallen out of Bethany's salad, and dropped it on her pizza. "So, do you like to party?"

"I can hold my own."

"Good. I'm having one Saturday night. You should come."

"Maybe. I'm moving into a new apartment over the weekend."

"You gotta come." Valerie's statement was more fact than question. "There'll be a few people from work and a bunch of friends."

"I can't make it that night." Rhonda's eyes crinkled with her warm smile. "I'm meeting some buddies for dinner." She patted Valerie's arm. "You know I love you."

"She's a God person." Valerie let out a dramatic sigh. "But don't worry, she's okay."

Rhonda flicked a crouton at her. "That's what you call me?"

"Well, yeah, because you have this pipeline to the big man upstairs or something." Valerie munched a stolen carrot from Bethany's plate. "If she says she's going to pray for you, watch out. She's prayed me out of several relationships. Okay, they were slime, but man, they were cute."

Rhonda shook her head. "Girl, if you didn't have God watching out for you, no telling where you'd be."

"*Your* God is not on speaking terms with me, but it's good to know someone's got my back." Valerie dipped her pizza into Rhonda's salad dressing container.

Rhonda pushed the container toward Valerie. "You keep it. You girls want anything? I'm going back for some muffins."

"Yeah." Valerie snatched several croutons off Rhonda's plate. "Could you get me some jalapeños?"

"You and your cast-iron stomach. I'll see what I can find."

Valerie waited until Rhonda left. "Now on to office politics."

"Wait." Bethany held out her hand. "I really don't want to hear any rumors."

"They aren't rumors, merely facts. Jason is the brains, and a nice guy, a little too nice for my taste, but oh well. Warren's kind of cute and okay for a klutzy genius. And, you met Alex aka Luscious 'Lex. He'd sell his soul to the devil for a high commission. And with those looks, it's rumored he has. Have you met Nicole? Well, watch out for her. She thinks she's the boss and will do anything to get ahead. And I do mean anything."

"Val!" Shaking her head, Rhonda rushed back to the table. "Let her make up her own mind about people."

"I'm just making sure she knows the score." Valerie took the jalapeños off Rhonda's plate and snagged two muffins in the process. "Bethany, stick with us, and you'll do fine."

Back in the office, Bethany studied the computer's updated diagrams and laid another finished portfolio in her outbox. Thank goodness, she had interned between school sessions. Even for a first day, she didn't feel lost. And with Valerie around the office, days would never be boring.

Movement in the hallway drew her attention.

A leggy blonde in a tight skirt, low-cut blouse, and spiked heels stood, or more posed, in her cubicle doorway. "I'm Nicole." She didn't offer her hand. "You must be Bethany. Feel free to ask any questions. I stay updated on all projects." She took a step closer and lowered her voice. "By the way, I've noticed several of the men stopping to check you out. Just remember, intra-office dating is frowned upon by management."

Bethany bit back a smile. "I'll keep that in mind."

Her first work day successfully under her belt, Bethany shut her cell phone and stepped out of her car. The phone discussion with her dad went better than anticipated. Thankfully, he didn't push her to carry a gun, and only slightly pressured her about bodyguards. He backed off when she offered to take the cute one. She could take care of herself. No way she'd live in fear. Her car remained a source of contention, but she couldn't give it up—not yet.

She stopped to say hello to the evening nurses at the retirement home and check on her grandfather's progress. For the past two years, his dementia slowly separated him from the family. Maybe tonight he'd have a spark of recognition and they could talk. Grateful she could visit more often, Bethany hurried to his open door.

His personal furniture and belongings decorated the small, tidy room. Family pictures adorned the dresser and walls. He sat in a chair with his back to the window, his best suit loose on his thin frame. The nurse always dressed him for her visits.

"Grandfather?"

He stared at the blank television screen.

She kissed him on his forehead lined with creases of time. "How are you today?" When he didn't acknowledge her presence, she sat next to him. "I move into an apartment on Saturday, and I've started a new job. Most of the people are really nice. Some of them are rather interesting. One girl is a firecracker. I've never seen anybody with so much energy."

"Stocks are down." He clicked his tongue. "I told them to take out the dog."

She searched his eyes, longed for his presence. "My office is on the fourth floor, and it has a window. Well, not much of a window, but I can see the grass if I stand on my tiptoes." She paused as he became restless. "Mom and Dad are doing well."

"Who?" His gaze held no recognition.

"It's okay." Trying to ignore the ache in her chest, she reached into her purse. "I brought you some strawberry jam."

With a shaky hand, he set the jar on his dresser.

Bethany waited, steeped in her memories of the grandfather who always made time to listen and always had a word of guidance and love. Her favorite picture of her smiling grandparents early in their marriage panged bittersweet emotions. Their relationship could have been in the movies—sassy, fun, and always sweet.

Grandfather rubbed his hand over his face and spoke quietly, "Anna?"

Bethany blinked back tears. After three years, he still missed her. "She sends her love."

He hung his head, closed his eyes, and slowly rocked. "Gold hair, warm smile."

She patted his arm, wished she could comfort him, and waited for him to return. "It's a beautiful evening."

His rocking stopped. He struggled to his feet, his eyes aglow lost in another time and another place. "Anna. Dance?"

Bethany again played the familiar part. "Oh, Harold. I would love to dance with you."

Smiling, he took her hand as she rose. "You're beautiful."

"And you are as handsome as ever."

They swayed to the music playing in his head, the pure bliss of the moment covering his face. "Paris."

"Paris is beautiful this time of year." The picture of her grandmother watched from the dresser as they glided past. If only time could be replayed.

His voice strengthened. "Italy. I'll buy you a villa."

She tried to steady her voice. "On a hillside with a vineyard?"

He twirled her. "Yes, and travel the world."

She kissed his cheek, repeating the words her grandmother, Anna, said to him every night before she died. "Harold, you gave me the world when you loved me."

Chapter 4

Bethany thanked and tipped the delivery men before crashing on her new soft-white couch with bright red throw pillows. Dad insisted she make a clean start in her new apartment with all new furniture and even demanded the bill. She'd been more than happy to comply, even if the gesture was thinly veiled bribery to get her to stay.

She'd already organized what she and her parents brought earlier in the day. Only a few more boxes of odds and ends remained in her car, and they didn't need to sit any longer in the hot sun. With a groan, she pushed off the couch. After a quick reassuring pat for Jedi, she grabbed her keys and stepped out the front door.

Footsteps on the sidewalk drew her attention. A black-haired man, maybe mid-30's and wearing faded blue jeans, walked toward her. "Hi. Just move in?" He hooked his thumbs in his front pockets.

"Yes." Though he smiled, she checked again to make sure her door locked behind her.

He glanced toward the parking lot and then looked over her shoulder. "Not many people here yet."

"No, I guess not."

His smile faded, and he leaned toward her. "It's kind of quiet here in the woods. You have to be careful of spiders."

Spiders? The trees surrounding the complex didn't look

as inviting as earlier. She moved back and swallowed the dirt clod in her throat. "I guess so."

"I'm Clint. I live over there." He pointed toward the next building.

Bethany made a mental note to avoid him and that area forever.

A Corvette wheeled into the place next to her car.

Grateful for the distraction, she scuttled past Clint. "I need to get a few things from my car."

"Do you need help?"

"No." *Never in a million years.*

"It was nice to meet you, Bethany."

A wisp of fear serpentined down her spine. She never gave him her name. Focusing on the Corvette, she refused to turn around. Right now, she just wanted to get away.

The Corvette owner, a silver-haired man close to her dad's age, stepped out of his car. He closed his door and smiled at her. "Moving in?"

"Yes." She popped open her trunk, ready to grab a tire iron if anyone else made her feel as uncomfortable as that Clint guy.

"I'm Andrew. I live in 5E." Dressed in shorts and a golf shirt, he kept a respectable distance. "Need a hand?"

Bethany peeked to check the sidewalk. Thankfully, creepy Clint was no longer in sight, but an escort to her door sounded like a good idea. "Sure. That'd be great." She handed Andrew one of the boxes and gathered the last remaining items from her trunk. "I appreciate the help."

"You new to the area?" He kept in pace, but not too close, as they walked back to her apartment.

"Yes and no." She scanned the lot. Maybe moving into a new complex wasn't such a bright idea.

"Just moved back, then?"

Way too perceptive. She glanced his direction. "Where are you from?"

"Moved here three weeks ago from Texas."

The slight twang in the accent had already given him away. She stopped outside her door. "Thanks for the help."

"No problem." He placed his box next to her and stepped back. "Need help with anything else?"

"That's it for now, thanks." She hesitated and glanced back toward the trees. "Do you know the guy who was standing near me when you drove up? His name's Clint."

He scratched his chin. "No, I've never seen him before. But I might not have met everyone who's moved in."

Bethany thanked Andrew and hurried to get inside. She locked the door and gathered Jedi in her arms. Why was she getting paranoid over some weird guy? She shuddered.

Spiders.

She hated spiders.

Saturday evening, Bethany circled Valerie's block three times before gathering her nerve. Getting back into a party scene wasn't high on Bethany's list. Hopefully, no one she knew from her past would attend Valerie's party.

Bethany relaxed her grip on the steering wheel. The majority of the simple frame houses in Valerie's neighborhood had been restored in vibrant primary colors, giving the area an artsy feel. Large oaks lined the streets. While most yards were meticulously landscaped, others looked condemned.

Still sore from moving into her apartment, Bethany unbuckled her seat belt and rubbed her shoulder. Valerie's neon-purple, cottage-style house was hard to miss. Especially with the eclectic group of people gathered on the front porch and spilling into the yard. An orange, crooked-tail cat rubbed Bethany's leg as she entered the crowded house.

Valerie, beer in one hand and cigarette in the other, hugged her. "Glad you came. Hey everybody, this is my friend Bethany. She works at Sca."

Exuberant shouts, hellos, and a few toasts to *Sca* were made on her behalf.

Bethany waved off the offered beer. A few months ago, she would have happily accepted and challenged anyone to a drinking contest, but she'd learned the hard way. Partying away the past didn't work—it only left hangovers and more regrets.

Before she could move, she ended up in a discussion about the latest science fiction bestseller. And in this group, sci-fi seemed appropriate. One guy's extensive piercings could set off every metal detector in the county, and the girl clinging to his arm sported a tattoo of the Starship Enterprise across her ample chest.

"I owe you an apology," a male voice whispered from behind.

She turned. Tom Chambers wore jeans, a short-sleeve shirt, and a smile.

Bethany narrowed her eyes and deadpanned. "How well do you grovel?"

He stepped back, blinking rapidly. "I really am sorry."

"Let me give you some advice." She moved closer and kept her smile hidden. "Next time, just ask your questions. You might actually get an up-front answer."

"Would you have answered?"

"No way." Bethany grinned. "But I accept your

apology."

Tom's shoulders loosened as if he'd taken a muscle relaxer. "I liked the gopher."

"I thought you might need a reminder."

"No need to worry. You're unforgettable."

"Is that a positive or negative statement?" Only partially teasing, she couldn't tell from his tone.

"Definitely positive. For the record, I'm not here as a reporter. Valerie's a good friend."

The discussion around them grew intense. When someone began speaking Elfin from the movie *Lord of the Rings*, Tom tapped her shoulder. "You want to join me in the backyard?"

At this point, she'd join a hungry, grizzly bear to escape.

He smiled when she didn't respond. "Don't worry. I'm safe."

"I'm not worried." Bethany followed in his wake as he politely pushed through the crowd.

In the backyard, citronella torches cast an orange glow across the pathway. Overgrown rosemary, thyme, sage, and a variety of herbs and flowers rambled throughout what could have been an English garden. The disorganized yard, if trimmed, could be beautiful—but coming from Valerie, it somehow worked in an odd, quirky sort of way.

Bethany grazed her hand across the gardenia bush, releasing its sweet fragrance. She missed gardening. A nursery wasn't far from her apartment, maybe something would grow on her balcony. Better yet, Valerie might let her take some cuttings since most of the plants needed a trim. Bethany knelt to stroke the soft leaves of the Lamb's Ears.

"You're really enjoying yourself." Tom's voice brought her back to the present.

"I love gardening."

"I'm surprised. You don't seem the domestic type."

"Why?" She stood and faced him. "What type am I?"

Even in the low light, his face reddened. "Something more entertaining."

Forcing herself not to react, she bent to pull some weeds. "Digging in the dirt is similar to a reporter researching a story. It's satisfying to see the rewards of your labor." She wiped her hands as she straightened. "I love flowers this time of year. Let's just hope there are no gophers in the ground so I don't have to blow their heads off."

He blinked several times and didn't move.

"There you are!" Valerie hurried toward them and took Bethany by the arm. "Come back inside. I want you to meet more of my friends."

Before Bethany could resist, Valerie hustled her into the living room and into a political discussion. Within five minutes, she wished the science fiction group would call her over. When offered another drink, she hesitated. *This could be a long night.*

The next morning, Bethany wandered through the aisles of the up-scale grocery store tasting samples. Much to Valerie's chagrin, Bethany left the party early after several men made advances. Cute guys or not, she needed to be good. She already had enough regrets to fill a dump truck. Forcing that thought aside, she stuffed another gourmet item into her overflowing basket. She might live alone, but she'd enjoy herself.

Turning past the cereal aisle, her heart and feet froze when she spotted the last two people on earth she wanted to see. *Why today?* A quick glance at her watch summed up the problem. Church had let out. She backed away and hurried to produce. Anything to get away from the two who'd caused her so much grief.

Sickly sweet voices called her name.

Bethany cringed. She pasted on what could hopefully pass as a pleasant expression and turned to face the tormenters from her previous life. "Cindy. Joelle. How are you?"

As always, both women wore the latest fashions. *Isn't there some saying about a gold ring in a pig's snout?*

Cindy tilted her head as if deep in thought. "Why didn't you tell us you were back?" Her overly white teeth sparkled.

"I haven't been in town long." Bethany gripped her basket, wishing she had worn something other than jeans.

"Are you staying with your parents?" With Joelle's tall heels, a stiff wind could send her and her designer dress toppling.

"No, I have my own place."

"Oh?" Joelle sounded surprised. "Are you working?"

"Yes." Bethany offered no details.

Cindy rested her left hand on her neck, her ring finger twitching. The large marquis-cut diamond sparkled in the florescent lights. "Now that Neil is in hospital administration, we bought a large home in Breckenridge. You know, the new upscale neighborhood."

Bethany rummaged through the oranges. "I'm not familiar with it."

"Oh, you poor dear." Cindy's voice took on the tone of a mother trying to explain something to a toddler. "You definitely haven't been back long, have you?"

Joelle stared at Bethany's hands. "You're not wearing a ring. You haven't met anyone else? Did you know Gavin and Linda are having a baby? They live in Ohio and are so happy together."

Bethany bit her tongue to avoid a profanity-filled response. The last thing she needed was to hear about her ex-husband. No way she'd let these gossip mongers get to her. With effort, she remained stoic. "I wish them the best."

Joelle patted Bethany's arm like she was a child. "We didn't see you at church."

"No. I'm looking."

Cindy's overly arched eyebrows slid upward. "I can't believe you wouldn't come back to your home church."

Bethany considered smashing a cantaloupe into their faces. Instead, she forced her best imitation of a sweet smile. "Why would I? To give you more gossip and lies to spread?" She turned away without waiting for a response.

Gavin having a baby? She wanted to slam her cart into something, scream at the top of her lungs, grab a bottle of wine and drink herself into oblivion. He didn't want kids—probably because he was too busy with his affairs. She honestly didn't love Gavin anymore. The pain from his lies carved a valley so deep she didn't think she could ever love again.

Monday morning and work brought a welcome distraction. Why did she promise she'd move home? Bethany sipped her coffee as she studied the latest drawings with Jason.

She forced herself to concentrate on the job. Jason meticulously reviewed every detail, and any ideas or suggestions she made were met with positive reinforcement. Although the work relationship was enjoyable, a wall remained between them on anything personal.

Most people could talk non-stop about themselves. Not

Jason, and right now that was fine with her.

Alex entered without knocking. "Bethany, I discovered we have a mutual friend."

"Really?" She couldn't imagine, nor did she want to know.

"We have much to discuss." He shot a smirk at Jason. "I'm taking Bethany to lunch. Call my cell if you need us."

"Fine." Jason's look said otherwise. "I didn't realize it was lunch time."

Before she could object, Alex took her by the arm and led her to the door. "I know just the place."

She pulled away when they got in the hallway. "Who is this mutual friend?"

"I'll tell you when we get to the restaurant."

"Why don't you tell me now?"

His smile twisted into the epitome of smarminess. "Trust me. A quieter place would be better."

A boulder lodged in her stomach.

Jason grabbed fast-food and went back to the office. Why did it bother him that Alex took Bethany to lunch? Other than knowing Alex was a slime ball, why did he care?

Because Bethany's a knockout. Intelligent, turquoise mischievous eyes, incredible body. Jason raked his fingers through his hair as though he could remove his less than honorable thoughts. He had to keep praying about the incessant attraction and stay focused. She ran in different circles than he did—Valerie's party and now lunch with Alex.

Jason wouldn't, no *couldn't*, slip back into his wild ways. He was a changed man. He had to prove that to God. He *would* prove it. His life remained on a different course than years before, and he planned on staying in the right direction, even if it meant being alone the rest of his life.

Bethany picked at her salad. Alex talked non-stop, ranting about himself and his accomplishments in grandiose terms. The way he talked, he could singlehandedly climb Mount Everest, sky dive several thousand feet, then ski the rest of the way.

She was ready to smack him. "Who is this friend?"

He sat back, ice and fire colliding in his deep blue eyes. "You remember Ken. He said you were quite the party girl in college." He placed his hand on top of hers. The heat from his fingertips scorched to her soul. "I like that in a woman."

She jerked away. "I've mellowed."

"Really? I doubt that. You have quite a reputation."

Bethany clenched her hands ready to shove the table into his gut. "You shouldn't always believe what you hear."

"Don't be so sensitive." His smile reminded her of a hungry crocodile. "He didn't say anything bad about you. On the contrary, he was *very* complimentary."

She studied the crimson stain imbedded on the tablecloth in front of her. Even bleach couldn't clean up the mess she made of herself after the divorce. Shame someone didn't sell regret and shame remover.

Feigning a serene look, she tried to think of something to say that wouldn't add more fuel to an already lit fire. "You know, Alex, I think what you need is to attend Bible study. Maybe that would give you a chance to see the world from another angle." Not that she would go, but the confused and

44

dazed look he gave her provided the reprieve she needed. His slimy legs were cut out from under him.

Glancing at her watch, she mustered up a smile, and stood to leave. "We better get back to work." She placed enough money to cover her portion of the bill. "I'm going to powder my nose. I'll meet you at the car."

After a quiet ride back to the office, Bethany threw her purse on her desk and slumped into her chair. She couldn't win. Maybe she should move to China or Timbuktu. A big city like New York looked better every day—a place to get lost in a crowd. No one would ask questions, and no one would care about the past.

"Can I come in?" Rhonda waited in Bethany's doorway.

"Sure."

"Is everything okay?" Rhonda pulled a chair next to her.

"I guess." Telling the truth meant revealing the past. At this rate, she might as well take out a billboard or go on a talk show.

"We don't know each other well, but I'm here if you need to talk." Rhonda's caring tone tugged on her heart. "Don't let the bad ones get you down. Alex makes a play for every female. He's great at his job, but management has his number when it comes to women. They won't let him step over the line." Rhonda hesitated and then wagged her finger. "He didn't step over the line, did he? I'll give him a piece of my mind if he did."

"It's okay. I can handle Alex." She would have preferred more painful methods than talking about Bible study, but on the way back to the office he'd remained quiet. Who would have thought that mentioning church could actually be a good thing?

"Can I pray for you?" Rhonda's voice jolted her back to

the present.

Bethany shrugged. "Sure." She'd take all the help she could get.

"You got it."

Fortunately, Rhonda didn't bow her head right then. *Way too embarrassing.*

Rhonda studied her a moment. "Would you be interested in helping stock our food bank on Saturday? I lend a hand at Cornerstone, down on Glenview."

"That's where I used to help." Tension eased as fond memories drifted back. "That'd be nice. What time?"

"Seven o'clock. Is that too early?"

"No, that'd be great."

Rhonda patted her shoulder and gave a gentle squeeze. "I'll meet you there." She turned and almost ran into Alex standing in the doorway.

He didn't acknowledge Rhonda, but moved closer to Bethany. "If you're going somewhere fun, call me." His smarmy smirk made his intentions obvious.

Rhonda put her hands on her hips. "Don't you have work to do?"

"I'm always working." He wagged his eyebrows at Bethany.

"Stop pestering that girl."

"I just want her to feel very welcome."

Rhonda shoved him into the hall, all the while lecturing him on proper workplace etiquette and how to treat a lady. Their voices faded as they walked away.

Bethany glanced at her calendar and counted the days. She couldn't wait to leave behind the petty mind games of the past. Soon, she'd escape Southburg, but her reputation was a self-made monster destined to haunt her for life.

Chapter 5

Saturday morning, Bethany parallel parked between Rhonda's van and a pearl white SUV. Cornerstone's two-story historical brick building looked the same and always made her smile. The name of the original owners remained embedded in brick and mortar since 1943—Anderson, Powel, and Egbert. *Who would name their firm with the initials APE?*

Cornerstone held happy memories. Too bad Brad was in Peru. He was the one person who really understood her.

A hint of chlorine cleanser lingered in the air as she walked down the back hallway to the open door of the mini-warehouse. Donated bags and boxes of nonperishable items waited to be categorized and stacked on aging, stainless steel shelves.

Rhonda juggled an armload of canned goods. "Hey, girl, glad you made it."

Bethany hurried to help. "You here alone?"

"No, the others are upstairs. You said you volunteered here when you were younger. When was that?"

She picked up some cans and stacked them on the shelf. "My brother, Brad, and I helped Mr. Collier get the building converted when we were in high school. We came by most weekends to help stock." She checked the concrete floor by the side door. Sure enough, the gouge remained from seven years ago when the scaffolding fell. Thankfully, Brad landed safe and unhurt. He never again tried his incredible, epic, double acrobatic move. She could imagine their laughter still bouncing off the walls.

Rhonda smiled as though reading her thoughts. "What brought you back to Southburg?"

"My parents live here."

"That's sweet. I hope my babies stay close when they get older. I've been so blessed with my children. They're good kids—not perfect, but good." Rhonda pushed another bag toward her. "Your parents must be proud of you. Graduating with a 4.0 is amazing."

"Books are easier than real life."

"I hear that. My brilliant ex-husband would get lost going to the store. At least that's the excuse he made when I found out he was cheating on me."

Chalk another up for the jerks. "I'm sorry."

"It's okay. I'm blessed." Rhonda methodically sorted the green beans and corn. "Forgiveness goes a long way, and God takes good care of me and the kids."

"God isn't the problem." Bethany cringed, sorry she'd voiced that thought.

Rhonda stopped and studied her. "You want to talk?"

No, she didn't want to talk. She didn't even want to think. "I found my ex-husband in bed with my best friend." Heat shimmied up her neck. She couldn't believe she said something that personal. What was wrong with her? She grabbed an armload of cans and shoved them onto the shelf.

"I'm so sorry."

"I'm over him. It's just that others won't let me forget." Being back in a familiar, safe environment, made her talk way too freely. She should've stayed in bed.

Rhonda nodded. "I know that's true. People, who make

trouble by throwing the past in someone's face are bad news."

"That's an understatement." Bethany tossed a dented can without a label into a separate bin. "The worst were in our church."

"The church should be a safe place."

"I haven't been back since."

Rhonda stopped. "Girl, you need to be in church."

Here comes the lecture. "No thanks. It's full of gossips and hypocrites."

"You're right."

Bethany almost dropped a can. "You agree?"

"Honey, the church is full of sinners. It's a hospital for the sick, and God is the Great Physician. We can't expect perfection from his children. Or those who *say* they're his children. Only God is perfect. People may fail you, but God never will."

They worked in silence while she pondered Rhonda's statement. Not everybody in church was rotten. She knew that. But going back didn't seem worth the effort. Why should she spend her time with people who wore pasted-on idyllic expressions and spouted biblical platitudes? A shame more people weren't like her grandparents—honest, sincere, and loving.

"Bethany?" Her old friend, Nancy Miller, bounced across the room, and threw her arms around her. "Flipping pancakes, it is you! It's sooooo good to see you."

Bethany untangled from the mass of Nancy's long, blonde hair. For a hundred and ten pound person she could pack a wallop. "Good to see you too." She meant the statement. Nancy hadn't changed a bit in the years they'd been apart.

"What are you doing here?" Nancy held her hands as though they were school girls. "You look great. I heard your dad was in the hospital. Is he okay?"

"He's fine and back full-throttle at work."

"Good. I was praying for him." Nancy paused, her hazel eyes shimmering. "I've missed you. I left several messages before you moved away."

"I was kind of shell-shocked." *Wounded, hurting, hung out to dry, emotionally bleeding on the side of the road, thrown to the wolves.* "Life goes on."

"I can't wait to tell Don you're back. He'll be glad to know you're doing well. You are doing okay, aren't you?"

"Sure." *In a cosmic sort of way.* "You're still with Don?"

Nancy held out her left hand. The small diamond glistened on her ring. "We married a year ago. You know, Don wanted to beat Gavin to a pulp."

Best news she heard in a long time. "I knew I liked Don."

"How about we all do lunch?"

Bethany glanced at her watch. *Where did the time go?* "Didn't you just get here?"

"No, I was working upstairs. If I'd known y'all were here, I would've come down sooner."

"You know Rhonda?" Bethany pulled several more cans out of a sack.

"Of course. She's one of my prayer partners."

"I met Nancy last year in Bible study," Rhonda said. "I can't make it for lunch today. I've got to get some things done around the house."

Nancy tugged on Bethany's sleeve. "I'll grab you at eleven. Please come with me. I really want to catch up. There's a great Mexican restaurant not too far from here. We'll get high on salsa. Just like the old days."

Maybe she should have stayed in touch. Friends and salsa buddies throughout high school left memories of some great times. She couldn't resist Nancy's smile. "Lunch sounds good."

At the restaurant, Bethany studied the fabric hanging from the antler horns on either side of the restaurant windows. Kind of a buckskin look. *Chamois.* Cut, distressed, and made to look like old fabric. Tan stucco walls and a picture of a white buffalo hanging above the stone fireplace created the perfect Mexican restaurant ambience.

The true test would be the salsa. She scooped a generous portion on her chip. The flavor of roasted tomatoes and peppers danced on her tongue. She let a small moan escape. There were some things that made life worth living—salsa being one of them, second only to dark chocolate.

Nancy dipped her chip in guacamole. "Where are you living?"

"I'm in the new apartments on Lee Road." Bethany relaxed as the mellowing of the salsa worked its magic.

"The new ones? Those are awesome. Are you working for your dad?"

"No way. I couldn't handle that much stress. I'm working for Smith, Canton, and Associates."

"Oh, that's where you met Rhonda. One of my friends has a brother who works there."

Bethany's stomach flip-flopped. "He isn't Alex, is he?"

"No! Oh my goodness. I've heard about Alex. That man needs prayer. Kelly's little brother is Jason."

"Jason's somebody's little brother?"

"Kelly teaches our women's Bible Study at church. He goes there too. Their parents died in a car crash when Jason was in high school and she was in college. She took over raising him."

Maybe that's why he kept to himself. At least she didn't

need to worry about Jason. "He's married, isn't he?"

"No, way." Nancy chuckled. "Kelly's been trying to fix him up forever."

"But I saw pictures of kids on his desk."

"They're probably Kelly's. Jason's helping out while her husband's overseas working with the military."

Jason moved up a notch in her estimation for being involved with family. But for a single guy, why did he put up so many barriers? And why on earth didn't he date with those gorgeous eyes of his? She'd definitely pay more attention now that she knew his available status.

Nancy waved her hand in front of Bethany's face. "Are you with me?"

"Oh, sorry, I was just thinking."

"Have you been back to church with your parents?"

"I ran into Joelle and Cindy at the grocery store."

"Ugh, I'm sorry." Nancy grimaced. "How did it go?"

Bethany took a long drink before she answered. "As fun as ever. They haven't changed."

"Don and I left the church right after you did. Too hard to worship there after what they did to you."

A lump worked in her throat. *Get a grip.* Getting sentimental was a sign of weakness, and she'd blown it with Rhonda. "I didn't know anyone else knew what happened." Bethany grabbed a chip and piled high the salsa.

"Lots of people know Gavin lied. You left before most people could reach out." Nancy placed her hand on top of Bethany's. "I'm really sorry that happened. I can't imagine how alone you felt. I'm sorry I wasn't a better friend during your marriage. I just thought you two would be busy getting acquainted and wanted time alone."

"You didn't know." *Nobody knew.* "We got acquainted,

and it wasn't pretty."

The waiter placed Nancy's taco salad in front of her. Dark green Romaine piled high, red tomatoes, cheese, and meat, back-dropped with a fan-shaped shell, a true work of art. Bethany's chicken fajitas enveloped her in a cloud of smoke, swirling like her thoughts.

Nancy broke off a corner of her shell. "Do you remember when we used to drive around on Friday nights? I'll never forget the time you raced Roger."

Grateful for the subject change, Bethany rolled her fajita. "Having my car souped up was worth every penny. Nothing more fun than having a run-of-the mill car with a fast engine."

"Poor guy couldn't hold his head up for weeks. Losing to a girl just about did him in."

"I'm sure he got over it." She hadn't thought about Roger in years. He had been cute.

"I heard he works with one of the NASCAR drivers in the pit crew." Nancy stirred guacamole and salsa into her salad. "He's still single and handsome as ever."

Bethany met Nancy's amused gaze. "That just might make a road trip worthwhile."

"Can we?" Nancy bounced in her chair. "I haven't had one in years. I've really missed getting out and doing crazy things. Life hasn't been the same since you left."

Maybe time had come for the old Bethany to play again. Road trips with Nancy had been fun. "Okay, we'll do something. You're sure Don will let you?"

"Don loves when I go places since it gives him an excuse to go fishing. I'm thrilled you're back." Nancy patted her arm so hard her fork flipped, flinging lettuce onto Bethany's blouse before landing in the chip basket.

Nancy gaped. "That's a three-pointer, don't you think?"

Bethany grabbed her napkin as they broke out laughing. Making another month or two might not be so hard.

Chapter 6

Thursday evening, Jason couldn't wait to get a hard workout to get rid of the week's stress. He opened his locker, emptied his gym clothes onto the bench and pulled off his shirt. All the company projects were on schedule and moving smoothly. Bethany's input had been invaluable, which he found surprising for someone new to the team. He'd be grateful for her presence, if it weren't for *her presence*. Why did she have to be so good-looking?

Finished dressing, he slammed his locker. *And smart, quick-witted, and pretty.* Why did she have to have all those qualities?

Bethany didn't seem to be involved in church. He couldn't be attracted to her, and he wouldn't take the chance. At least the gym provided safety since no one from work came here— except Valerie. And Valerie would never be his type.

The gym was nice as Valerie promised. Bethany adjusted the bike settings to random and settled in for a long ride. Getting back into a workout routine would help occupy her evenings.

Jason remained friendly at work, but no questions were asked about personal life. Which still seemed odd, but in a way refreshing. Occasionally, he displayed a quirky sense of humor, but he seemed almost embarrassed to show any side of him that non-stoic and work-related. She definitely couldn't figure out Jason.

The bikes lined the back wall and faced the free-weight area. Bethany ignored the televisions hanging from the ceiling and enjoyed the view. Two power lifters grunted and moaned as they grappled with ever-increasing weight. She made a mental note of the cute, blond guy. Stocky but not fat, and incredibly strong. She overheard his name, thanks to the girls on the bikes next to her who talked about him and drooled over his progress. His lifting partner's shouts echoed off the mirrored walls.

"I didn't know you came here." The male voice coming from behind her sounded rather annoyed.

He stepped in front of her vision. *Jason.* He looked good. Who knew he had all those muscles. How long had he been standing there? Heat roasted her cheeks. "Valerie invited me."

He blinked several times as though unsure Bethany was real. "She teaches yoga," He paused. "I … I lift weights."

"Oh." She didn't know what else to say.

He studied the carpet, mumbled. "See ya," and walked away. When he reached the weight section, he picked up forty-five pound dumbbells and pumped arm curls.

Valerie jogged toward her, blocking the view. "How's it going?"

"Great. I've ridden thirty minutes."

"I'm impressed. Why don't you yoga with me? I've got another class starting in ten minutes."

"Maybe next time. I'm more the kick-boxing type."

Valerie pivoted and threw a kick. "I'd teach if they'd let me put up a mannequin with a picture of my old boyfriend's face."

"The class would be full." A loud groan followed by weights clanking to the floor drew her attention. "I didn't know Jason worked out here."

"Yep, but he stays to himself."

"He stopped by. Didn't even say hello, just said he didn't know I came here. Does he always work out that hard?"

Valerie watched Jason complete a set of bench presses. "No. But he's never seen you in your exercise outfit."

Bethany shook her head. "He doesn't know I exist."

"He's a guy. He *knows*."

After dinner, Jason taped a Happy Birthday banner for Elizabeth's party across the entryway to Kelly and Matt's dining room. He still couldn't believe his niece turned eight.

Kelly frosted the two-layer cake in shades of pink. "How's the new girl working out?"

"She came to the gym." He stared at a pink balloon. Why did everything have to be pink? Bethany's outfit had been black and pink and very form-fitting.

"And?" She gave him a curious look.

"I don't want to talk about it."

"Why?" Kelly arranged eight candles and added ballerina decorations. "Is she doing her job well?"

He shrugged. "Yes."

"So, is she attractive?" She washed and dried her hands but kept her gaze leveled on him.

"Yeah." *Way too attractive.* Drove him crazy.

"And that's a problem?"

"I don't need distractions." He punched the balloon tied

to the back of the chair. "She went to lunch with Alex and to Valerie's party. And you should have seen her exercise outfit."

"Was it inappropriate?"

"No, but on her it was."

Kelly chuckled. "Wow, sounds like she's getting to you. You've lunched with Alex, and you've been to a party at Valerie's house. I've never heard you complain about someone's clothes before."

"It's different." He tried to tie several balloons together. His finger stuck in the string. Several angry yanks shook it free. "I don't need someone around who parties."

"Gee, I remember someone who used to live a wild life." She set the finished cake on the table.

"That was then." Why did he get so worked up? He had to control his emotions. "I don't need anyone in my life like her."

"Excuse me?" Kelly's eyes narrowed as she took a step toward him. "Do you even know what Bethany is really like? Have you already judged her? Jay, you throw back anyone I set you up with, because they're too boring, too good, or too something. You always have an excuse. What are you afraid of?"

He avoided her stare. "Nothing."

"Why won't you trust God to move in your life how he sees fit? Not just in your narrow-minded thinking."

Jason grabbed a balloon and squeezed hard. "I'm *not* narrow-minded."

"Yes, you are. You're holier-than-thou." She took the object out of his hand. "You were a mess, and if anybody needed grace, it was *you*." She shook the balloon in front of his face. "Now, you won't give anyone the time of day, and you withhold grace from everybody you meet. You *can* be good without being obnoxious."

He stormed out the front door. His sister didn't need to tell him how to live. The other girls just weren't his type. Bethany was different, and that's what scared him. She drove him crazy—at work, the gym, his thoughts, and last night in his dreams. He kicked the tire on his car. Maybe he *was* going crazy.

Obviously, his old ways had managed to resurface. Constant prayers hadn't stopped the thoughts about Bethany. No way, he'd let someone like her in his life. Because of his wild past, he'd have to do penance by living alone or marrying some homely girl. A woman like Bethany would be …. Well, he just couldn't go there.

Maybe he'd talk to the pastor or work out harder. Worse case scenario, his physique would improve.

Jason yanked open his car door. Elizabeth's party started in thirty minutes. He couldn't leave. Not now. He had to get his act together. *Please don't let me go back to what I was before.*

When he returned, Kelly waited in the doorway, her brown eyes full of apology. "I'm sorry. I'm on edge with Matt not being able to come home. I shouldn't have attacked you." She held out a balloon. "Friends?"

"Yes." Jason accepted. "I just don't want to mess up."

"You're going to be okay." Kelly squeezed his arm. "Please try to lighten up on yourself and everyone else. God knows you love him. Enjoy your life. It's okay to have fun."

Chapter 7

Bethany chose the *Save the earth, it's the only planet with salsa* mug and finished her breakfast bar as she walked to the break room. Getting in early at work had advantages. At least the coffee would be fresh.

Valerie, hunched over like a mad scientist, stood at the break room counter dropping some unidentifiable fluid from an eyedropper into a cup.

Bethany tried to see over her shoulder. "What are you doing?"

"Feeding a science experiment. A dollop of buttermilk and a touch of sugar, and this baby's ready to go. Several of us take turns feeding Warren's mug. He hasn't touched or noticed the thing in four weeks." Valerie held it toward her.

Bethany recoiled at the green, furry, foul-smelling mass growing at the bottom. "That is sick."

Valerie snickered. "It's great. Maybe we'll create a new life form. You want to join the betting pool?"

"No thanks."

"Suit yourself, but I'll win fifty bucks if he sees it this week." Spouting an evil laugh, Valerie hurried out of the room.

Bethany leaned against the white linoleum counter and waited for the pot to brew. The groan in the hallway told her someone else saw Valerie's concoction.

Jason shook his head as he came in the door. "Man,

that's disgusting. You're not in on this are you?"

"I could barely look at it without feeling queasy."

"I must admit, it is funny." He smiled and pointed to her coffee cup. "I like your mug."

She found herself in uncharted waters. Jason actually seemed pleasant talking about something other than work. Was it the early morning? "Thanks. You like salsa?"

"Sure, but it needs to be hot." He set his mug on the counter. "There's a place on the south side of town that has great salsa and bean dip."

Who was this guy? Couldn't be Jason. *Body snatchers had to be the answer.*

The pot gurgled as it finished brewing. She filled both cups and reached to give him his. Coffee sloshed during the handoff. Liquid spilled down both their shoes. She jumped back. "Yikes. I'm sorry."

"No problem. Spills happen." Jason grabbed several napkins, knelt, held her ankle and wiped off her shoe.

She stared dumfounded.

He finished wiping off his shoes, deposited the trash, and turned toward her. The realization of what he'd done seemed to smack him as his face grew crimson. "Bethany, I am so sorry. I must be spending too much time with my sister's kids. I went on autopilot. I didn't think. I'm sorry I touched you without permission."

She choked on her laughter. "You always ask?"

Jason blinked several times. "Work," he croaked. "I gotta go work." He picked up his half-empty mug and hurried from the room.

With a chuckle, she added creamer and sugar to her coffee. Jason was human after all.

###

Jason splashed cool water on his face and stared into the bathroom mirror. *Idiot. Real smooth. Grab her ankle.* Her silky smooth ankle. He raked his hands through his hair. *God, how do you expect me to be good if you keep tempting me?*

A glimmer of hope flickered as he dried his face. Soon, he'd be out of town on business—without women, without Bethany. Meetings would fill his morning, then lunch. He checked the hall before rushing to his office. Thankfully he didn't have to see her until late in the day. By that time, maybe he could regain a shred of dignity.

###

At eleven o'clock, Bethany closed her computer file and stepped across the hall. "Anyone ready for lunch?"

Valerie glanced her way. "Can't. Have to pick up my alimony check."

"You were married?"

"Not to Alvin. He and I adopted Bill the cat last year when we lived together. He promised to take care of him. We're meeting for lunch."

"You're meeting Alvin?" Rhonda peeked around the corner. "Girl, don't do anything rash."

"You worry too much." Valerie shut down her computer.

Rhonda hurried toward her. "Are you sure you don't want us to go with you?"

"I'll be okay." Valerie rummaged through her purse and pulled out her car keys. "You're worse than my mother. I can take care of myself you know."

"I know." Rhonda took a deep breath and shook her head. "That's why I worry."

"Fine." Valerie growled. "We're meeting at Roma's if you have to keep an eye on us."

The restaurant, located in a strip shopping center, pleasantly surprised Bethany. Each table stood draped in a white tablecloth, cloth napkins, polished silverware, and a small crystal vase with a cluster of wildflowers. A mural depicting the Tuscan countryside adorned the walls. Tantalizing aromas of garlic and baking bread surrounded her as the waiter led them to a table.

Rhonda and Bethany were seated close enough to watch, but not near enough to hear the conversation between Valerie and her lunch partner.

Bethany smoothed her napkin on her lap. "So who is this guy?"

"He's some sweet-talking college professor."

"The cat's father is a professor?" Not bad looking, not handsome either. He did look older with his graying temples against his brown hair. Distinguished? No. She couldn't decide what category he would fit. He studied the menu, only occasionally glancing at Valerie. "I don't like him. He doesn't look at her."

Rhonda shook her head. "I can't say any more. It would be gossiping. I'm just going to pray."

"Right here? Now?"

"Don't worry." Rhonda picked up the menu and stared blankly. "I'll pray in my head with my eyes open. Jesus hears me no matter how I pray."

Her face showed the intensity Bethany's grandmother called storming the gates of heaven. She really wanted to know why this guy bothered Rhonda so much.

Prayer time over, Rhonda relaxed and put down her menu. "Do you know what you're going to have?"

"I'm going to try the chicken scaloppini." She'd skip dinner. "How about you?"

"Better stay with the soup and salad."

Bethany followed Rhonda's gaze back to their workmate.

Valerie stared adoringly at Alvin. He smiled but seemed to focus beyond her—perhaps to the blonde at the next table. *This guy doesn't need prayer. He needs a swift kick in the rear.* Bethany fingered her fork and wondered how far she could throw. "I really don't like that guy."

A tall, thin waiter with an Italian accent dropped off a basket of fresh rolls and took their order. After he left, Rhonda leaned back in her chair. "I had a dream about you the other night."

Bethany buttered a roll. "You did?"

"Yes." Rhonda's eyes crinkled in pleasure. "You were a happy woman. Married to a good man and blessed with children."

"*What* did you eat last night?"

"It wasn't what I ate. I was praying for you."

She nibbled on her melt-in-the mouth treat, not sure she wanted to hear the rest. "Why?"

"I see something special in you." Rhonda leaned closer. "God can heal that broken heart if you let Him."

"I tried. He didn't."

"Maybe you should give Him another chance."

"You don't understand." Bethany put down her roll and crossed her arms. "It's a big mess."

"Honey, God is a *big* God."

Bethany wanted to reply but couldn't think of a

comeback. When the waiter brought their meals, she breathed a sigh of relief. At least she could eat and not answer. She knew God existed. But after Gavin, she ran so far she didn't think she could ever return.

Jason purposefully arrived late for the meeting. Everyone on the team was present, except Warren. Nicole laughed much too loud as she leaned far too close to Alex. Bethany sat between Rhonda and Valerie as the three checked over the latest architectural drawings. Bethany didn't look up.

Jason closed the door behind him and strode to the front of the room. Chairs squeaked and papers shuffled. Avoiding eye contact, he concentrated on the back wall. "As you know, the project is on schedule. I want to thank each of you for your hard work. Next week, Warren and I will travel to the customer's site." He fumbled with his handouts. "I have the latest schedule."

The door opened, and Warren hurried to a chair. He settled in his seat, raised his mug. *The* mug to his lips, and drank.

Rhonda gasped.

Nicole paled, clasped her hand over her mouth, and excused herself.

Bethany groaned and laid her head on the table.

Valerie pumped a fist in the air and laughed hysterically.

Warren cocked an eyebrow. "Did I miss something?"

Chapter 8

Bethany wiped her tears as she left her grandfather's room. He seemed to be fading, more fragile. *Why did anyone have to get old?* She said goodnight to the nursing staff and glanced up to see her parents coming down the hall.

"How is he?" Mom's eyes were moist and red.

"He looks so weak."

"Go on ahead." Dad said to Mom. "I'll be there in a minute. I want to talk with Bethany." He waited until they were alone. "It's time to sell the car. We had another tip from security. I've assigned Scott to watch you."

Things were serious if he would relent on her choice of bodyguards. But selling the car, the last reminder of her grandmother was too much. "Please let me keep it."

"I understand how much her car means to you." His voice lowered. "You can park it in our garage. I'll buy you another one. Your choice, as long as it's something more common … less standout, with no bumper stickers."

"Can I wait until next month?"

"No. Tomorrow, after work, start looking." Tonight, Dad's eyes held a hint of sadness, or concern. She couldn't tell which. Either way, something had happened to worry him, and that knocked the fight out of her. "My choice?"

He didn't blink. "Call me before you sign the papers, and I'll come or send my lawyer."

The creepy factor just went up. Bethany resisted looking over her shoulder. "Can you tell me what's going on?"

"No. But when I tell you to be careful—I mean it. Be careful."

She resisted the urge to salute. Instead, she did the unthinkable and hugged him.

He stiffened for a moment and then returned her hug. If things hadn't been so serious, she would have smiled. Hugs were rare occurrences.

"I love you." He whispered under his breath. "Be careful."

She almost fainted.

Bethany checked her surroundings as she crossed the parking lot. Moonlight flicked eerie shadows from the stand of trees to the left. The click of her high heels on the pavement echoed, bringing unwanted attention. Suddenly feeling small, she glanced back at the front doors where Dad waited and watched—his presence reassuring.

The lights blinked on a black sedan. Scott was ready.

She hated to admit Dad was right about her car. She might as well drive a neon light. Bumper stickers lined the back and the rear window. Tonight they looked like targets. She trembled. As soon as she got home, she'd surf the net for the best deal.

The next morning, Bethany slumped in her office chair and tried to concentrate on her project. Most of her night had been spent online. Fortunately, a dealer nearby had the perfect model. During lunch she'd close the deal.

"Are you okay?"

Bethany flinched when she heard Rhonda's voice behind her. "Yeah, fine."

"You? Jumpy? What's up?" Rhonda pulled a chair next

to her. "Want to talk?"

"No. I'm fine, really." She moved papers aside and knocked over her bottle of water. She grabbed the container before too much damage. Thankfully, nothing spilled on important documents or her computer. "I'm okay."

"Uh, huh." Rhonda handed her a handful of tissues and helped her clean the mess. "Could you use some prayers?"

"Yes."

"Goodness girl, with that quick reaction, I'll make sure I pray extra hard. You don't need to give me specifics. You do know you can call me anytime." She wrote down several numbers on a sheet and handed it to her. "And I do mean anytime."

Bethany finished cleaning her desk. She had to get her thoughts focused. "You don't know anything about buying a car, do you?"

"Not much."

Valerie dashed into Bethany's cubicle. "Did I hear car shopping? Can I come, huh? Please? I love watching salesmen squirm."

Rhonda stood. "I do *not* want to watch. Val helped me buy my car. She got me a great deal, but her interesting negotiating tactics just about did me in. I think I'm still having heart palpitations."

On the way to the dealer, Bethany shared with Valerie what make, model, and price she wanted, the automobile high on the green list for environmental friendliness. A deal was already negotiated through the dealer's Internet sales department.

When they arrived, three salesmen wearing white shirts, dark ties, and dark slacks huddled on the front steps of the dealership.

"Buzzards waiting for their next meal." Valerie muttered.

"They're just trying to make a living." Bethany opened her door and almost knocked over a clean-cut salesman with the face of a choirboy.

He stepped back and flashed a perfect, white, no-cavity smile. "Welcome ladies. How can I help you today?"

"I need to see someone in the Internet sales department." She took a quick peek at the hybrid car she wanted.

"Are you sure?" He stayed with her. "I'd be glad to help. Probably get you a better deal. Would you like to take a test drive?"

"I don't need to take up your time. I'm sure they can help me."

Valerie grabbed the salesman's arm and moved close against him. "She means we would *love* to take a test drive."

His face reddened and his Adams apple bobbed with a swallow. "I'll be right back with the keys."

Bethany waited until he left. "He won't get a commission since I've already got a quote. All I have to do is sign the papers."

"Either way, you need to give the car a good look. Plus, he's kind of cute."

"You're interested in the salesman? He looks like he just got out of high school."

Valerie leaned against the car with a smile that said trouble was brewing. "I'm ready for someone younger. You know, train him."

"He's not a dog."

"No, but somebody as cute as he is surely could learn to sit and play. He might even fetch me a few things."

"Just make sure your puppy has shots. Trust me, I know

these things."

An hour and a half later, Bethany drove her new car back to the office, and Valerie had a date scheduled for Friday night. Thanks to smooth negotiations, her dad agreed to the price and all details were arranged over the phone.

Strange how life seemed to be falling into place. In just a few months, she worked at a good job, made contact with her old buddy, and had a new car, a new apartment, and new friends. Valerie blew huge gum bubbles and pulled the resulting goo off her face. Some of the friends were unique, but that made life interesting.

What was she thinking? Soon, she'd be out of Southburg and starting a new life. She stared at the road. For some reason, right now, the idea didn't sound that appealing.

Jason checked his flight arrangements, notes, handouts, and architectural drawings for tomorrow's meeting. Everything seemed to be ready, but he still needed to check. He rounded the corner to Nicole's cubicle. "Have you seen Warren?"

She turned in her chair, obviously posing her low-cut red blouse for the maximum effect. "He called in sick. He's covered in poison ivy from working in his yard. I've got the data if you need to go over anything."

Jason averted his eyes and rubbed his forehead. "Let me find out how bad it is."

A quick phone call told him there was no way Warren could join the trip. Needing guidance, Jason hurried down the hall to George Canton's office.

"Come on in." George gave him a smile of anticipation. "Are you ready for tomorrow's meeting?"

"We've got a major problem. Warren can't come."

George's smile faded as he twirled and clicked his pen. Twirl and click, twirl and click. The pen stilled. "Take Nicole. I'm sure she can fill in additional details."

Jason inwardly groaned. Gone were his plans for escape from women. At least their flight left early in the morning, the meeting would take the day, and then they'd return late that night. No problem.

The next morning, Bethany settled in for her day. She couldn't believe she actually missed seeing Jason in his office. Such a strange emotion—and one she couldn't afford.

Valerie carried a clipboard as she entered Bethany's work space. "Would you like to sponsor me?"

"Sure, what you are you raising money for? The society for creation of strange coffee mug life forms?"

"No." Valerie propped herself on Bethany's desk. "I want to fly to Aruba. James and I need some time away."

"James?"

"The car salesman." Smugness laced Valerie's smile.

"No information please. If I give you a dollar, will you go away?"

"Five and you won't see me the rest of the day."

Bethany couldn't believe she handed over five bucks, but watching Valerie skip back to her cubicle made the loss worthwhile.

Aruba sounded great. Bethany leaned back in her chair. Would she ever meet someone to enjoy life with? The last time she was on a beach was her honeymoon. Her stomach churned. That memory threw a damper on her disposition. *Gavin.* The man she had adored and fallen in love with. The man she saved herself for and who promised to love her forever. So much for that promise.

The fairy tale evaporated on the honeymoon. In the warm sunshine, Gavin's dark sunglasses rested on his perfect, roman nose as he pretended to read. His eyes never met the pages—instead they kept focus on every woman who walked past.

She shoved back from her desk and hurried to the break room for a shot of strong coffee.

Jason said a silent prayer as he drove to the airport. Dark thunderclouds boiled in the evening sky, but even they couldn't dampen his mood. The meeting had been a huge success, and a lucrative contract waited in his briefcase. The customer seemed pleased, and Nicole answered every question directed toward her with surprising professionalism.

Raindrops smacked with the velocity of water balloons. Shame he didn't pack a wet suit. He dropped Nicole and their drawings at the terminal and drove to the rental car return. Rain or no rain, with the flight leaving soon, there was no way to make it gracefully. He charted his course, grabbed his briefcase, and dodged puddles the size of Lake Erie.

By the time he made it inside, his new suit stuck to his skin like tree frogs on a window. Why couldn't humans shake off like a dog? He slogged toward a foot-tapping, glaring Nicole.

"You aren't going to believe this." She shook her red-clawed finger in his face. "They've cancelled our flight."

"No problem." Jason peeled off his jacket. "We'll take

another airline."

"No. You don't understand. With this storm, every flight is cancelled. Not that a dinky airport like this would have much to offer. We're stuck." She pulled out her flaming red cell phone. Her angry voice echoed louder than the rumble of thunder.

He collapsed on a bench. Too far to drive home, and in this weather not an option, trapped in an airport with an irate woman. What a mess.

Nicole snapped closed her phone. "I'm *not* staying in an airport. The company can put us up in a hotel. We passed one down the street."

Tension squeezed at the base of his neck. Staying in a hotel with Nicole? Not a pretty picture. He dialed George Canton's number and explained the predicament. Getting the contract made George's day. He insisted they find a nice hotel, stay the night, and have a big dinner on the company.

Nicole held out a map. "Here are the directions to the mall. You'll have to drive me, since I'm without an overnight bag. I need to pick up a few things."

A great day ruined by a thunderstorm. And from the look on Nicole's face, his evening would not be pleasant. Convinced there wasn't a dry spot on his body, he didn't bother to run to retrieve the car from the rental lot or later when he parked at the mall. What was the use? He couldn't get any wetter.

Nicole, still perfectly put together, frowned as he slogged in the door of the department store. "I'll meet you in forty-five minutes at the perfume section."

Jason left a trail of waterlogged footprints as he grabbed a pack of underwear, jeans, shirt, socks, an umbrella, and some casual shoes. At least his sister would be pleased he went clothes shopping.

After paying for his purchases, he changed clothes in the men's room. He waited at the perfume counter, waving off the saleswomen, and trying not to get ill from the overpowering smells. If he'd been with Warren, they'd have gotten a steak and hung out at the huge sporting goods store. He leaned against a chair next to the cosmetics counter and stared at the floor.

"I want to buy one more thing for tonight." Nicole's breathy voice whispered in his ear.

He cringed as he faced her.

Her smile broke him out in a sweat. "You can help me pick something."

Warning bells clanged in his head. Trying to keep his attention from her new tight jeans, he said a silent plea for help as he followed her down the corridors of the mall.

She stopped in front of the lingerie shop. "I'll let you choose."

He gulped and backpedaled. "No. You're on your own. I'll meet you at the car."

Chapter 9

At five o'clock, Bethany washed down two aspirin with half a bottle of water and attempted to fumble through their latest project. If Jason were here, she'd pick his brain. His office had looked so dark and empty. The guy was only gone for one day, and she missed him. The thought sent a flutter of surprise up her spine. She couldn't think that way, not with a co-worker and not with somebody nice like Jason.

Valerie waved five dollars as she sashayed into Bethany's cubicle. "Come on, I'll buy you a drink."

"I thought I wouldn't see you for the rest of the day."

"You didn't. It's officially evening. James and I are meeting some friends for dinner and drinks."

"Wait a minute. Are you using the money I gave you?"

"No way. That's tucked safely in my wild-and-crazy spending fund." She patted her chest. "Come on, you'll have fun. Get out and enjoy life."

Bethany smiled at the irony. Just a few months ago she had pushed Nadia, her college roommate, to have fun. Those days were over, and being back in the hometown made things more difficult. Mom wanted her to get back to church, find a nice guy, settle down, and raise a family. That option only left a shredded heart and kept the gossips busy. Bethany cleared off her desk and gathered her things. "Give me directions, and I'll meet you there. I need to run home and walk my dog."

###

Jason focused on his meal—the steak wasn't too bad for a hotel restaurant. Nicole's conversation became animated and much more suggestive and aggressive after she finished her third glass of wine. The last thing he needed was trouble. With food still on his plate, he signaled the waiter for the check.

"What's the hurry?" Nicole's hand rested on his as she leaned closer, her low-cut sweater barely covering....

He cleared his throat, pulled away, and fixed his gaze on her forehead. "We've had a long day. I need to look over a few things for work."

"I've got a few things you can look over."

Jason stood. A few years ago he would have jumped at the opportunity to be with Nicole. Why was doing the right thing so blasted hard?

She rose and stumbled against him. "I seem to be a little dizzy. Would you help me to my room?" She giggled. "I guess I had a teensy bit too much wine."

The waiter handed Jason the check. "Have a nice night."

Fighting the urge to knock the smirk off the waiter's face, Jason over-tipped so he wouldn't have to wait for change.

Before he could move, her body pressed tightly against his arm. He swallowed hard. *I don't need this. I don't want to be like I was.* He had to get out of this mess before he did something he'd regret.

The hallway to their rooms lengthened to a mile. He tried to keep himself steady while Nicole babbled incessantly about him being strong and handsome. Sweat trickled down his back, and he stifled the urge to curse. He stopped in front of her door.

She leaned her back against him as she searched through her handbag for her room access card. Her soft blonde hair tickled his neck. "Here it is."

The door opened with a click.

She wrapped her arms around him. "Please stay."

Why not? He had been good for a long time. Didn't that count for something? He helped her into the room and sat her in a chair. "I need to leave. You're drunk, and we work together."

Nicole stared at the carpet. "You're right." Her shoulders drooped. "I'm sorry I came on so strong. I'm getting a major headache anyway. Do you have any aspirin?"

"No, but you can probably get some from the front desk."

"Would you mind getting it for me? I would hate for anyone else to see me like this." She blinked her eyes at him. "Jason, thank you for being such a sweet guy, it means a lot to me."

Against his better judgment, he nodded. "I'll be back in a few minutes."

Bethany checked her rearview mirror for the third time. *Still no sign of Scott.* Maybe Dad gave him the evening off. Surely bodyguards wouldn't be watching for all twenty-four hours of the day. No time to worry about that right now. The dog needed a walk, and she needed to change.

Jedi and his hyper-active wagging tail met her at the door. Dog toys strewn about the den showed the path of his playfulness during her absence. She spent time petting him before she put him on his leash. If she ever found someone as loyal and loving as Jedi, she'd marry him in a heartbeat. At least her faithful, furry companion would never leave.

Bethany followed the prancing dog as he sniffed his way around the grassy area. She surveyed the latest additions to the parking lot. Being one of the first to move into the complex did have advantages. She could match each car with an apartment. The Corvette belonged to Andrew in 5E. The black pickup truck matched with creepy Clint. The BMW went with 3C.

The only unidentified car was a blue sedan in the last parking space. Strange. How many people sit in a car to read the newspaper at dusk? Maybe he was waiting for someone. Just the same, she hurried Jedi back to the apartment and peeked out the window.

The car hadn't moved, nor the guy. Was he trouble? Should she call someone? Or take a baseball bat and beat the truth out of him? Okay, maybe she shouldn't have watched that action movie last night. Unfortunately, Jedi wasn't a Doberman. She smiled at the thought of putting a healthy dose of whipped cream on his little Shih Tzu face to make him look like a mad dog.

She changed into jeans and a casual top and knelt in front of Jedi. "I want you to bark really deep and loud if anyone knocks." He wagged his tail and licked her nose. *So much for that idea.*

She checked the parking lot again. The man remained in the car, paper down, staring her way.

A tingling sensation prickled her scalp. Without the options of a baseball bat or a big dog, she phoned Scott.

Tylenol bottle in hand, Jason rehearsed his good

intentions on the way back to Nicole's room. Had he just passed some cosmic test? Throw the good-looking girl at Jason and see what happens. He may have wavered, but he didn't fall. Surely that counted for something. All he had to do was toss her the meds and lock himself in his room for the night.

He stopped outside her door. Maybe he could shove it under and run. What an idiot, she could barely stand. If anything, she'd probably be passed out on the floor. He knocked. "Nicole, it's me."

"The door's open."

Tension dug into his shoulders. *Throw her the pills and run.* The only light came from a candle flickering on the nightstand. He closed the door behind him. Nicole lay across the bed in her lingerie like someone posed for a centerfold.

His feet cemented to the floor as he tried not to stare. *So much for passing the test.*

"I've been waiting for you." Her soft, breathy voice stirred his emotions.

"No." He shook his head, needing to run but wanting to stay.

"What do you mean?" She sat up. "Don't you want me?"

He focused on the carpeting. "No, I won't do it."

She said nothing until he looked at her again. Her face hardened. "No one turns me down."

Willing his feet to move, he turned toward the door.

"You'll be sorry, Jason. *Nobody* turns me down."

Bethany peeked through the blinds to check the parking lot. The mystery car sat in the same spot but now without a driver. She checked her watch. Scott told her he was already there and would report with information in ten minutes. Twenty minutes had passed. Trying to stifle her growing imagination, she rubbed the goose bumps pebbling on her arms.

Why so nervous? Last year, she single-handedly wrestled a purse snatcher. Now she cowered in her apartment. Maybe she needed a large, healthy dose of chocolate.

A deep throaty growl from Jedi made the hair on her head stand at attention. She prayed for help and then chided herself for praying. Conversations with the man upstairs halted years ago. Would he even remember who she was? Then again, he probably did and would squash her like a bug for her misbehavior after the divorce. Either way, she hoped he'd listen now.

A knock on the door flipped her heart. Jedi barked hysterically and hid behind her legs. On tiptoes she checked the peep-hole. *Scott.* Relief made her legs wobble. Ugh, weakness was for sissies. Composing herself, she opened the door with a smile.

Scott raised an eyebrow as he entered the apartment and shut the door behind him. "I had a little talk with your stalker."

"My stalker?"

"He *was* watching the building."

"Really?" Bethany perched on the couch as Jedi sniffed Scott's legs. "Why?"

He crossed his arms on his muscular chest. "Are you familiar with Donna Martin?"

"Donna? The girl next door?"

"That was her boyfriend waiting for her to get home."

Total and absolute humiliation. Heat emanated from every pore of her body. "I guess I owe you an apology. Sorry to make you come over."

A smile flickered across his face then disappeared. "You did the right thing. With your dad's business, you can't afford to take chances."

Unsure if his comment made her feel better or not, she gave Jedi a good petting, grabbed her purse, and locked the door behind her. She needed a drink.

Jason flipped on the television. Why did he turn down Nicole? She might not be his type, but she was attractive and available. Who was he kidding? He didn't even know what he needed anymore. Maybe he could have placated Nicole with some line about dating someone else.

Right.

The only females he hung around with were his sister and niece. He hadn't been on a date in five months.

Three choices. Get to bed and try to forget about it. Go back to her room. Or, find the military channel and try to relax by watching something get blown up.

He raked his hands through his hair and turned toward the door.

Bethany weaved her way through the crowded restaurant bar until she found Valerie perched on a stool in a sea of desperate-looking men.

"I thought you chickened out on me." Valerie reeked of alcohol.

"Just needed to take care of a few things at home." Bethany sat next to her friend and ignored the leer of the middle-aged man hovering nearby. "Did you eat already?"

"Yeah, I've had some nachos, peanuts, and a couple of drinks." Valerie pushed the remnants of the appetizer toward her. "James is in the bathroom. I don't think the nachos agreed with him."

Bethany signaled a waiter, ordered a drink and Buffalo wings.

Valerie nudged her. "Lots of guys checking you out. There's a real cute one at the table over there. All you'd have to do is smile."

"No thanks." She did glance over her shoulder. Being back home made her feel caged, unable to relax. Not that letting go of inhibitions had gotten her anywhere while away at college.

Valerie lit a cigarette and studied her. "What is it with you? I don't see you as the prudish type, so I figure you've been burned."

"More like toasted."

"Toasted? That's major. Who did that?"

Bethany gulped her drink and instantly regretted the decision. The alcohol set her throat on fire. Four months without hard liquor sure changed her stamina. She coughed to regain her voice. "My ex-husband."

"Sorry about that. Ex's can be bad." Valerie took a long drag on her cigarette. "I've been there done that. We were both eighteen and ran off on the night of our high school graduation. Made it through the summer, until we realized we still wanted to go to college in different states. Neither of us would budge, so he took off with our stuff while I was at work and left me with the bills—including some for expensive gifts to a girl he had on the side. My dad had the Zucchini brothers visit him."

"The Zucchini brothers?"

"Yeah, my ex hated zucchini. So the two men told him that was their names when they went to *talk* with him." Valerie laughed far too loud. "I bet he hates that veggie even more now."

"Shame I didn't know you a few years ago. I could've given the brothers another job."

"They would've helped. They love their work." Valerie glanced toward the restrooms. "I better go check on James. I'll be right back."

Bethany smiled to herself at the thought of Gavin receiving a *talk*. Unfortunately that wouldn't have changed what happened. She pushed her drink away and ordered a coke.

"You from these here parts?" A young man wearing a cowboy hat, jeans, western shirt, and a little-boy grin stood next to her.

"I grew up in the area."

"I'm not from here." He took a swig from his beer bottle and wiped his mouth. "Just passing through."

"I might've guessed that."

"Yeah, everybody says I have an accent. But a part of me will always be back home. You can't forget your raisins."

"Raisins?"

"You know, how your parents raised you. They make you a better person. Funny talking about this in a bar though, ya know? Maybe we should be sitting in the restaurant area." He pointed with his bottle.

"That's okay. I'm fine here."

"No problem. We can stay." His shoulders fell, and he scuffed his well-worn boot on the floor. "Anyways, I guess I'm thinking hard about this 'cause my grandma passed away last night. Makes you more aware of family and such. I've even been trying to get back on the right track." His eyes moist, he blinked and sniffled. "I'm on my way back home."

Bethany placed her hand on the young man's arm. "I'm sorry about your grandmother."

He swallowed hard. "Thank ya. She was a good woman." His voice cracked, and he cleared his throat. "Well, I best be going. Take care of yourself."

"I will. You too."

Valerie returned and shot a curious glance at Bethany as the stranger walked away. "I leave you for a few minutes, and you pick up a baby cowboy? What were you talking about?"

"Raisins."

"Wow, you really do need to get out more often."

Bethany drank her coke and shrugged to stave off her whirling thoughts and emotions. "I'm not sure what I need anymore."

James didn't recover, and the evening plans were cancelled. Since sitting in a bar alone wasn't high on her fun list, Bethany parked her car and glanced at the time. Ugh, not even ten o'clock and already back home.

College life had been easier. Classes, studying, or partying filled the days and nights. Self-medication with booze kept away bad memories. Getting her life together started before graduation, when her roommate shared a past secret. Bethany needed to be strong then for Nadia. Now Bethany wasn't sure what to do. She couldn't even take a drink or hang out in a bar without somebody talking about something spiritual.

What if she turned into a boring person?

In the bright moonlight, she half-heartedly checked her apartment parking lot. Jedi met her at the door, his tail wagging with the intensity of an airplane propeller. At least he found her fascinating.

She grabbed his leash for one final walk. Maybe a little fresh air would regain her perspective on life.

Jedi pawed and sniffed his way around back to the pet enclosure. The blue car was gone and in its place sat a black paneled van. No way she'd get paranoid again . . . even if someone sat inside . . . someone big. She picked up Jedi and marched back to her apartment. That did it.

Tomorrow she'd buy a stun gun, mace, pepper spray, a baseball bat, or take the gun her dad had offered.

Chapter 10

Jason placed the briefcase on his office desk and collapsed in the chair. The morning couldn't have been more uncomfortable. Nicole didn't say a word at breakfast, during their wait at the airport, or on their flight. At least back in his own territory he remained safe. She could be avoided, and hopefully she'd set her sights on some other victim.

His conscience, for the most part, remained clean. Did they give out gold stars in heaven for turning down attractive girls? *Not bad for an ex-reprobate.*

He focused his attention on the stack of waiting papers and a note from Bethany. A realization immediately deflated his ego. If Bethany had been on the trip, he would never have walked away.

###

Hunger pains called, Bethany checked Valerie's office. A handwritten *Out to lunch* sign covered her computer screen. With Valerie, that could mean just about anything. Rhonda had already left for a doctor's appointment. Bethany's stomach growled for the third time. She really wanted to try the new Mexican restaurant, but didn't want to go alone and didn't want fast food.

Jason. Maybe he could go. She knocked and stepped

inside his office. "Want something hot?"

He blinked, stared at her like she was some strange being. "You mean lunch?" His voice broke.

"There's a new place that opened this week. I hear the salsa's great. I know you just got in from your trip, but I do need to ask you a few things on the project."

"Right. I got your note." He moved a stack of papers aside. "Lunch sounds nice."

Bethany turned and almost ran into Nicole.

"You two going out?" Nicole swayed over to Jason and kissed his cheek. "Thank you for last night."

Jason's face ignited red. He gaped for a moment then composed himself. "Anytime you need aspirin after you drink too much, I'll be glad to help."

Nicole's glare could have charbroiled a steak. With a huff she stomped away.

Bethany bit her tongue to keep from laughing. "Looks like your trip was interesting."

He didn't look amused. "Nothing happened."

"You don't need to explain. If anyone knows what it's like to be misunderstood, it's me. Let's just leave it at that."

Jason stared at Bethany. Maybe he should give her the same benefit of the doubt she gave him. Either way, he needed to talk to someone before the situation with Nicole got out of hand. "Give me a few minutes. I'll meet you downstairs." Taking two steps at a time, he hurried to talk to the one person who would understand, the man who led him to a relationship with Christ two years ago.

George Canton smiled and offered his hand. "Great job

on the meeting. You should have taken the afternoon off."

"I wanted to get a few things done." Jason closed the door. "I need to tell you something."

"Looks serious."

"The meeting was a huge success. Nicole did a great job, but ..." Jason sat and tried to formulate the words. "Can you turn around your boss collar and talk as a friend?"

"Sure." He flipped the end of his tie over his shoulder. "What's going on?"

"I don't want to spread anything negative. Nicole celebrated with a few drinks and got a little too friendly. I helped her to her room. She asked for aspirin which I went and got. Beyond that, nothing happened. I don't want this to affect work or our reputations."

George leaned back in his chair. "Okay. So, nothing happened. As a friend, I'm proud of you. As a boss, I'll be watching to make sure this doesn't become a problem."

"I understand. I just wanted you to know."

Bethany tried to sort through her emotions as she waited in the lobby for Jason. Why did she care if something happened on his business trip? It wasn't like they were dating. And why on earth were her nerves jangling? No big deal, lunch with a co-worker. A handsome, hunk of a co-worker. But all the same, they worked together. They couldn't date, could they?

Jason smiled as he strode toward her, and a tingle crawled up her spine. Shame she didn't have a Taser, she'd use it on herself. A good jolt of electricity would end this schoolgirl attitude.

He palmed his keys. "I'll drive, if you show me the

way."

"It's a deal."

He led her to a Honda Accord and opened her door. A small baseball glove and bat rested on the back seat. Not exactly what she pictured a guy like him driving. Something tougher, like a Jeep.

He looked apologetic as he buckled his seat belt. "I bought the car to drive my niece and nephew around."

Did he read her mind, or was her surprise that obvious? "Your car's nice. Just thought you'd drive something more rugged."

"I sold my Dodge Viper two years ago." He grimaced and gripped the wheel as though reliving a painful memory.

"Do you know the days and hours since you let it go?"

Jason glanced at his watch before he pulled into traffic. "Sixteen months, five days, and fourteen minutes."

"You're joking, right?"

"I may be off by a few minutes." His smile made her face heat.

Grateful for air conditioning, she adjusted the vent. What was *with* her? Girls her age didn't have hot flashes. Why did he affect her this way? If only she could get in his head and find out more about him.

"You had some questions?"

He *could* read her mind. She contemplated jumping out of the car.

"You needed some information for the project?"

"Oh?" Bethany couldn't remember the questions. "Sorry, I think I need to eat. The brain is running slow."

At the restaurant, Bethany scooped salsa on a chip and let the mellowing begin, something about the blend of tomatoes, onion and cilantro calmed her soul.

Jason shoveled in a healthy portion and erupted in a coughing fit.

She kept her grin at bay. "I thought you liked it hot."

He chugged his water. "Must have gone down my windpipe."

"You can have mine." She moved her untouched glass toward him.

"Thanks, I'll be fine."

Totally content, she finished her salsa and looked longingly at Jason's still-full bowl. If only her straw would reach, she'd suck down that spicy concoction in a heartbeat.

The waiter took their orders and refilled her empty one. She didn't hesitate to have more.

Jason chewed on a chip. "I'm impressed. How did you get such a cast-iron stomach?"

"Two older brothers into challenges and a dad in the military. I received training on the battlefield."

"Must be some interesting stories from your childhood."

"Definitely. How about you?"

"One older sister, so there's not much to tell." He shifted in his chair and finished what was left in his glass.

Interesting. He looked as uncomfortable as she did talking about the past, which only ramped up her curiosity. "Where did you grow up?"

"In Raleigh. Not too far from where you went to college."

Bethany choked on a chip. He lived in the same area? *Please don't let it be at the same time.* "When did you move away?"

"It's been five years. I worked in the Chicago office."

Good. Their paths probably wouldn't have crossed. "I wanted to work in Chicago, even sent off a resume, but life got in the way."

"Mind if I ask what happened?"

Probably Karma from not living right. "My dad had a stroke."

He leaned forward. "Is he okay?"

"He's doing well. He's not one to let anything stop him."

The waiter delivered their order. Grateful for the interruption, Bethany rolled a fajita and tried to think of something to say ... anything that wouldn't get too personal. Subjects before age eighteen were okay. The next few years, Gavin's presence stamped a dark hole void of time and full of pain. College memories left self-inflicted regrets. She scooped some salsa onto a chip. The past was over.

"You okay?" Jason searched her face, his expression curious.

The mind reading thing had to stop. "Must have gotten a hot bite." She peered around the room and screeched to a stop. Tom Chambers sat two tables away wearing a mischievous smile. Is he here for lunch or as a reporter?

She jerked her vision back to Jason and almost laughed when she spotted her bodyguard at a table across the restaurant. Maybe she should send Scott to check on Tom. *Nah, he's harmless.* So many men, so little time.

"Are you sure you're okay? Too much salsa?"

"You can *never* have too much salsa."

Jason rubbed his chin, and cleared his throat. "Since you grew up in the area, do you have a church home?"

Quick and very uncomfortable subject change. Bethany focused on the drops of salsa trailing from the bowl to her plate. "My family's been involved in the same one since we moved here." He didn't need to know she avoided their church like the plague.

"That's good." He seemed relieved. "Church is good."

Smart, great-looking, with a sense of humor, and religious—a deadly combination. The last guy who fit that description took her heart and ripped it to shreds. "We better get back to work."

In the evening light, Bethany balanced her sack of groceries and fumbled with her keys. Shopping on an empty stomach added at least fifteen items. She'd stayed late trying to get ready for tomorrow's meeting, plus work kept her mind off Jason. Not as much as she hoped but any distraction helped. She unlocked the door, and placed her bag on the kitchen counter. "Jedi?"

No response.

She checked her bedroom and closet. Everything looked the same but something felt odd. Jedi's toys remained in his basket in the corner of the den, his food and water untouched. Why was the bathroom door closed? Strange. It always remained open when she wasn't home. She grabbed her purse, pulled out her Taser, and cell phone. If somebody hurt Jedi, she'd zap the offending party until his hair fried.

She froze, head cocked, ears straining at a noise inside the bathroom. *Call Scott.*

Ignoring the thought, heart thumping, she crept forward. Lungs begging for oxygen, she drew in a breath and reached for the knob.

Taser ready to fire, she swung open the door.

Her gaze swept the room. Empty, except for Jedi sprawled on the floor next to a half-eaten chew bone. He whimpered and opened one eye. His tail rose to half-mast, quivered in a wag, and fell to the floor.

She rushed forward and cradled him in her arms. *Where did he get that bone?* Fighting back tears, she held him close and called Scott.

Twenty minutes later, Bethany paced in the lobby of the animal hospital. The veterinarian didn't think the substance on the bone was poison, but the poor pup would be looped out and sleepy for a few more hours.

Who would do such a thing? Her mind whirled through a mental list of the things in her apartment. What if it wasn't the workman? No, she wouldn't get paranoid again. Management did have workers checking the appliances.

First thing in the morning, everyone would be questioned by Dad's security team. As a precaution, Scott made sure her locks were changed and the windows bolted. Maybe she'd buy a Doberman as a guard dog for Jedi.

Fortunately, Dad moved Scott next door. She could probably bang on the wall of her kitchen, and he'd come running. That might be a problem if she started dating again. Ugh. Why on earth did she agree to move back home?

"Miss Davis?" The female vet assistant carried Jedi. "He's ready to go home."

Her furry baby's tail wagged as Bethany took him in her arms. "He looks better. Did you give him a strong drink of coffee?"

The girl laughed and stroked his fur. "Nothing quite that pleasant. He may be a bit hungry since we made sure nothing remained in his stomach."

"I'll take good care of him."

Bethany drove home with Jedi curled on her lap. She'd take him to work with her if she could. Maybe, put him in a little pouch like a papoose. Thank goodness he'd be okay. At the thought of losing him, she realized someone else needed to be thanked for his protection. "Thank you, God, for letting Jedi be okay." She couldn't believe she actually prayed, much less out loud. Praying for someone else was always easier.

Jedi's tail wagged and he looked at her with those sweet, trusting, puppy dog eyes.

Maybe God hadn't given up on her.

Chapter 11

Thirty minutes late, Bethany hurried to her desk. She couldn't bring herself to leave Jedi this morning without giving him a thorough petting and double-checking the doors and windows. Scott promised to call by noon if they learned anything about the work crew. If she ever got her hands on the jerk who did that to Jedi, she'd tear him to pieces.

"Good Morning." Rhonda handed her a report. "Are you ready for the meeting?"

"Yikes. I totally forgot. Let me grab my things." Bethany rushed to find her paperwork and then joined Rhonda in the hall.

"Is everything okay?" Rhonda fell in step beside her on their way to the conference room.

"Somebody came in my apartment and drugged my dog."

"What?" Rhonda stopped. "Is he okay? Are you okay? Did they take anything?"

"We're both fine. It may have been a workman. I don't think anything is missing." She tried to tamp down the rising suspicion of something more sinister.

"If you ever need me, call. My son's a big guy. He's planning on going into law enforcement when he graduates." Rhonda placed her gentle hand on Bethany's arm. "I'll pray for your protection."

"Thank you, I think we can both use it." Ignoring Alex and Nicole, Bethany sat next to Valerie at the rectangular table.

Valerie leaned in close. "What's going on? Why do you need prayer?"

"Somebody drugged my dog."

"What?" Her spiky hair trembled. "Oh man, I would feed somebody like that to sharks. Do you know who it was?"

"Not yet."

"You need me to call my *friends*?" Valerie's eyebrows danced up and down.

Bethany grinned. "You mean the former Zucchini brothers who could now be called the SBCA brothers? The Society that Beats the Crud out of Animal Abusers?"

Valerie laughed out loud and high-fived Bethany. "Oh yeah."

Rhonda held up her hands, amusement dancing in her eyes. "Girls, I'm going to start praying right now if you don't behave."

"Are you ready?" Jason cleared his throat and pointed to the whiteboard filled with dates and project notes. "We have lots to go over."

She didn't even realize he was in the room. *Whew, he looks good.*

Wearing a smile, he stopped at her chair. "You have some notes on the Bradford project?"

He even smelled good. Shave cream, soap, and some kind of spring-smelling fabric softener on his clothes. *Nothing like a clean man to help forget problems.*

"Do you have them with you?" He held out his hand.

Papers. Files. Focus. She gave him the folder.

"She's probably thinking about her dog." Valerie said. "Somebody drugged him."

A look of concern flashed across Jason's face. "Someone was in your apartment?" He picked up a pen and scrawled numbers on a piece of paper. "This is my cell and home number. Don't hesitate to call if you need anything."

Bethany took the note. She could hear a pin drop. Heat rose to her face as everyone just sat there staring.

Jason's face glowed red. He positioned himself at the front of the room and focused above their heads. "We have two weeks to get phase one done. Alex, you're scheduled at the end of next week to visit the customer. Nicole, you and Warren need to be finished by this coming Wednesday. Bethany, Valerie, and Rhonda meet me back here after lunch today. The rest of the schedule is on this handout or on the board." He passed out the papers and left the room.

Nicole shot looks at Bethany that could cut through steel.

Bethany gathered her papers. *What an interesting predicament.* Was Jason being nice or did she notice something more? And if so, would that be a problem?

Jason splashed cold water on his face. *I'm always in the bathroom, trying to recoup after an idiotic move.* He dried off with a paper towel and stared in the mirror. He might as well have broadcast on the loud speaker he liked Bethany. Why couldn't he have waited and done that in private? Noooo, he had to hand her his numbers with everyone on the team watching.

He could see it now, like some court martial, George Canton stripping away his title. *Back to the rank and file Jason, you've once again become a heathen.* Two years of being good and Bethany walks into his life and he throws in the towel.

Then again, he offered his number because he cared. He

hadn't done anything wrong. She was attractive and being attracted to someone wasn't a problem. Who was he kidding? He'd give Bethany his apartment key if she wanted.

The bathroom door opened, and Alex strode toward him. "Interesting meeting, Jason. You're getting quite the reputation around here."

"What are you talking about?"

"First the incident with Nicole, and now you're passing out your numbers to Bethany. I thought you said you didn't do those sorts of things since you're a Christian."

Jason clenched his fists and considered hitting Alex. *Great. Someone challenges my faith and I think about bashing in his face.* He did a quick count to ten.

"Nothing happened with Nicole, and giving my number to a co-worker shouldn't be a problem for you or anyone else."

Alex shrugged. "Right. Whatever you want to believe."

Jason waited until Alex left and then returned to his office. Absolutely no way to win, he collapsed in his chair and considered his options. Something had to give. He couldn't live like this. People would talk no matter what he did.

The facts were that Bethany's family attended church. That meant stability and hopefully the same belief system. He couldn't deny the attraction. What did he have to lose by asking her out?

He pushed out of his chair. *Might as well take the plunge.*

Bethany stopped by the break room and grabbed a cup of coffee. Jason's sweet concern only made things more difficult. She liked him but didn't want to. Someone who seemed nice could have ulterior motives. Dating jerks was easier, definitely not better, but at least you knew what to expect. She checked her watch. If only Jedi could answer the phone.

Valerie waited in the hall. "You've been holding out on me."

"What do you mean?"

"Look on your desk."

Bethany turned the corner and almost fell over at the sight of a dozen red roses in a crystal vase. She fingered the card not sure she wanted to know.

Valerie peeked over her shoulder. "Come on, who are they from?"

Bethany opened the envelope. *Would love to see you again. Give me a call. Tom.*

"Who's Tom?"

"Just a guy."

"A guy who sends roses. You must be doing something right." Valerie smiled and sashayed back to her office.

Not sure what to think, Bethany stared at the card. Why would Tom send her flowers? The last time they talked would have been Valerie's party. The smile across the restaurant didn't merit an expensive bouquet. She tossed the note onto her desk and glanced at the doorway.

Jason stared at the roses. Without saying a word, he walked away.

Why did he give that sad look?

Her phone rang and she grabbed it on the second ring. Scott told her the latest. They found the name of the guy who had been in her apartment. He'd only worked for the crew two weeks and was now missing. The address given to his employer was merely an empty lot. Dad was livid she might be in danger and wanted her back under his roof.

The theme song for *Mission Impossible* played in her head. She couldn't go home with her parents. Scott would be close by and she carried a Taser. Shoot, she'd even consider a gun. Nobody would force her out before she was ready. She'd stay in her apartment. If trouble called, they'd find more than they bargained for.

Right now, she needed to give Tom a call, thank him for the roses, and find out why he sent them. If he wanted information on her dad's business, he wasted his money. If he wanted a date, she'd take the idea under consideration.

Chapter 12

Five o'clock on Saturday morning and wide awake. Jason stared at the clock on his nightstand. How had life spun into a rhythm of boring monotony? Next month, his brother-in-law would return from overseas, and Kelly and the kids wouldn't need him in their lives. *Finally get the nerve to ask Bethany out, and she's already dating someone.* He kicked back the covers.

Life as a dull monk had to end. *I need some help here, God. Show me a sign. What am I supposed to do?* Preferably, something besides work and the gym. Cornerstone could probably use his help more than once a month. A long jog to clear his head, read the paper, shower and shave, and he could get there early enough to help the food bank stock for the week.

Three hours later, Jason pulled his car into the parking lot. Nancy and Rhonda were already there. He whistled his way down the hall, and both women greeted him with smiles.

"I'm surprised to see you." Nancy said. "Is Kelly coming this morning?"

"No, she's getting ready for Matt's return."

"At Bible study the other day, I thought she'd pop from being so happy. Their kids have to be thrilled."

"Yeah, it's wild around there. Matt will be shocked at how the kids have grown."

Rhonda pushed a box of canned goods in front of him. "I

know you're glad for them, but how are you dealing with all of this? You've been involved in their lives for a long time."

"I'll keep busy." He avoided her perceptive stare, grabbed some cans, and placed them on the top shelf. "Nancy, what's Don up to these days?"

"He's out on the bay fishing with Barry from church. You ought to join us for a fish fry this evening at six thirty. If they don't have any luck, we'll order out. Barry and Karen will be there too. I'm sure the guys will have some wild tale from their adventure."

"Thanks, I may take you up on that."

"Jason," Rhonda said. "Can you get a hand truck and bring the latest shipment from the back? We've been blessed with a new supplier, and we were wondering how we were going to get all of that in here."

"Sure, I'd be glad to."

Rhonda's voice echoed off the warehouse walls as she broke into song. Nancy added harmony. If his voice didn't sound like a dying frog, he'd join them.

Bethany sat staring at the cars in the Cornerstone lot. *Is that Jason's car?* Hopefully not. After last night's fiasco of a date with Tom, she just wanted to talk with friends.

Singing greeted her as soon as she stepped in the doorway. Rhonda's soprano gave her goose bumps. She'd recognize Nancy's alto anywhere. Thank goodness, it was just the two of them. Nancy signaled for her to join in. Bethany stood between her friends and harmonized to the sweet hymn she hadn't thought about for years. Funny how some things stayed in the brain forever.

When they finished, Nancy gave her a big hug. "I've missed that. I'm so glad you're back in town."

"Me, too, even if life is strange and interesting."

"Sounds like you need to talk."

Rhonda handed Bethany a list and a sack to be packed with groceries for a needy family. "Did you ever find out who drugged your dog?"

"Yes. But nobody knows what happened to the man."

"What's going on?" Nancy put her arm around Bethany as though in a huddle.

Bethany filled them both in on the apartment situation. "Plus I went on a disaster of a date last night with Tom Chambers, the reporter who sent me roses. He promised no discussion of Dad's business and instead asked all sorts of questions. Plus, he stayed focused on my chest more than my eyes."

"Wow, you *have* had a wild ride the last two weeks. Why didn't you call me? Don and I could help."

"Dad stays on top of things. He's made sure I have a Taser in my purse and a body guard watching my every move."

"You're kidding?" Nancy scanned the room. "I feel like I'm in a spy movie."

Rhonda patted Bethany's arm. "You know I really am praying for you."

"Thanks. I'll be honest, all this kind of creeped me out at first, but now I'm just mad."

Nancy chuckled. "Good. That means you'll be fine. You need to tell Rhonda about what you did to the captain of the football team."

Bethany laughed at the memory. "Nobody messes with my friends. The guy was a real jerk. He started spreading rumors about lots of girls." She stopped and reformulated her next thoughts before she shared them with Rhonda's tender ears. "Let's just say he soiled some reputations. I told him to meet me on the football field at midnight. Of course, he thought I wanted to do more than talk."

Rhonda held up her hand. "Do I want to hear more?"

Nancy nudged Rhonda. "It's really a great story. She didn't scar him for life, not too much anyway. He's now a preacher in Texas."

Deep laughter carried from the back.

Bethany tried to see over the boxes. "Who's there?"

Still laughing, Jason waved a white napkin. "Please don't turn me into a preacher."

Molten lava flowed through her veins. "How long have you been listening?"

He stepped back. "Not long. I just heard the story about the football captain. Nothing more."

She moved in front of him. Sweat glistened on his forehead, upper lip, and arms. He worked hard and still smelled good. *Shoot.* Every time she got around him, her thoughts went crazy. Should she hit or kiss him?

She kissed him. Planted a big one on his lips. His amazing lips. "There, let that be a lesson." On weak knees, she attempted to remain unfazed by the sparks that had to be blasting around them. "Don't ever eavesdrop again."

Jason looked momentarily shocked, glanced at the two other women, grabbed Bethany, and gave a kiss that made her every hair rise in awe. By the time she regained her senses, he was gone.

Nancy clapped and laughed like a hyena. "Woo hoo! I would love if you two got together."

Smiling, Rhonda shook her head. "Mmm, mmm, mmm.

Goodness, I'll be praying for both of you."

Ignoring a coy smile from Rhonda and giggles from Nancy, Bethany pretended to focus on her work. She moved over the biggest box she could find and got busy. What happened to Jason? He went from avoiding her like the plague to giving her a kiss that still made her loopy. He snuck the last kiss but she was bound and determined to win this battle or have loads of fun trying.

Jason puffed his chest as he walked to the back. He had asked God for a sign and he got one in the form of a kiss. Maybe the years of penance finally paid off. Now he needed to calculate his next move. Nancy extended the invitation for a fish-fry this evening. Perfect. No time to waste. Bethany was one woman he wouldn't let get away. He picked up a box and made his way back to the women.

Bethany smiled. "Need more?"

The box slipped, but he quickly regained his grasp. He turned his attention to Nancy. "Does your invitation for tonight also include Bethany?"

Nancy chuckled as her eyes flitted back and forth between Jason and Bethany. "Of course. I think that's a great idea."

He moved as close as he could without touching Bethany. "If you're brave enough to give me your address, I'll pick you up at six."

She brushed her lips against his cheek, her breath against his ear. "514 Lee's Road, Apartment 4B. Don't be late."

###

Two hours later, Bethany's smile remained. She waited outside her apartment while Scott checked to make sure everything was clear. Her next door neighbor, Donna, said hello as she passed on her way to the parking lot.

What did the neighbors think about this interesting ritual? Not that it mattered. Right now, she needed a shower and to find the perfect outfit for a sparring match with Jason. If he kept up with this surprising behavior, she would definitely need to stay on her toes.

She thanked Scott when he finished and told him about her date this evening. Scott entered Jason's name and information in his PDA. At least Jason wouldn't be questioned, or have the stuffing beat out of him when he dropped over. Somehow the whole situation seemed way too familiar, like being back in high school with Dad checking her dates. It did keep her unstained by the world, until her marriage with Gavin—he made sure to take every bit of her innocence.

Tail wagging profusely, Jedi waited in the entry with a stuffed animal in his mouth. If only she could find a man as honest and loving. She pushed her answering machine playback and sat on the floor to pet her baby.

Nancy's voice and laughter spilled from the speaker about Bethany's date with Jason. Nancy and Don knew him from church and approved the match. If Nancy had anything to say about the matter, they'd be married and start a family within the year.

Bethany leaned against the wall. She wasn't against marriage, just against getting back into a situation that would destroy the remaining fibers of her heart. The little left had to be protected at all costs.

Something was different about Jason. He seemed to

wrestle with life as much as she did. Passion bubbled under the surface and mingled with a sweet, gentle side. *Shoot.* Every time she thought about him, it made her mushy.

A shower, makeup application, and fourteen outfit changes later, Bethany collapsed on the sofa. What made her so compulsive about this date? It took forever to find what to wear … coy, revealing but not too revealing, just enough to make Jason sweat. He *could* kiss, and seeing his sense of humor made him all the more interesting. She had to have the upper hand and keep him off-kilter.

Jedi growled and pounced on his toy squirrel. The thing didn't have a chance. And if she had anything to say about the matter, neither did Jason.

He picked her up precisely at six, looking and smelling better than a man should. He wore jeans and a teal-blue polo shirt that looked custom fit. Even his car was immaculate. *Rats.* So much for the upper hand.

On the drive to Nancy's they small-talked about work and Cornerstone. He seemed more confident and sure of himself. If a kiss was all he needed, she would have been happy to comply on the first week of work.

When they arrived, Nancy greeted them with hugs and led them to the back deck where Don hovered over his obviously homemade fish fryer. The contraption looked like it had been built in his garage. And knowing Don, it probably had been.

Don did a quick double-take. "Bethany! Man, you look great."

"You don't look bad yourself." He was still cute as ever and the perfect guy for Nancy. His crazy personality matched her bubbly one. "Marriage agrees with both of you."

"I would've married her sooner, if she'd accepted my

proposal when we were in seventh grade."

Nancy draped her arm across his shoulder. "I would have, if you had given me more than a plastic ring."

"Hey, I mowed two yards to get that."

"You do spoil me."

Smiling, Don handed Nancy his cooking utensils and extended his hand to Jason. "Glad you could make it. Always nice to see friends outside the church hallways." He pointed toward the couple sitting at the picnic table. "Check out Barry's hand. He's got a heck of a story from this morning."

Jason grinned and with a light touch on the small of Bethany's back, guided her toward the table. "Barry and Karen, this is Bethany. Barry teaches the men's group at church."

They settled next to the attractive middle-aged couple.

"You going to tell us what happened?" Jason pointed to Barry's bandaged left hand.

Barry leaned toward them. "It was a dark and stormy morning."

Karen shook her head. "You mean a beautiful morning." She gave Bethany a sly smile. "Get ready for a whopping fish tale."

"Honey, please. It's my story." Barry stood as though addressing congress. "It was a *somewhat* sunny morning. Don and I were out on the Chesapeake Bay. Both of our rods were cast and secure. I was busy cutting bait, when a wave crashed against the side causing my knife to slice down to the bone."

Karen cleared her throat.

Barry gave her a sideways glance. "Okay, it was deep. Maybe not to the bone, but it was close. Anyway, at the same time, my reel started whirring and my rod's bending. Don gets action too, and we're both grabbing, trying to bring in our fish. No way, am I going to let some major injury keep me from catching the big one, even if blood was spurting all over the place." Karen rolled her eyes at his statement. He nodded at her. "It *was*."

"Hey." Don called from his station in front of the fryer. "I wanted to let mine go and help Barry, but he wouldn't let me."

"True." Barry said. "He did offer to help, but some things *are* more important. We struggled for probably an hour."

Karen's eyes narrowed.

"Fine, not really an hour, but it seemed that way. By now, I'm getting woozy from lack of blood, but I'm not letting go. My rod is bending like it's a big one, some Moby Dick-like creature. When the battle finally came to an end, Don reeled in a twenty-five pound Rockfish, but mine ..." he puffed his chest, "is a big, fat, monster. The biggest. Thirty-eight pounds."

Don carried over a serving platter heaped with fried fish. "After a trip to the emergency care clinic for twelve stitches, then drop off Barry's fish at the taxidermist, it took an hour to clean up the boat. Barry's fish will be on his wall in a week and mine's dinner."

Jason patted his full stomach. Dinner had gone better than expected. Bethany seemed to enjoy herself and be at ease with everyone. Several stories about Nancy's and Bethany's high-school antics had come out in conversation, which made her all the more intriguing. Her sense of humor and that mischievous twinkle in her eyes drove him nuts. She almost seemed too good to be true—Christian, fun, and gorgeous.

Don tossed him a football, ran into the yard, and waited for a return pass. "Send me a spiral."

Jason threw the ball with ease. Catch with his four-year-old nephew was fun, but nothing like a hard and fast one to an adult.

Don returned his throw.

Bethany shoved Jason aside and caught the ball. She smiled and thumped his chest. "I told you I could play the game."

"I never doubted that fact." He leaned toward her, close enough that her hair tickled his face. "So how fast can you run?"

"Faster than you, big boy." She kicked off her shoes, tucked the ball under her arm, and sprinted past him.

He started to hold back and give her a big lead, until he saw how fast she could run. The girl was lightning. Puffing hard, he got close enough to grab her shirt.

She squealed and wiggled away. "You'll never take me alive."

No way he'd let her beat him. He kicked into high gear and got her by the arm. She still wouldn't stop. He tugged, and she pulled. Giggling and twisting, she made a quick move to extricate herself.

With a scream, she crumpled to the ground and grabbed her leg.

His stomach dropped with her as he fell to his knees. "What happened?"

"My knee." She writhed in pain, sweat glistening on her forehead. "My knee's out of socket."

Helping a guy with an injury and helping a female were totally different. He choked down the acid rising in his throat. "What can I do?"

Bethany groaned and pulled on her leg. "I can't get it back in. You'll have to help."

"Me?" He sucked in air and glanced at the group hovering over them. They shook their heads and took a step back. "I'll try." He took her calf in his hands but couldn't allow himself to put any pressure.

Tears trickled down her face. "Please you've got to do this." She gripped the grass like a lifeline. "Just pull straight out and my knee will go back in."

He took a deep breath and pulled.

Pop!

Every bit of blood rushed from his head. He collapsed next to her to avoid passing out. "Did you hear that?"

She grimaced and wiped the tears from her face. "I'm usually too busy screaming to hear anything."

"Man, that has to hurt."

"The pain gets better when it's back in the socket. It's an old football injury."

"Football? The team captain?"

"No." She sat up, her color returning. "My brothers and I played. I thought I could be as strong as them. I held my own until the day of the infamous dog pile. With my brothers, everything was infamous or epic."

Seeing her in less pain, his stomach settled. "How many stories do you have?"

"Probably a million. I haven't led a boring life." She struggled to her feet.

He offered his arm. "Let me take you home."

She gave him a sly look as she steadied herself against him. "I've heard that line before."

Bethany wished she could crawl under a rug. Everybody

stared at her like she was some feeble female. Nancy was white as a ghost, Barry held his hand as though her pain had transferred to him, Don talked about the logistics of building a stretcher, and Karen just kept calling her a poor baby and whispering prayers.

Dumb knee. "I'm not helpless, you know." She huffed at Jason.

"I know." His gentle voice and smile made her want to swoon. *Swoon?* Who even thought of a word like that? If her knee didn't hurt like crazy, she could stand here in his muscular arms forever. Ugh, even her thoughts were sickeningly sweet. *No way another guy would get close again.* Her heart couldn't take the hurt. She put pressure on her bad knee and let the pain bring her back to sanity.

Jason tightened his grip. "Let me help." His firm tone made her stop. Plus, she couldn't walk right now and calling in Scott would be downright embarrassing. *Fine.* She'd play the helpless woman, but if Jason got out of line, she'd Taser him.

After hugs and goodbyes, he held her close as she hobbled down the driveway.

Scott sat in his car across the road, pretending to read a map. A double tug on her left ear signaled all was well. He nodded, his expression curious.

Not exactly the evening she planned. But being with Jason had turned out to be enjoyable—good-looking, fun, a terrific kisser, nice, probably too nice for someone like her. She buckled her seatbelt and reached for her cell phone, which showed a missed call.

Swallowing hard, she listened to the message from her mother. *Come quickly, Grandfather's fading fast.*

Chapter 13

Jason kept his grip tight around Bethany's waist as he helped her hobble down the hallway to her grandfather's room. Having her next to him, his arm around her felt natural and right. From her reaction to the phone call, this would not be an ordinary visit. She obviously fought to remain composed even though an occasional sniffle escaped.

A sophisticated looking middle-aged man with salt-and-pepper hair stepped outside the room. Standing military rigid, the man's dark eyes scanned both Jason and Bethany. "What happened?"

Bethany slipped from Jason's grasp and held onto the doorway, her usual confidence withered. "I hurt my knee."

The man's eyes narrowed as he studied Jason. "I'm Bethany's father, Charles Davis." He held out his hand. "And you are?"

"Jason Ross." He shook her father's firm grip. "I work with Bethany."

"On Saturday?"

"No sir, we were having dinner with friends."

"Dinner?" Mr. Davis' questioning gaze fixed on Bethany.

She gave a little shrug. "Fish fry at Nancy's. Jason was kind enough to give me a ride."

He turned toward Jason. "Thank you for getting her here safely. We'll make sure she gets home."

Feeling like a private being inspected by a general, Jason nodded, kept his arms by his side. "Yes, sir."

"I'll be there in a minute." Bethany waited until her father closed the door behind him. "I'm sorry about that. He's kind of protective."

"I don't blame him, you're worth protecting."

Emotions that he couldn't read flickered across her face. Confusion? Pain? Gratitude? "Thank you. I'm sorry our evening ended like this. I really did have a nice time."

"Same here. Could we get together next weekend?"

She stared at the floor for a moment before looking at him. "I don't know that I'm ready for a relationship."

He held up his hands. "I'd just like to get to know you better."

"Jason, I'm not sure you want—"

"One day at a time. No pressure."

"I need to go."

Unfortunately a kiss didn't seem appropriate. He shoved his hands in his pockets. "I'll be praying for you and your family."

Tears welled in her turquoise eyes. She nodded, opened the door, and limped inside.

Jason drove along the interstate. Prayers for Bethany's family were interspersed with thanks for the opportunity to date someone like her. She didn't say yes, but she didn't say no. Too antsy to go home, he drove toward work.

Bethany closed the door behind her. Jason's arms wrapped around her made her heart ache. If he knew who she really was, and what she had done, would he run? And if he didn't, could she risk allowing someone behind the protective walls she'd built?

She hugged Mom and then stood by Grandfather's bed. His chest rattled as he struggled for air. He looked so frail and helpless. *Does he even know I'm here?*

If only she could bottle up the memories—the fishing trips, sitting on the dock dangling her feet and talking for hours. Regardless of what she wanted to discuss, he was always ready to listen. Even outside, working and sweaty, he smelled like sunshine. She still had so much to say, things she wanted to know and tell him. She leaned close to his gaunt face. "Grandfather, I love you. Please don't go."

Mom sat in the chair on the other side of his bed, her lips moving in silent prayer. Dad paced like a caged animal, his normally strong expression replaced with the look of a helpless little boy.

Bethany gently rubbed her grandfather's vein-lined arm, his skin thin, almost see-through. She choked back a cry. Who would be here for her now? *God, please don't take him. Not yet.*

Guilt washed over her. Did she even have a right to pray? Praying for others came easier. They deserved help. She didn't.

His eyes closed, Grandfather coughed, and gasped, his breathing growing more and more shallow. She clung to his arm, wishing she could pass her strength to him. *I'll be good, God. Please just keep Grandfather here.* She cradled his hand and scrunched her eyes shut to keep the tears from falling.

So long ago, he had velvet hammer strength—gentle, yet tough, with an undercurrent of deep calm, rooted in rock. His favorite verse ran through her mind. *God, create a pure heart in me. Give me a new spirit that is faithful to you.*

She needed a new heart. The shredded vestiges of what

remained beating in her chest had been walled in a cage of steel.

Until now. Jason's attention, her parent's love, new friendships, and Grandfather lying helpless, cracked and shattered the protective barrier. She *was* tired of running, of making bad choices, screwing up her life because of what happened with Gavin.

Is saying you need help admitting defeat? Or is it grabbing onto a lifeline?

Is it too late?

Dad's strong hand squeezed her shoulder.

Mom's arms came around Bethany, holding her close. "I love you, honey. I love you so much."

Did she say out loud what she was thinking? It didn't matter. She did need help. All the hurt, disappointment, and anger that had hounded her the last few years, flooded out, spilled down her cheeks, and dotted the floor. *God, please take me back. I'm sorry for the way I've behaved. Please forgive me.*

Bethany didn't even care what her parents thought about her tearful breakdown. It felt good to release the pent-up past.

Grandfather gagged, his chest heaved and fought for air. He had struggled so long. It wasn't fair to ask him to stay. Composing herself, she placed her cheek against his and whispered in his ear. "If you need to go, we'll be all right. Grandmother is waiting for you. I'll always love you." Her tears fell on his face, and she wiped them away. "I'm home to stay. I'm back home with God."

Grandfather gasped, sunk into his pillow. In an instant, he was gone.

Weeping, she fell to her knees and pressed his lifeless hand against her cheek. "Oh, God...."

but his throat bobbed as he swallowed repeatedly. Mom's tears restarted and she patted Bethany's arm almost as though she was the one crying.

The organ music swelled, and the crowd rose to its feet. *"Amazing Grace."* Emotions swept through her as they sang the familiar hymn. If only Grandfather could be here with them right now. He loved the song, and he would be so proud to have her back home.

Please, God, tell Grandfather and Grandmother I miss them.

She couldn't even croak through her tight throat as the music continued. Grief mingled with comfort, joy with sorrow, and regret with relief.

The preacher announced his sermon topic as the return of the prodigal child. Bethany coughed back a chuckle. If Grandfather had been here, he would have busted out with a laugh and a loud hallelujah.

When the service ended, Bethany waited in the lobby as her parents continued to accept condolences.

"Bethany?" Joelle, wearing spiked heels, teetered toward Bethany with Cindy following close behind. "I'm surprised to see you here." Joelle nudged Bethany with her perfectly tanned, bony elbow. "The sermon must have been rather uncomfortable."

"Actually." Bethany smiled and kept her voice even. "I enjoyed it thoroughly."

Confusion crossed Joelle's face, and her bracelets tinkled as she patted her overly sprayed, bleached blond hair. "Well ...." Joelle glanced at Cindy, then back at Bethany with a condescending smile. "We would ask you to lunch, but we only have four reservations at the country club."

"Ladies." Dad's firm voice came from behind Bethany. "If you'll excuse us, we have plans at La Rochelle for lunch."

He held his arm toward her.

Surprised looks with a hint of jealousy passed between Cindy and Joelle. The restaurant Dad mentioned happened to be the finest in town. Feeling like royalty, Bethany straightened her shoulders as he led her through the doors and to safety. Out of earshot of the gossip twins, she leaned toward him. "Thanks for the rescue."

"My pleasure." He stopped and faced her, his dark eyes shimmering. "Bethany, you don't have to put with those kinds of people. We're glad you're back. But feel free to find your own church home."

Mom nodded in agreement.

The sincerity of his words panged Bethany's heart. "Thanks. It *really* is good to be home."

Jason helped Kelly clean the kitchen after Sunday lunch while the kids played out back. He scrubbed at the blob of ketchup on the floor. *How could two well-behaved munchkins make a mess with hot dogs and chips?*

Of course, he had made an absolute mess of his life. Just his luck, he'd fall for a girl with a bad reputation. More proof he hadn't changed. "I've lived a reprobate, and I'm going to die a reprobate."

Kelly stopped loading dishes in the dishwasher. "What?"

"I've tried to change." He ran a frustrated hand through his hair. "I've tried to keep away from women. I've stopped drinking. I've stopped messing around. And I'm still screwed up."

"Does this have to do with Pastor John's sermon this

morning?"

"I went out with Bethany last night. Actually, I met her at Cornerstone and then Nancy invited me to a fish fry, so I took Bethany."

"Really?" Her eyebrows danced up and down in pleasure. "How did it go?"

He unclenched his teeth. *No wonder my jaw hurt.* "Great. It went great."

Kelly closed the dishwasher and rinsed her hands. "That didn't sound positive." She turned and studied him, waiting for his next reply.

"I really liked her. She's incredible, gorgeous, has a great sense of humor, and an awesome personality."

She shook her head and sighed dramatically. "You have *such* terrible problems."

"It *is* a problem." He didn't mean to raise his voice. He threw Kelly an apologetic look, and tempered his tone. "After my date, Alex told me she's been married before and has a past that probably shames mine."

"You got your information from him?" Kelly glanced out the back window checking on the kids and then settled in a chair at the kitchen table. "Doesn't that make you wary?"

"No." Jason pulled out a chair, but instead chose to pace. "If anybody should know about loose women, it's him."

"Wow, you're being pretty hard on this girl."

"Look, I only asked her out because I thought she was a Christian. I was trying to do the right thing." He ignored the nagging memory of the kiss, her looks, her personality, everything about her.

"*Is* she a Christian?"

"I doubt it. Not with what Alex told me."

"So if somebody told Bethany about who you used to be,

what would she think?"

Heat crawled up his neck. "You're not helping."

"And *you're* being judgmental."

Jason ignored the barb. "I knew it was too good to be true. God's still mad at me. I asked for a sign and got one, and sure enough it was just like dangling an awesome gift in front of my face and jerking it back."

"What sign did you get?"

He coughed into his fist trying to think of something to deflect that question. Right now, the kiss didn't sound like a proper sign. "Never mind. I obviously misread something."

"You've got to get over your past." She shook her head as she stood and moved to the back door. "And you've got to let others move on from theirs. Find out the truth about Bethany, and then we'll talk."

Jason stared at the floor when Kelly left. It wasn't like he was raised on the streets and didn't know better. He willingly chose to make a mess of his life. Losing his parents gave him an excuse, but he still had been the one who made the choices.

Grace was so blasted hard to comprehend. How could forgiveness be given without expecting long-term payment or a thorough beating? Jason picked up his Bible and searched for notes from the church service. He stared at the last statements. *God tells us that forgiveness comes after true repentance—right then, not later, not after years of penance. God's touch is instantaneous.*

If only he could get that truth into his thick head.

###

After church, the house filled with relatives and friends in preparation for Grandfather's funeral on Tuesday. In an attempt for some quiet time, Bethany sat on the boat dock on her parent's property. Chase and his wife had driven down from D.C. Chase acted as pompous as ever. Living near the Capital had only inflated his big head, but when he greeted her something unfamiliar sparked in his eyes. A moment of tenderness she had never seen before. Based on all that had happened, she couldn't argue with the feeling that moving home had saved her in many ways.

A breeze tousled her hair and sent a ripple across the water. The familiar scent of bay air melted away the tension. Grandfather would enjoy a day like today. Even during her wild years, he accepted and loved her. He knew the cause of her running, and he prayed and waited patiently for her return. Now she was home, physically and spiritually.

Brad was due to arrive from Peru before the funeral. His job with the Peace Corps kept him away from home far too often.

With Grandfather gone and Dad better, why should she stay? This morning's church service had proven that her past would be a constant sore point.

Footsteps drew her attention. "I hope you don't mind." Nancy's sandals flopped on the wooden deck. "I'm so sorry about your grandfather."

Fresh tears stung Bethany's eyes as she rose to accept Nancy's hug. "I'm really going to miss him." *Probably forever.* "At least he's out of pain and safe in Heaven with Grandmother. If only Heaven had a phone line that you could call and say hello to loved ones. Please, pray I know what to do." Without him here, did she need to stay?

Nancy pulled away and gaped at her. "Did you just ask me to pray for you?"

Gee, does everybody think I'm a lost cause? "Yes. Don't act so surprised."

"I'm sorry." Nancy smiled, shook her head as though clearing her thoughts. "I'm just so happy to hear you say that."

"I always needed prayer. I was just too stubborn to ask. I'm back with God."

Nancy let out a squeal and almost smushed the breath out of Bethany with another hug. "I just knew I was supposed to come out here today. I'm so happy I could do the Snoopy dance."

"Don't let me stop you."

"All right. I will." Nancy threw back her head, hummed the song from the Peanuts cartoon, and gave the best rendition of a Snoopy dance Bethany had ever seen.

Bethany found herself laughing and crying. How could so many emotions be mixed together?

Dance over, they sat next to one another, their legs dangling over the edge, just like old times—laughter and someone who was comfortable enough to allow for quiet moments.

The sun lowered on the horizon, painting melon and strawberry hues into the evening sky.

A light flashed as though a mirror or something shiny caught the sun's reflection. Bethany studied a boat anchored on the opposite inlet shoreline as a lone person ducked behind the windshield. *Odd.* A man alone on the water without fishing gear? The bay normally stayed busy with fishermen, families, or tourists. No reason to worry. Maybe he was just looking around or enjoying the evening. A weird tingle pricked at her neck. If only she had binoculars, she could check.

"What is it?" Nancy hunched toward Bethany. "Something suspicious?"

"Probably not. If anything, he saw you dance and ran for cover."

Amusement played in Nancy's eyes. "Speaking of interesting moves. You and Jason looked like you were enjoying yourselves yesterday."

"I'll admit we had a nice time. He has certain attributes I find appealing." *Terrific kisser, handsome, fun, gentle, makes me crazy.*

Nancy nudged her. "You are smiling from ear to ear."

"We work together. It would be way too awkward." Bethany tamped down her feelings for Jason and focused on the boat. Probably a twenty-foot Boston Whaler. The guy still hadn't reappeared.

"I don't know. I'm sure if it's meant to be, something will work out."

"You've got to stop trying to marry me off. I've done my time, and it wasn't pretty."

"Not everybody is a jerk like Gavin. There are good guys out there, and I happen to know Jason is one of them."

"Good guys aren't usually attracted to someone with my past." She swallowed a lump of regret and looked at her friend. "I left here thinking everybody hated me and thought I was a tramp, so I basically lived like one."

"You can't change yesterday. Gavin tried to spread lies about you, but we knew the truth. Word got out after you left that he was the one having the affairs."

"Tell that to Cindy and Joelle."

"Those two are always looking to drag up dirt on people, then they don't have to face their own messed up lives. Bethany, it doesn't matter now. You're home. Really home."

The boat's engine started. Still the guy was nowhere to be seen. The bow turned, and the boat drifted forward.

Who is that, and when did it get so dark? Bethany got to her feet and helped Nancy up. "Maybe we need to get inside."

"You're starting to scare me. You're worried, aren't you?"

"I'm probably just being paranoid. The bay's always busy."

Running lights off, the boat's engine revved, lifting the bow out of the water as it raced toward them.

Chapter 15

Icy fingers tickled Bethany's neck as the boat roared toward her. "Let's get to the house."

Nancy stared wide-eyed, ditched her flip-flops, and barreled off the dock. "Scared. Walking." She gripped Bethany's arm like a vise. "Walking really fast. My stomach feels like it's full of frogs on caffeine."

"Frogs on caffeine?" *Did a hysterical friend make everything more fun or more frightening?* "The boat can't come on land. We've got a good three minute lead on him from that side of the inlet. It takes two to get to the house."

"I'm praying. Screaming on the inside. Running." Nancy's arms flailed, her voice rising in octaves with each word. "How do you know we have a good lead?"

Bethany kept going but glanced over her shoulder. "Gavin. And if it's Gavin now, I'll personally dismember him." She tripped over her running feet but got back in stride without losing too much ground.

"Stop talking and run faster!"

Where is everybody? Flood lights flashed on as they ran onto the patio. Thank goodness, for sensors. Someone moved in the trees on the right.

Nancy screamed, sending vibrations of pain through Bethany's eardrums.

Grabbing Nancy by the arm, she shoved her to the back

door. Nobody would mess with her friend.

Two men with flashlights dashed past them toward the dock.

Security. Bethany took a deep breath of relief and glanced at her friend. *Wow, knees really can knock.* "It's okay, those are the bodyguards."

"Why weren't they here sooner?" Nancy broke down in sobs, her body quaking. "This scared me to death."

Enveloping her friend in a comforting hug, Bethany strained to see through the darkness. Security, in her dad's ski boat, sped off in hot pursuit. Gavin used to pull stunts like that as a joke. But tonight *wasn't* funny. *Besides, Gavin's married and living in another state.*

Isn't he?

Jason focused ahead as his sneakers pounded the pavement. Sweat dripped off his forehead stinging his eyes. He wiped his face with the back of his hand and continued praying for Bethany and her family.

When he had returned from Kelly's house, he found that Nancy had left him a message on his answering machine about Bethany's grandfather. His chest tightened thinking about her loss. The feelings ran deeper than sympathy, for some reason he felt tied to her. The problem was, would she make him sink back into his old ways?

Kelly was right. He couldn't just take Alex's word about Bethany. She deserved the benefit of the doubt.

Long and dark shadows covered the winding park pathway. He needed to get home. Maybe a shower would clear his thoughts. He could always swing by the florist and take flowers to Bethany's apartment and offer his condolences. Then again, he probably needed to take a long, cold shower before he went by her place.

###

The back door opened and Bethany's mother ushered them inside the kitchen. "What happened?"

Tears hung on Nancy's lashes. "A bad guy was after us."

Dad rushed over and focused on Bethany. "Are you both okay?"

"Yes." Bethany almost stepped back at Dad's concerned look. "A boat raced toward us. Maybe kids were playing a prank."

He glanced over his shoulder at the family and visitors remaining in the den. "Let's step into the study. I want to know what happened in detail." He patted Nancy's shoulder. "We'll get you a ride home, and make sure you're safe, okay?"

Nancy nodded, fear still in her eyes.

Bethany hugged her friend. "Everything's going to be fine. We both had a great run and some fresh air. Just like old times, huh?"

"Please be careful." Nancy's voice quivered. "I'm really worried."

"I'll be fine." After one final hug to her worried friend, Bethany walked down the hall to her dad's study. She closed the door behind her and faced her father sitting at his desk, Bluetooth in one ear, cell phone in the other, and the speaker phone crackling with conversations from security. *How on earth does he listen to all those things at once?*

He motioned for her to sit. "How could you let him get away?"

She swallowed hard. "I—"

He didn't look at her. "I expect better or I'll hire someone else." He crossed to the window and stared outside. "I want a full report on my desk in the morning." Snapping shut his cell phone he turned his attention to the speaker. "I want you in my office at seven in the morning, and you *better* have some answers." He clicked off both the speaker and his headpiece. "Tell me exactly what you saw and heard."

Her heart skittered at his intensity. "I was just sitting on the dock with Nancy when I noticed a flash, like a mirror or something. It came from a boat on the other side of the inlet. I, uh, think it was a Boston Whaler maybe a twenty footer."

"Good." He nodded. "What else did you notice?"

"Someone on the boat ducked when I started looking. I think he had on a ball cap. I thought maybe it was my imagination or I was being paranoid until the engine revved and he started coming toward us. It was probably kids, even Gavin used to do things like that for a joke."

His eyes narrowed, he held up a finger in her direction, opened his cell phone, and speed dialed a number. "I want a detective tailing Gavin Marks…. Yes, Bethany's ex…. I want to know what he's been up to lately and where he is…. Not in the morning, now!"

Invisible ant feet pricked across her shoulders. "Dad, what's going on?"

He sat at his desk and shut the phone. "Since the company signed this latest contract, we've been receiving threats. Not just at work, but on our family."

Family? Fire pulsed through her veins. "What kind of threats?"

"I can't give you details. The weapon we've developed will be used for peaceful purposes by our country, but others are trying to get us to release information. Security isn't the only one watching our backs, several government agencies are on alert." His fingers drummed the desk. "We're close to the final stages. Another two months and the weapon will be in the hands of the government. But, the knowledge came from our company. I don't think they will lose interest anytime soon." He leaned forward. "I want you back home."

Air seeped from her lungs. Threats were bad enough, but being under the same roof with no means of privacy or escape sounded worse.

"Please let me stay in my apartment."

His jaw worked and dark red stained his neck. "Girl." Shaking his head, he pushed away from his desk. "I just got my baby back." His voice thickened. "I don't want anything to happen to you."

Her vision blurred as she fought to swallow the lump caught in her throat. If she had been a little girl, she would have thrown herself into his big arms and buried herself against his chest.

Bethany followed Scott to her apartment. Two hours of begging and her parents finally agreed to allow her to return to her own place. Part of her wanted to stay at their house ... especially after Dad's statement. He really did care. It made her stand a little taller and feel braver.

During the conversation with her parents she had prayed, and for some reason felt she needed to be home. Maybe being away from family would actually help. They'd be safe on the estate, and if anyone came after her, they'd leave her parents alone.

131

Mom and Dad agreed, but only if Scott slept on her couch. If this whole thing wasn't so creepy, she'd laugh at the absurdity of her parents making sure a man stayed in her apartment.

Tonight, she needed to get back to her place and Jedi. The poor pup would be desperate for a potty break.

Questions jumbled and ran through her head. Since yesterday, she had a great date with Jason, until the knee incident. Life was so blasted confusing and painful. Grandfather's death, and now weird things continued to happen. The defense industry opened up all sorts of negative and very unappealing possibilities when it came to threats.

Waiting outside her apartment while Scott checked, she sent up prayers for protection for her and her family.

Jedi happily danced, wagged, and followed him during this nightly routine.

Her neighbor Donna and her boyfriend walked arm and arm on their way to the parking lot. Strange how she seemed to see Donna almost every time she came home.

Scott returned. "All clear."

"Thank you." She put a hand on his shoulder. "I'm sorry to make you stay tonight."

He smiled, more business than pleasure. "We'll make sure you're safe." His eyes narrowed at a car passing through the parking lot.

Not hesitating a moment, Bethany scooped Jedi into her arms and hurried inside.

Jason smacked his hand against the steering wheel and glanced at the flowers he had purchased for Bethany. He swerved, barely missing a car hiding in the shadows on the side of the apartment entrance.

Idiot! He was a complete idiot. Fifty lousy bucks and all he had to show for it was nauseating flowers and knowing that some guy was staying with Bethany.

God, why don't you take these feelings away or just shoot me?

Chapter 16

Bethany groaned and forced open her scratchy eyes. By the look of her messy covers, it appeared that an army had parachuted in and attacked her bed. Sleep had been fleeting between her overactive imagination, praying like crazy, and strange noises outside her window. Even Jedi stayed on edge all night, and when he did sleep, his dreams were punctuated with muffled growls and barks.

At six, Scott hummed a military tune in the shower. Funny how nice that sounded, knowing no guilt or regrets came with hearing a man in her bathroom. Smiling, she rolled over and hoped to snatch a few more minutes' rest.

The alarm jolted her from bed at seven.

Jedi stretched, gave her a quick wag, and ambled toward the door.

Yawning, she forced herself upright. Every movement seemed like being under water—slow and laborious. Work was out of the question, even if being around Jason would be a nice distraction. She dialed his work number and left a message. After she showered and ate breakfast, Scott escorted her to her parent's home. Jedi loved the ride, stretching his head high enough to see out the car window. She took no chances this time. Her baby would stay by her side.

Within an hour of being home, she grabbed Jedi's leash and took him outside. Chase and his wife, Andreitta, daughter of a foreign diplomat, had talked nonstop about their fancy dinners, and their children's involvement in the finest schools. Goodness knows the kids couldn't take time off from their studies, even if they were only ten and twelve, and it was summer.

Having the kids around would've been a nice distraction. Thankfully, Brad should get in soon. He'd reduce the tension hanging in the air. His tenderhearted and fun personality brought out the best in people.

She considered sitting on the dock but instead settled in the glider on the back patio. Jedi jumped up and lay next to her. Scott and security roamed the premises, watching with binoculars every boat that passed.

"Hey, kid!"

Brad's familiar voice put a smile on her face. She stood and almost knocked into him.

He hugged her, stepped back, and whistled. "Wow, you look great." Tiny lines appeared around his eyes when he smiled.

"You too. A little older though."

"Working outside for twelve hours a day will do that." He leaned down and gave Jedi a belly rub. "Hey, boy, good to see you."

"I'm glad you're here. I've missed you."

He sat down and patted the seat next to him. "I've missed you, too. So fill me in. You behaving yourself these days?"

"Actually, I am."

"Really?" No condemnation, just humor. "Either you have a decent new man in your life, or you've returned from the dark side."

"You don't pull punches."

"Never did. Never will." He smiled and bumped her with his elbow. "I think you're back, aren't you?"

"Yes, I am." How could a brother be so perceptive? "It really is nice."

He poked her. "Told you."

"You're such a pest." She punched him on the arm.

"See, you really did miss me." The moments passed in comfortable silence. He kicked with his heels starting the glider in motion and stared toward the inlet. "Mom said you were there when Grandfather died."

"Yes." Her voice cracked as the ache returned at losing the only man who loved her unconditionally. "I told him I was back."

He swallowed hard, nodded. "He was waiting. He wrote me when he was able and never failed to mention how much he was praying for you."

Tears stung her eyes as her throat tightened. "I'm sorry it took me so long. I did some rotten things while I was away. I'm amazed I can be forgiven for the things I've done."

Brad nodded. "That's why it's called grace. Yep, grace even for rotten, little wayward sisters." He tossed a mischievous smile over his shoulder. "Last one to the house has to tell our big brother they love him."

Fate worse than death.

She grabbed Brad's arm, battled and clawed him all the way to the door. They both jammed in the doorframe with Jedi trailing behind.

"Ha!" Brad scooped up the puppy. "You, my little furry friend, must do the dirty deed." Wagging profusely, Jedi licked Brad's nose. "Looks like he won't mind a bit."

###

Jason rearranged the files on his desk for the fourteenth time. His projects kept stacking up, and still his brain refused to cooperate. The viewing for Bethany's grandfather started in an hour. Rhonda, Valerie, Nancy, and Don would meet him there.

He hated funerals, and hated seeing Bethany again knowing that she had been with some guy, hated that he and Bethany didn't have a chance, and hated that he still wanted to see her.

He kicked his desk, sending his empty coffee mug clattering to the floor and pain shooting through his foot.

Rhonda peeked around the corner. "You okay?"

"Yes." Ignoring his aching appendage, he grabbed his cup and set it back on his desk. "Just trying to get some things done."

"Uh huh." Her eyebrows rose. "Want to talk?"

"No thanks." All he needed was another female trying to sort out his problems. "I'm fine."

"I know Bethany will be grateful to see us tonight. God knows she'll need comfort."

Jason rubbed the back of his neck, trying to squeeze away the tension. Why wasn't he the one to provide her comfort?

###

Bethany stood next to Grandfather's casket in the viewing room. Grief rolled inside her, like waves, frothing, ebbing and flowing. His favorite hymns played through the sound system. Flower arrangements from friends lined the walls, filling the room with a sweet aroma.

She rejoiced he was in heaven, but looking at the shell

that had been Grandfather, the man who loved and never gave up on her, now lay alone in a casket. She'd miss him. Forever. Who would dance with her? Who would love her unconditionally like he did?

You are loved unconditionally.

Grateful for the thought, she pinched the bridge of her nose to keep from crying. But still she longed for human contact.

Brad stayed close beside her, his presence providing comfort. Keeping what she hoped was a pleasant expression, she shook hands and thanked those who came.

At the entrance of the room, her parents accepted condolences. Mom kept a brave face, but often her hand would search out Dad's, and a gentle squeeze would pass between them.

Chase and Andreitta graciously spoke to each person. Chase, ever the politician, worked the crowd with ease.

From the corner, Scott surveyed each person. Other security personnel watched and mingled among the guests. Would this be their life from now on? Bodyguards and never any privacy?

Relief washed over her at the sight of her friends. Rhonda, Valerie, Nancy, and Don hurried toward her and smothered her in a group hug.

Rhonda's gentle hands lifted Bethany's face and wiped off her tears. "I'm so sorry for your loss."

Nancy hugged her tight.

Bethany choked on her tears as she soaked in her friends love and concern.

###

Jason hung back, watching the outflow of affection between his co-workers and friends. The guy from Bethany's apartment glared at everybody like some Special Forces bodyguard. *Jerk, doesn't even look interested that she's crying.*

"Jason?"

He faced Bethany's father. "Mr. Davis. I'm very sorry for your loss."

"Thank you." His appreciation appeared friendly and genuine. "I want you to meet my family."

Jason introduced himself to each member until he found himself in front of Bethany. What could he say? He'd already asked her out for this weekend. Not that she really gave an answer.

The guy in the corner narrowed his eyes. Jason wanted to punch him. If jerkface really cared for her, he'd be with her.

Bethany looked at him with those tear-filled turquoise eyes, and his heart melted, puddled right to his feet. It didn't matter if the whole world watched. Something, and he hoped that something was heavenly based kept pulling him toward her. He enfolded her against his chest and whispered in her ear. "I'm sorry. I'm really sorry about your grandfather."

She clung to him, and in that moment the world faded, just the two of them standing there, lost in each other's arms.

Valerie snapped her fingers in front of his face. "Break it up, or I'll call the fire department."

Heat still rising, he stepped back but didn't dare look around the room. He couldn't imagine what people thought. It didn't matter. He wanted to read Bethany's mind. What did she think? Her expression flickered with something he couldn't read, as if a million thoughts ran through her mind.

###

Bethany hugged her arms against her chest, mainly to keep from jumping back into Jason's embrace. Was it her imagination or were they like magnets, drawn to one another? Those brief moments they connected left her reeling, with static sparks shooting in all directions.

Her heart, already raw, soft, and tender, fluttered with emotion. And now, he looked like he expected her to pledge her love. And what was worse, she could. Just throw all those fears in the air, grab him by the arm, and run away from life.

She willed herself to focus. This was Grandfather's viewing.

Glancing at her friends, she thanked each one. She paused at Jason, held out her hand. "Thank you for coming." At his touch, her knees weakened. She squeezed his fingers, hoping he would understand what even she didn't. His gaze locked with hers and he returned the pressure.

It took all her strength not to kiss him.

Bethany stared out the limousine window, trying to ignore Brad. He hadn't said anything about Jason, but her brother's smirky smile told her he couldn't wait to make some snide remark. She couldn't stand it anymore. "Go ahead, say it."

"Who is he?"

"Jason?" She hoped to sound casual. "We work together."

"Right." He drew the word out with a sarcastic tone. "That's it, just work together." He pushed a button, and a mini-bar appeared in front of them stocked with sodas. "Traveling in style does have advantages." He handed her a drink and popped one open for himself. "Jason, huh? I'll have to ask Dad since he made sure to make introductions. Jason must have passed inspection."

Part of her wanted to scream about lack of privacy and the other part reared a curious head. She hadn't thought about the fact that Dad actually made sure Jason knew everyone. Was that good or bad? One of those reverse psychology things? Parents acting as though they like someone so you'll run screaming, or did they really like him? And if they did, why? What did they know?

She leaned toward Brad. "If you find out anything, tell me."

"I knew it." He sat his drink in the cup holder, leaned back, and placed his hands behind his neck. "You like him."

"Maybe."

"*Maybe?* You practically crawled inside his suit coat."

She cringed. "That obvious?"

"If I found sparks like that, I'd marry the girl in a heartbeat."

"Brad, this scares me. Jason doesn't know who I am. I come with major baggage, and I can't go through another bad marriage."

"Well, if Jason's a good guy, he could be the right one for you, or maybe you just needed to know that there are caring men out there. Have you prayed about this?"

"Maybe, kinda ... I don't know. It's not like I've been back in God's graces for long."

"There is definitely a major attraction going between you two. You can't afford to get messed up in something that will drag you back down into a bad lifestyle."

"Ouch, this could be tough. If we date, we probably

ought to take a chaperone."

"Yep, and Jedi doesn't count."

The limo pulled off the freeway and u-turned, heading back to the city. Brad knocked on the divider. "What's going on?"

The glass slid down. "Your father called and said to take you both to Bethany's apartment. There's been a break-in at the estate."

Heart racing, Bethany flipped on her cell phone and waited impatiently as it came to life. *Finally.* She punched in Dad's speed-dial. A busy signal beeped in her ear. *Strange.* She dialed Chase's number and his went straight to voice mail. "I can't get anyone to answer."

"This is driving me nuts." Brad practically crackled with impatience. "I shouldn't have left my phone at the house."

She tried Scott. He answered on the first ring and didn't wait for her questions. "Bethany, I'll meet you at your place. Your family is fine. No one is hurt. They're checking the premises. I'll answer any questions when I get there."

The line clicked dead.

Chapter 17

Eons passed before the Limo stopped. Bethany strained to see out the tinted window. Why were they parked in the mall parking lot? She banged on the glass to get the drivers attention. "Why did you stop here?"

The intercom switched on. "There's a problem at your apartment. We're to wait here until we know more."

What now? Why didn't Dad let her and Brad take her own car? She punched numbers like crazy. Again, Dad's phone didn't go through, neither did Chase's. Frantically, she tried Scott's cell.

He answered on the third ring. "Bethany, I'm sorry for the delay. Someone's been in your apartment. Nothing seems to be missing." He hesitated. "However, there is one item we're concerned about."

Spider tingles rippled down her spine. "What?"

"They left you a message written in red lipstick on the bathroom mirror. Leave Southburg, or else."

Air seeped from her throat. *What's going on? Who's doing this?* Thank goodness, Jedi wasn't there.

Brad signaled for her to talk to him.

She waved him off. "Scott. Before you hang up. Is Jedi okay back at Mom and Dad's?"

"Affirmative. Your dad wanted to make sure we told you. We'll let the driver know when it's safe to bring you

143

home." The line went dead.

Numb, she sank in her seat. *Safe?* When would she ever feel safe again?

Brad shook her arm. "Tell me what's happening?"

"Someone left a message on my mirror. Leave Southburg, or else."

The limo restarted and pulled into traffic, traveling in the opposite direction. The divider window rolled down. "I'm to take you back to the estate. We've received the all clear."

She wanted to crawl into the front seat and throttle him. "What about my apartment?"

"No details as of yet. You'll be notified of the progress." The divider whirled back into place, leaving them in silence.

The limo weaved through government vehicles and police cars parked on both sides of the winding road leading to Mom and Dad's house. Every light on the estate burned bright, the grounds crawled with Dad's bodyguard force, along with those wearing FBI and Homeland Security jackets.

Bethany clung to the door. "FBI *and* Homeland Security?"

Wide-eyed Brad stared out the window. "Helps to have friends in high places. Dad's project must be bigger than we thought. At least I hope that's all it is."

Before she could question him, the car door opened and a security agent motioned for Brad.

Payne Tanner, Dad's main bodyguard, escorted her into Dad's office. He signaled for her to sit, closed the door, then balanced on the edge of the desk. "I need to know the names of anyone who might be considered your enemy."

Mind reeling, she gulped air as his dark eyes studied her. With a name like Payne, thank goodness he was on their side. "I guess Gavin."

He ran a hand through his silver slicked-back hair. "We've got him covered."

Covered? Smothered would have been a better analogy.

"Anyone else?" His pen tapped impatiently on his paper. "Anyone you can think of, male or female. I need names."

"I don't know. I haven't been back long. Alex and Nicole at work probably don't like me too much, but they wouldn't do anything like this. If Alex broke in, he'd be bringing champagne."

His scowl made her cringe. *So much for attempts at humor.* "There's Tom Chambers, the reporter. He wasn't too happy with me on our date last week. I wouldn't give him information about Dad's contract."

Payne made a note on his pad. "Anyone else?"

She shrugged. "Back at college, I probably made some enemies. A guy I dated named Ken. Ken Stober. He wasn't very nice."

Without looking up, he scribbled a note. "We know about him." He coughed into his fist. "And the rest."

If Payne and security knew, did her parents know? Melting into the carpet would be good right about now. She fanned herself before self-combusting from embarrassment. The room faded and she gripped the arms of her chair. She couldn't pass out now. *Focus. Breathe.* No wonder her parents were glad she was back. "How long have you guys been watching me?" Her words came out far too needy.

He looked at her, and his expression gentled. "You've never been out of your father's care."

The way he said it, brought tears to her eyes and a lump the size of Chicago lodged in her throat. She hadn't been watched to find out what she was doing wrong, but for her safety. If only she could go back and make some changes.

"Tell me about Nadia Minsky."

Hearing her college roommates name jolted her. "Nadia?"

"Doesn't she have Israeli connections?"

Bethany flew out of her chair. "Don't mess with Nadia. She's been through enough."

He held up a hand. "Whoa there, missy, I'm not making accusations, we just need to cover all our bases."

"Nadia is happy now." She pointed a finger at his barrel chest. "Don't you dare upset her. There's *no way* she's involved in any of this. If anything, I want somebody making sure she's okay." She marched to the door. "I'm talking to Dad."

He jerked up from the desk and cut her off. "Just a minute. We're not through. I need you to think. Is there anyone else you haven't mentioned?"

"The only other people I can think of are Cindy and Joelle, the gossip twins."

He made several notes and paused. "Either of them wear red lipstick?"

"I'm sure they do. All women at one time or another have probably bought and worn red lipstick. It could even be a man. It doesn't have to be a woman." Pulse pumping in her ears, Bethany pushed past her interrogator and stomped down the hall.

If she ever got her hands on whoever was doing this, she'd rip them apart. And to add insult to injury, security had the audacity to question her about Nadia. If they so much as harassed her, even for a second, they better get ready for a

Bethany Davis beating. Probably not a very Christian thought, but the fact her friends and family were in danger brought out her fighting side.

She found her family huddled in conference around the dining table. Chips, crackers, and cookies sat in silver platters, evidence of Mom's care to always make sure all needs were met.

Upon entering the room, Brad looked up and grinned. "Look out. Wild-cat on the prowl."

"Dad." Bethany stopped at his chair. "Don't you dare let security contact or harass Nadia. She does not need any more trauma in her life."

He patted her arm like she was a wayward child. "Nadia's not a suspect. They're looking at every angle, especially since she has connections with Israel."

Trying to control her anger, Bethany plopped in a chair. "You know she wouldn't have anything to do with this."

Chase huffed. "Grow up, Bethany. We've all been questioned."

Andrietta nodded in agreement.

Bethany stared at the table, wishing she could do something, anything. Tension hung thick, like layers of spider-webs, and all she could do was sit.

"Honey, I promise she'll be okay." Mom offered Bethany a cookie. "We're all going to be fine. With our prayers, and so many officers looking, they'll find whoever is doing all of this."

"Mr. Davis?" A Homeland security agent entered the room. "Could I see you for a moment?" He nodded toward the family then looked squarely at her father. "In private."

Dad squeezed Mom's shoulder and left.

Brad nudged Bethany. "Grab a cookie. I want to show you something."

Curious, she picked up Jedi and followed her brother up the stairs to his old bedroom.

He closed the door behind her and gave her his trademark, mischievous smile. "Sit down and make yourself comfortable until the storm blows over."

"I thought you were going to—"

Brad held up his hand. "Wait for it, don't be so anxious." After rummaging through his closet, he produced a suitcase. With a flourish, he popped open the latches, removed a stack of clothes, snapped off the inner lining, and pulled out a legal-sized envelope. "This, my dear sister, is a treasure map."

"Right, and Jedi is a Doberman."

"You don't believe?" He opened the envelope, and carefully removed a yellow, tattered parchment. "I'm meeting with an expert Thursday morning to have this analyzed."

She hitched a breath as she stared at the unfamiliar markings of what looked like an ancient map. "You're kidding, right?"

"No." His serious expression made her stomach roll.

"Have you told Dad? Could this be the reason somebody is after us? Brad, people get nasty when it comes to money." She collapsed on the bed. "I thought you worked for the Peace Corps."

"I did."

"What do you mean, you *did*?"

"I quit last year."

"Dad is going to have your hide for this. Does anybody else know about you leaving the Corps? Or about this?" She pointed at the map as if it would bite.

"You're going to have to trust me. I promise I'm not doing anything illegal."

"If you take treasure from a foreign country, they'll do

more than tan your hide. You've got to tell Dad, or security, or somebody about this."

"It's not safe to tell them. It could put them in danger."

"Then why did you tell *me*?" Bethany stared at the map. Should she hit him or run to Dad screaming? How could Brad put their family in such a dangerous situation? Weren't there enough problems? Somebody already wanted her out of Southburg.

Curse words popped into her mind and she batted them away with a quick Bible verse. *May the words of my mouth and the meditation of my heart be pleasing in your sight.* How did she even know that verse? God, please *help me not kill my brother.* All those years of drinking, partying, being wild, and when she finally gets back on track, her brother sends her over the edge of sanity.

Since strangling him was out of the question, she shot him her hardest look. "What were you thinking, bringing this thing here? And after Grandfather's death. On top of that, why did you show me the stinking thing?"

"I'm sorry. I had to." He sat next to her, giving her his trademark innocent-brother look. "Do you still have the artifact I sent you last year?"

Realization buzzed through her brain. Her throat dry, she swallowed hard. "You sent something that is now on full display to every person who sets foot in my apartment. Did you even think that it might get me killed?"

"I honestly didn't know it was important when I sent it to you, until we found this on our latest dig."

The vile, yellowing paper smirked at her in some obscure language, calling out to the bad guys to tear apart their home, her life, and any chance of happiness. She picked up a pillow and smacked him. "What happened to you? You used to

149

be the smart one."

"Bethany, trust me. I'm not doing something stupid. There's more going on than I can tell you. I promise, in a few days this will all be over. I'll be back in Peru. Everyone in our family will be fine. Believe it or not, I have prayed about this."

"What did you pray? God, make me rich?"

The twitch in his expression showed her comment wounded him. "You know that's not what I would do. I ran from the money, remember?"

"Then what are you doing with a treasure map?"

He carefully placed the paper back in the envelope and returned it to its hiding place. "It's not mine. I'm working for—"

Growling, Jedi lunged off the bed and stopped at the door.

A hard knock made them jump and Jedi lunging for the safety of Bethany's arms.

Brad threw his clothes in the suitcase, stuffed it in the closet, and sat next to her on the bed. "Come in."

Payne Tanner surveyed them and the room. By the look on his face, he knew they were up to something. "We need you both downstairs."

Brad looked as casual as ever.

A neon sign stamped *guilty* probably blinked across her forehead. She followed her brother into the dining room. Agents and security rimmed the outer walls, standing in military fashion, arms by their side, legs slightly spread. If she hadn't turned a new leaf, she would have thought she had died and gone to heaven with all those well-built ex-soldiers.

Dad stood at the head of the table. "Bethany, security will run you back to your apartment to look for anything missing, and then I want you back here tonight. Tomorrow, after the funeral, Chase and Andrietta will return to Washington with an extra bodyguard assigned to them." He nodded to the black-haired agent then addressed the family again. "Brad is scheduled back in Peru at the end of the week. Prints were found at Bethany's apartment, and Payne is running them through several agencies."

Brad waved his hand like a schoolboy. "I'd like to go with Bethany to check her place."

Dad's right eyebrow raised. "Fine. I want you both back here as soon as possible." He turned to address security. "Payne, you and your men are dismissed for a few minutes." He waited until the room cleared and then sat next to Mom. "I know it's late. But there's one more thing we need to do as a family." He bowed his head. "Let's pray."

Dad praying? And it's not dinner or church. Bethany closed her eyes. Her heart stepped up a beat. His voice, thick with emotion, gave proof the situation had turned deadly serious.

Bethany surveyed her apartment. *What were they looking for?*

Nothing seemed out of place, but a presence remained — palatable and oppressive. The knowledge someone had been here, looking, touching, and walking among her belongings freaked her out. She checked each room, security pummeling her with questions. Everything seemed tainted, violated.

She released a frustrated breath. Where did these guys get their crime scene training? Fingerprint dust covered the doors, windows, table tops, counters, even her bathroom sink and mirror. From the looks of things, they would have dusted Jedi if he'd been home.

Brad, holding the ceramic artifact he'd sent her last year, sidled next to her in the bathroom. "Found it."

"What's so special about that thing? It's been sitting on my mantle since I moved in."

"Right here." Pointing to the headpiece adorning the small black and red figurine, he threw a wary glance at the security officers in the other room. "These..." He lowered his voice to a whisper. "These markings match the map. With this, we should be able to discern a more precise location."

"If that's what they were after then, why they didn't take it?"

"Whoever was here wasn't looking for an Incan artifact." He pointed to the warning scrawled on her bathroom mirror in red lipstick. "Somebody else wants you out of Southburg."

Back at the estate, Bethany, half-asleep in her pajamas and robe, sat on the floor and leaned against Brad's bed. Jedi snored soundly in her lap. Brad studied the map and artifact while making notations in a leather-bound notebook. If Jedi were awake and mean, she'd have him growl. "It's late, and I'm tired. Are you ever going to tell me what's going on?"

"Just give me another minute."

Stifling a yawn, she stared at the clock. *2:15.* Only eight hours until Grandfather's funeral. Tears stung. She'd miss him so much. "I really need to get some sleep."

"Okay, okay. It'll be worth the wait, you'll see. I promise."

She picked up Jedi and collapsed on the bed. "Wake me when you're ready to talk."

"I got it!" He jumped to his feet and plopped next to her. "Based on my notes, this map shows the gold is not in Ecuador but still in Peru."

"Great, that narrows it down to a thousand miles."

"True, unless you happen to know the landmark for this symbol." He pointed to weird marking on the map. "I know where this is. Thursday, I'll confirm with my contact at the Smithsonian and then call my boss."

"Indiana Jones?"

"No. I work for the Peruvian government."

She sat up. "*That's* your boss?"

"Yep, they asked me to help track and recover their treasures before thieves cleaned out the country. You should see some of the pieces we found."

Thieves are plundering Peru and she's sitting on the bed with a map leading to who knows where? "No telling how many people are after that map. Brad, you need to tell Dad. Security should know about this."

"Nope. The more people who know, the bigger the mess."

"At least tell Dad and then let him decide."

Brad gathered everything up and carefully placed it all back into his suitcase. "I don't know. I think it's still too big a risk."

"And hiding a map in the lining of your suitcase isn't? If the love of money is the root of all evil, you just stuck a lightening rod in your closet."

Chapter 18

Tuesday morning, Jason settled into the pew next to his co-workers and strained to catch a glimpse of Bethany. Dignitaries from DC and the surrounding area filled the sanctuary of her home church. She sat with her family, head down as though praying, her grandfather's casket open at the front. How could one woman look so strong and yet vulnerable? Her whole family sagged with exhaustion.

Scanning the room, Jason spotted the guy from Bethany's apartment standing stiff at the back wall watching each person who entered. If Jerk cared for Bethany, he'd be by her side. Just then, Jerk stiffened, stared hard, and signaled to a dark-suited man on the other side of the room.

Dark Suit rushed forward and stopped a well-dressed man approaching Bethany's family. With a hand on the man's elbow, Dark Suit led him to the back.

Wait a minute. Jason made a mental note of possible security personnel. The place practically crawled with them. What an idiot, he'd been. Jerk-face probably wasn't her date. He was part of a security force. But why would she need a bodyguard?

He leaned close to Nancy. "Where does Bethany's father work?"

She gave him a curious look. "He owns his own company and works in the defense industry."

A thousand questions ran through his mind but there was no one to ask. Not right now. He had to talk to Bethany.

The church service and ride to the grave passed in a blur. Though Bethany sat under an awning with her family, sweat trickled down her back as the preacher gave his final words. Her folding chair listed toward Chase, who stared impassively straight ahead. Andrietta, careful not to smear her makeup, dabbed her eyes. Dad kept his arm around Mom. Grandfather's casket waited to be lowered into the grave.

Everything felt surreal and in slow motion. Funerals were so final and so empty. Nothing to take home but memories. She had no more tears to cry, and after last night, fatigue stole her ability to feel. Her emotions shut down with everything hitting at once like pummeling relentless waves.

At the end of the service, Bethany stood by Grandfather's casket. "I'll miss you." She glanced heavenward and swallowed hard. "But you better behave until I get up there."

A hand rested on her shoulder. Thinking it was Dad, she laid her cheek on the fingers.

"I'm sorry for your loss." The voice belonged to Jason.

Her heart and stomach skittered in unison. *So much for lack of emotion.* She drank in his green eyes and tender expression. Every thought flew out of her mind.

He cleared his throat and shoved his hands into his pockets. "Is there anything I can do?"

Hold me, come riding on a white horse and carry me off into some safe and beautiful land. She stared at his lips. *Kiss me.* Straightening, she focused on his shoulder, something much safer than his handsome face. "No, but thank you. I'm glad you came."

He nodded. "Can I give you a ride?"

"I can't. We're going back to the church for lunch."

"I understand." He placed his hand on her arm. "Bethany, I'm here if you ever need me. Okay?"

I do need you. She stepped closer but movement caught her attention.

Brad signaled for her to hurry.

"I've got to get going. Jason, thank you." She turned, even though a hug would be nice right now. "I'll probably come to work in the morning."

"Don't rush." He walked next to her, matching her stride. "We'll be fine until you feel like coming back."

"Trust me, I need a distraction."

They stopped at the limo, the door open, with Brad sitting inside grinning like an impish kid.

Jason gently tucked a stray hair behind her ear, snapping her senses into high alert. "I'd like to see you this weekend if you're still free."

Yes, please. "That would be nice." She hurried into the vehicle before she said or did anything else she'd regret with her brother watching.

Brad snickered as they drove away. "You two definitely need a chaperone."

###

Wednesday morning, sympathy cards and a bouquet waited on Bethany's desk. The affection from her co-workers astounded her. Jason had taken the time not only to write a thoughtful note but also bought her flowers. She needed a cup of coffee to loosen her tightened throat. Blinking back the moisture threatening to escape, she grabbed her mug.

Valerie practically bowled her over to check out the flowers. "Who sent those? Reporter boy?"

"No, they aren't from Tom."

"Good, I didn't care for him."

"I thought you two were friends?"

Valerie, a look of disgust on her face, shook her head. "No way, I just met him the night of my party. He was downright rude to a friend of mine."

Bethany's skin pebbled. Was Tom the one to blame for the break-ins? Ignoring Valerie, she sat in her chair and searched the Internet for Tom's name.

Valerie leaned across her shoulder. "What are you looking for?"

"Maybe it's just my imagination, but I'm pretty sure Tom said you two were friends. It makes me wonder what else he's not been truthful about."

"What are you girls doing?" Rhonda perched on the corner of Bethany's desk.

Valerie pointed to a link on the computer. "I thought Tom was a greenhorn, this says he celebrated his thirtieth anniversary with the paper last month."

Bethany's veins frosted as she opened the article. At the top of the page, was a picture of a balding, overweight, middle-aged man named Tom Chambers.

She grabbed her cell phone and speed-dialed Scott.

Jason downed his fifth cup of coffee and tugged at his collar. He couldn't wait any longer. What did Bethany think of the flowers and his note? Steeling himself, he followed the chatter of voices.

Rhonda and Valerie hovered over Bethany as she talked on her cell phone. Valerie barked orders like a drill-sergeant, and Rhonda shook her upturned head in prayer.

He gestured for someone to notice him. "What's going on?"

Valerie glanced his way. "We've got problems. Tom Chambers is *not* Tom Chambers."

"What? Who?"

Rhonda shook her head. "That reporter is not who he said he was. Bethany is calling her bodyguard, and I'm praying for the Lord's protection."

Bethany's in danger? Adrenaline laced with a healthy dose of caffeine kicked Jason into overdrive. He squeezed her arm to get her attention. "What can I do?"

Still on the phone, she pointed to the computer screen as though he'd understand. He nudged Valerie. "What does this guy have to do with Bethany?"

Valerie let out an exasperated huff and told him the details.

Jason whistled. If he got his hands on Tom, or whoever the guy was, he'd throttle him.

Bethany hung up the phone. "Security is on the trail. Hopefully we'll know something this afternoon."

"I knew it. Tom, aka, mystery man, is a spy." Valerie huffed. "He's working for some terrorist county to find out details of your dad's latest weapon technology."

Rhonda put a finger to her lips. "Don't talk like that."

Bethany seemed unfazed. "I highly doubt he's anything sinister. Unless he's totally got me fooled, he's not smooth enough for that line of work."

Jason clenched his fists. "Well, he's obviously up to something, or he wouldn't be using an alias." All three turned toward him as though he'd appeared out of thin air. "What? I'm just trying to help."

"Well." Valerie toyed with Bethany's stapler. "I say we call my *friends* and let them *talk* to him." She smacked the stapler rapid fire.

Bethany grinned. "Interesting idea. Instead of delivering the paper, they could deliver the paper boy."

"By the time they finish, Tom'll be *red* all over." Valerie jabbed Jason. "Get it, red instead of read."

Rhonda tsked. "Shouldn't you girls be more serious? I don't like this one bit."

Jason nodded. "Bethany, I'll be glad to escort you to lunch."

Valerie's eyebrows raised and a mischievous smile played on her face. "I think Jason's right. You *should* have a man around for protection. We'll take Jason with us to lunch."

We? Not exactly what he had in mind. He attempted a positive expression. "Sure, that'd be great. I'll stop back around eleven thirty." Determined to find some answers on his own, he went back to his office.

Internet searches on Tom Chambers left only questions. Thankfully, she hadn't dated the married middle-aged guy in the pictures. Jason tried to switch gears to focus on work. He needed to get a report done for George before five o'clock.

Without a knock, Nicole sat in the chair in front of his desk. Leaning toward him, she smiled and batted her lashes. "I need your help." Too much flesh spilled from her low-cut blouse. "It's important."

Jason glanced at his clock. *11:15.* "Sure, I'll be glad to help after lunch."

159

She placed her red-nailed hand on his. "I really need your help *now*. Alex and my notes are waiting in my office. Do you mind?"

"Fine." He grabbed a file to get away from her talons. "I'll meet you there in a few minutes. I need to take care of something first."

He hurried down the hall. If Nicole didn't keep him too long, he could make lunch. If the situation took longer, maybe he could meet them at the restaurant.

Bethany sat at her desk, her head resting in her hand as she studied a diagram. Jason paused to enjoy the view.

A hard jab in his ribs snapped him to attention.

Smiling, Valerie squeezed past him. "We're ready for lunch."

He cleared his throat. "Something's come up. I'll meet you there in a few minutes."

"Maggie B's just opened downtown on seventh street." Valerie said. "The food's great, and they have live music."

"Sounds good." Bethany picked up her purse and moved next to him, close enough to make heat crawl up his neck. "I hope you can join us."

Stomach full of lunch, Bethany started her car. Even though the meal was enjoyable, having Jason around would have been a nice dessert. The annoying ding signaled that her passenger remained unbuckled. She shot a playful glare at Valerie. "You have to put on your seat belt."

"Fine." Valerie rolled her eyes. "Be a spoil sport, but if you'd snip a couple of wires that thing wouldn't be such a pest."

Rhonda covered her mouth in a vain attempt to hide a yawn. "Girls, after a big lunch like that, I could stretch out on this back seat and take a nap."

Valerie smirked. "Bethany should be tired too. She kept jerking her head around looking for Jason."

"Maybe I was just making sure we weren't followed." Giggles from both friends signaled their disbelief. *Rats*, she'd have to work on subtlety. She pulled into the flow of traffic and checked her rearview mirror.

"I am praying for you and Jason," Rhonda said. "He's a good man, Bethany."

"Thanks, Rhonda. I'm praying about a lot of things."

"Wait a minute." Valerie smacked the dashboard. "You *are* different. I want to know what's going on."

Bethany smiled at Valerie's disgusted expression. "I'll admit it, openly and without shame. I've gotten back with God."

"I *knew* it. At first I thought it was because of your Grandfather but now I can see it." Valerie huffed out a breath. "You've got that look."

"What look?"

"Like Rhonda. That contented, mushy look."

Bethany laughed. "Gee, that really sounds bad."

"It is for me." Valerie crossed her arms. "I lost another good-times buddy. Everybody's buzzing like flies to the light, getting zapped, and dropping off the fun wagon."

"What are you talking about? I can still have fun."

"Yeah, right. James got religion last week and said we can't keep sleeping together unless we're married. And now you ... *you* go and get what do they call it? Saved? Saved from what? I'll tell you *what* ... fun! You won't get to have any fun. No love and no good music."

Bethany turned up the radio volume and bobbed her head to the music. "I still like music, I still like fun, and I do *love* loving."

Rhonda fanned herself. "Goodness, I'll admit it, I love loving too."

Valerie blanched and did a 180 to face Rhonda. "I *can't* believe you just said that."

"Girl, I loved my husband, and I loved the times we spent together. And I would love if God brought me a good man into my life to marry. I miss having a man."

"Wow." Valerie faced forward, a look of utter confusion on her face. "This is the strangest conversation I've ever had."

Bethany nudged her and checked the rearview mirror. "Christianity and fun can go in the same sentence."

Valerie ran a hand through her hair. "I think I blew a gasket."

"Speaking of gaskets, is everybody buckled? There's a car tailing us. Hang on tight, I'm going to take a fast right at the next intersection. Valerie, get my cell phone out of my purse and speed-dial Scott. He should be behind us, but I haven't seen him."

Heart pounding, Bethany gripped the wheel, checked over her shoulder, and punched the gas. "The car looks like a blue Malibu. The guy driving has a ball cap and dark glasses." Heart beating double-time, Bethany clenched her teeth and turned the wheel. Her tires squealed in protest.

"Sweet Jesus, please protect us. Sweet Jesus...." Rhonda's whispered prayers bounced through the car as they fishtailed around the corner.

Valerie, completely nonchalant, braced one hand against the dash and with the other left Scott a message. "No answer. But I told him what's happening and where we are." She closed the phone and tossed it on Bethany's lap. "If he's not back there following, I'd demote him."

Bethany checked her rear-view. "He's probably behind us, I just can't tell in this traffic." At least she hoped he was there.

A stoplight loomed at the next intersection. The light changed to yellow. If she timed her speed right, they could make it through and stop him.

She tapped the brake just enough to slow down her pursuer then floored the accelerator as the light changed to red.

Horns blasted and tires screeched as the Malibu followed.

Valerie hooted. "You sure know how to make a point about having fun. Take the next turn. I know these streets like the back of my hand. Turn left." Valerie pointed right. "Turn left!"

"Do you want me to go the way you're pointing or the way you're saying?"

"I mean right. Now!"

Bethany cranked the wheel and almost flipped the car to make the turn.

Valerie giggled like a kid on a roller-coaster ride. "Quick, left into that alley."

Bracing herself, Bethany turned into a short alley lined with aged wooden fences.

"Aim between those driveways at the end."

"No way. The road stops at a hedge."

"It's not a hedge, it leads to an alley. Trust me. Think of Batman and his hidden cave."

"Jesus, help us." Rhonda's voice grew louder. "Jesus, help us."

Adrenaline coursing through her veins, Valerie's *woo hoo*

echoing in her ears, Bethany cringed and gunned through the foliage. The car sliced easily through a tangle of vines and screeched to halt behind a lilac garage.

Valerie drummed on the dashboard. "Oh man, that was fun."

Rhonda, pale, but smiling, leaned against Valerie's seat. "Thank you, Jesus. Thank you."

Bethany high-fived Valerie. "Don't *ever* let anyone tell you that Christians don't have fun."

Chapter 19

Nicole's problem could have waited. Acid burned a hole in Jason's stomach. He stifled the urge to curse and opened a pack of peanuts from his desk drawer. If something happened while he wasn't with Bethany, he'd throttle Alex and Nicole. It almost seemed as though they had plotted to keep him in the office. Why did everything go against him?

Jason needed to get the project done, but he couldn't concentrate. Should he continue to pursue Bethany? Even with the mutual attraction, if she didn't share the same values, it would only be a waste of time and a huge heartache.

He had to talk to her. Gathering his courage, he put down the file he'd been working on and went to her office. Outside the door he stopped.

Rhonda and Valerie chuckled with Bethany about something.

Valerie held up her mug in a toast. "Here's to fun, sex, and rock and roll."

A rock cemented in Jason's stomach. *Is that my answer?* He turned and trudged toward his office.

"Jason?" Bethany, still smiling, caught him by the arm. "Is everything okay? We missed you at lunch."

The dingy gray carpet matched his mood. "Something got in the way." Something would always be in the way. "I'll talk to you later."

165

"Wait. Thank you for the flowers and note." She stopped in front of him, her eyes shimmering. "That really meant a lot to me. I know Grandfather's in Heaven but I'll always miss him."

His pulse quickened. *If she knows about Heaven, does that mean?* "But you'll see him again, right?"

She gave him a curious look. "Not in this life—"

Valerie grabbed Bethany. "Hurry, Scott's on the phone."

"Sorry. I've got to get this. Talk to you later, okay?"

Jason yelled in his head—long, loud, and until his brain cells exploded. Why couldn't he find out what he was supposed to do?

Tom Chambers steadied his breathing as he rubbed his wrists. He'd watched cop shows. He could keep his mouth shut, ask for a lawyer, make a quick phone call to his dad, and he'd be back on the streets by evening. They may have caught him for tailing Bethany, but that was all they had. He wouldn't need to tell them more.

The interrogation room looked just as he'd imagined. A heavy table in front of him sat on the concrete floor. A single light bulb hung from the ceiling, suspended in a metallic cage. A one-way mirror covered the wall to his left, probably with cops watching and waiting.

He could do this, look cool, play the part, even if sweat did drip down his back and pool at his tailbone.

The door creaked opened and the tall blonde guy who'd cuffed and brought him in, sat in front of him. His steel-blue eyes narrowed. "Why were you following Bethany Davis?"

"I want my lawyer and a phone call."

"This is the last time I'll ask nicely." The man towered

over him. "Why were you following Bethany Davis?"

"I want my lawyer."

The man placed his hand on Tom's shoulder. Pain bolted through his neck where the man vise-gripped his top muscle. He cursed and squirmed to get away. "You can't do that! I have my rights."

"Who said you have rights?"

"You have to read them. Then I get a lawyer and can make a phone call." He tried to remove the rising octave in his voice. "Cops have to do that."

"Who said we're cops? I'll ask you again. Why were you following Bethany Davis?"

Moisture drenched his armpits and upper lip. "I don't have anything to say."

The man glanced at the mirrored wall and shook his head.

A few moments later, a silver haired man walked in carrying a car battery and jumper cables. With a thunk, he dropped them on the table. "I think it would be wise to talk to us."

Tom's heart plunged to his feet. "You can't do anything to me. You won't have a case. You'll be in big trouble."

Silver-hair shrugged. "No one has seen you come in, and no one will see you go out. Your only concern is will anyone ever see you again."

"I'll call the cops." His voice strained tight against his vocal cords.

"Go ahead. Call them." Silver-hair slid a cell phone toward him. "You call, and with them will come the FBI and Homeland Security." He picked up the cables and leaned toward him. "You don't have a clue who you're messing with and how much trouble you're in. If you cooperate, you can walk away. And then be grateful you can walk."

Why they couldn't talk to her on the phone at work drove her crazy. Ready to jump out of her skin with questions, Bethany perched on her couch with Jedi while Scott and Payne Tanner took the chairs opposite her.

"Here's what we know." Payne opened his notes. "Tom Chambers works for the paper as a copy boy. His dad is Tom Chambers, Sr., the reporter. Someone has been sending a cashier's check to Tom, Jr. to get information and then scare you to leave town. He doesn't know his contact, and we're working to trace that information. Junior followed you, drove the boat, and wrote the note on your mirror. He also paid one of the workmen to drug Jedi."

Bethany leaned back, a million thoughts ricocheting through her brain. "But why does someone want me to leave Southburg? I haven't lived here in three years. Did Tom break in at Mom and Dad's?"

"No. We've verified where he was that night. He has a receipt from the drug store to buy the lipstick and had a key to your apartment from his contact. There's no way he could have been at the estate."

"So we're still clueless on what happened at my parents, and we still don't know who's after me?" At her question, both men averted their eyes. "Are you sure he's telling the truth?"

Scott chuckled. "Yeah, when Payne brought out the car battery, Tom sang like a canary."

Payne shot Scott a glare and then returned his business-like gaze to Bethany. "I just happened to have bought a car battery from Sears for my wife's SUV and set it on the table."

She'd have done more than just put it on a table. "What happens next?"

Payne flipped to the next page in his notebook. "To lighten the charges against him, Tom has agreed to keep quiet until we find his contact. We have someone tailing him. If he so much as sneezes, we'll know. We've traced the location of the cashier's checks to a bank on the southwest side of town. He's due a check this Friday. We're also looking into how Tom's contact got access to an apartment key." He shifted in his seat. "Have you given a key to anyone?"

She straightened at the accusation. "No. Even Mom and Dad don't have one."

He nodded. "We'll have your locks changed. We'd like you to stay in the apartment and go about your regular routine."

"Have you talked to Dad? I'm surprised he'll let me stay here."

Payne shifted in his seat and cleared his throat. "He did take issue with a few things. We've assured him you'll be safe. Scott will stay close, and we've assigned other guards to man the outside stations. Any questions?"

"Only about a million. Do you think it's Gavin?"

"When we questioned him, he wasn't even aware you were back in town."

"You talked to him? Isn't he married and living in Ohio?"

"No." He tilted his head, his expression curious. "He's single and lives in Petersburg."

Vision tunneling, her chest turned to lead as she searched to find her voice. "Joelle told me he married Linda, had a baby, and lives in Ohio."

Payne flipped open his cell phone and motioned for

Scott. "Bethany, he didn't remarry and he doesn't have any children."

"But why would she lie?" Bethany pressed a hand to her churning stomach. "Just to hurt me?"

"I need you to fill us in." He closed the phone. "What's your connection with Joelle? You called her one of the gossip twins. "

"Cindy and Joelle used to hang out with Linda. We all went to high school together."

"Why isn't Linda mentioned?"

"She's the girl I found in bed with Gavin." She swallowed the acid rising in her throat. "I don't know where she is now."

His face softened. "I'm sorry we have to ask these questions. Maybe I can make this easier. I'll tell you what I know, you fill in the blanks." At her nod, he continued. "You married Gavin after he graduated from college, which was your sophomore year. The marriage lasted fourteen months, then you left town and continued your education in North Carolina. During that time, did you have any contact with Joelle?"

"No, other than when I came home for holidays. Joelle and Cindy started all kinds of nasty rumors about what happened while I was married to Gavin."

"Why?"

"I don't know. They hated my guts the minute Gavin asked me out."

"Did Gavin date any of the other girls?" He shifted and rubbed the back of his neck. "I mean before you were married."

"Gavin went out with all of them at least once." Tamping down the onslaught of unwanted emotions, she hugged a throw pillow to her chest. "I thought I was the special one when he settled on me. The only thing I got out of the marriage was a shredded heart."

He closed his notebook and stood. "I appreciate your openness. I may need to ask more questions later. We'll get to the bottom of this." He paused for a moment. "Bethany, your dad and I go way back." His voice thickened. "I'll do everything in my power to make sure you and your family remain safe."

Chapter 20

Bethany shoved her purse into the bottom desk drawer. Only a few people beat her to the office this morning. She couldn't have stayed in bed another minute. Last night had been miserable, sorting through old memories and looking for answers. Every clue with Joelle, Tom, Gavin, and the others only led to more questions. How did her life become such a mess? "Bethany?" Jason stood in the doorway, his eyes troubled. "Can we talk?"

At her nod, he pulled a chair next to her. "I need to know something. This might be an awkward question, but I really need to know. Are you a Christian?"

"Yes."

He blinked as though he hadn't heard her correctly. "A *real* Christian, you've asked Jesus into your heart?"

"Yes."

Jason's face softened and he swallowed several times. "We're still on for tomorrow night, right?"

"Yes, unless you're planning to feed me to the lions or something."

Smiling, he leaned toward her as though studying her for the first time. "I had to know. Is six thirty okay? I'd like to take you to dinner and a movie. Just casual, give us a chance to visit."

Before she kissed him, she better think of something to

say. "Gee, I don't know. My team leader is kind of tough. I'd have to leave right at five to make it home to get ready."

"Since we're ahead of schedule, I happen to know he's going to make sure the full team gets an early start on the weekend." He moved closer, so close every hair on the back of her neck stood at rigid attention as his breath smoothed across her skin.

Her ringing cell phone jarred her back to reality.

Jason, still smiling, squeezed her hand. "I'll talk to you later." With those looks and his smile, big-time trouble brewed for her heart.

After he left, she fanned herself and answered the call. Payne Tanner filled her in on the latest. Another check had been issued at the bank for Tom Chambers, but this time with a second one for an additional thousand. The security camera, showed a well-dressed woman paying in cash. They were on their way to talk with Joelle.

Bethany shook her head. Her life had become a total and absolute, weird mess. Jason's increased interest seemed more dangerous than being stalked. Physical peril she could handle. Emotional risks were a frightening matter.

Yes! Jason could lift a thousand pounds, run a one-minute mile, or climb Mount Everest without oxygen. A stick of dynamite couldn't remove his smile. Between prayers of gratitude for learning Bethany was truly a Christian, he plowed into his work getting more finished than he had in two weeks. All those years wasted and now he'd been given another chance. He wouldn't screw up this time. They could date for a decent period of time, get engaged, marry, and raise a family.

Whoa.

Maybe he should take this one day at a time.

How on earth was he supposed to date someone that physically attractive and still remain decent?

"Jason?" Bethany waited in his doorway. "Want to join us for lunch?"

"You bet." He jumped up, jostling his desk. The picture of Kelly's kids tipped over with a thud.

Her smile widened. "How does Mexican sound?"

"Oh, yeah. I'm in the mood for some hot stuff." Heat shot up his back and his neck. Could he possibly be anymore of an idiot?

She cleared her throat, but the giggle behind it was obvious. "Val and Rhonda are waiting in the lobby."

He followed her to the elevator and stepped inside. "I'll be glad to drive."

After punching the button for the first floor, he reached into his pocket to retrieve his keys. They stuck on the lining. A tug yanked the keys free, and they flew out and careened against the side of the metallic doors. So much for being suave and sophisticated.

She giggled and patted his arm. "Maybe we should go in my car."

When they reached the lobby, Rhonda and Valerie wore those female expressions—the ones that said they could read your thoughts and found them way too entertaining.

Bethany buckled in and glanced in the rearview mirror. Valerie and Rhonda grinned like cats watching caged canaries. What had she gotten herself into?

Valerie caught her eye and smiled. "I guess we shouldn't have the same discussion the last time we were in the car together. You know, fun and some major lov—"

Rhonda punched her. "Girl, don't you dare."

"Don't let me stop you." Jason turned toward Valerie and Rhonda. "Think of me as one of the gang."

"Gang?" Valerie huffed. "With you guys, I feel like a biker chick in a scooter world."

"I used to drive a Kawasaki Ninja, ZX-10, Stoic black, Metallic Raw Titanium." He looked at Bethany. "But I wasn't in a gang."

"I didn't think you were."

"Just wanted you to know."

"You don't have to explain."

Valerie smacked the car seat. "Oh, please! You two are disgusting just dancing around the issue. You're both gaga over each other. Just admit it."

Flaming with embarrassment, Bethany cranked up the air conditioning and focused on the road. In her peripheral vision, Jason grinned. Goodness, she was smiling too. No one warned her moving home would be this dangerous.

Thankfully, Rhonda and Valerie took up the mantle of conversation discussing something work-related. The ten-minute drive couldn't have taken longer. She wanted to talk with Jason, find out who lived in that hunky body of his, run her fingers through his hair, kiss those lips—.

"Bethany!" Valerie's irritated voice shot through her thoughts. "You missed the turn."

"Just making sure we weren't followed." Slowing the car, she backtracked at the next intersection.

Valerie chortled. "Nice cover up. Don't worry, Jason didn't notice, he's been too busy drooling over you."

At the restaurant, Bethany avoided looking at Jason, even if he did sit right across from her and looked cute enough to kiss. *Blast.* How on earth could they work together? And to top off the problem, Friday night, one more day, they'd be alone on a date. Or as much alone as one could get with a bodyguard. She glanced over her shoulder. Sure enough, Scott sat a few booths away, already enjoying chips and salsa.

"So, Jason." Valerie leaned back and studied him. "Tell us about yourself. Where did you grow up?"

Bethany almost felt sorry for him—surrounded by three women, and Valerie circling like a shark. Then again, rescuing or interrupting might keep her from learning something interesting.

He squared his shoulders as though facing an opponent. "North Carolina."

"The beach or the mountains?"

"Neither. We lived in Raleigh." He almost seemed amused by her questioning. "I prefer a hike in the mountains, but a long walk on the beach is nice."

"Brothers or sisters?" Valerie's purple-coated nails clicked on the table.

"One sister. She and her family live in the area."

"I've seen the pictures of the kids on your desk."

Valerie nudged Bethany. "Okay, your turn. You ask him a question."

The waiter dropped off a basket of chips and a healthy round of salsa, and took their orders.

A hike or a beach stroll definitely sounded tempting. She took a few bites while she thought of something to say. Oh my, Jason *would* look good in a bathing suit, or in a denim shirt, jeans, and hiking boots.

His foot nudged hers under the table, sending a jolt all

the way to the top of her head. He grinned. "You going to ask me a question?"

"Yes. Yes, I am." At least she would if her brain could get back in gear. "How much wood would a woodchuck, chuck if a woodchuck could chuck wood?" Okay, that had to be the absolute most stupid thing to say. If she could, she'd dive headfirst into a salsa bowl.

Everyone turned toward her. "What?"

Jason burst out laughing. "I know the answer. If a woodchuck could chuck wood, he would chuck 245 pieces of wood in two hours." His smile deepened revealing the absolutely cutest dimple in the world. "There are advantages to having an analytical nephew."

Valerie's mouth popped open as she shook her head. "You two are the strangest people I've ever known."

Rhonda chuckled. "Mmm, mmm, mmm. Work is never going to be the same."

With a sense of humor like that, Jason was practically irresistible. Bethany leaned forward. "Is there a question you *want* me to ask?"

###

Talk about a curve ball. Jason chewed on a chip. All three women stared at him. He should have known better than to put himself in this situation. Trying to navigate through female thinking could be hazardous to one's health. The waiter delivered their food. Maybe he could hide behind Bethany's fajita smoke screen.

Valerie flicked a chip at him. "We *are* still waiting."

What did he have to lose? Bethany's ice breaker with the woodchuck was great. He could ask her anything, and she probably wouldn't blink. "Would you prefer a long walk in the moonlight on the beach or a hike through the trail in the Smoky Mountains?"

"Neither." A smile tugged on Bethany's lips. "If I could choose, I'd take a hike in the Smokey's during the day, shower, then teleport to a beach and walk in the moonlight."

"Good answer."

Valerie smashed a chip on the table sending shards flying and drink glasses wobbling. "This is driving me absolutely nuts. Is this what we are going to have to live through for the next x-months or x-years while you two dance around questions? Why don't you just admit it, she finds you hot, you find her hot, and you guys want to hook up. But noooo, you can't."

Her eyes were wide and her spiky hair trembled. "You've entered the twilight Christian dating zone. No touching and goodness knows you can't talk about anything sensual." She glared at Rhonda. "Is this *really* what Christian dating is like?"

"It's okay." Rhonda patted Valerie's arm. "They can have fun. They're enjoying themselves immensely. Didn't you ever watch any of those old movies where the man and woman were interested in one another? Oh, girl, those movies were steeped in good times but nobody did anything bad. They didn't have regrets in the morning."

"Great." Valerie shoved back into her seat and crossed her arms. "This is going to be like watching a bullfight without a bull."

Bethany's ringing cell phone gave her a convenient distraction. *Payne Tanner.* She listened as his business-like voice related details. Security checked Joelle's place of employment. She supposedly left for a two week vacation on Monday to

Aruba. They were now working with the airlines to see if they could find further information.

His last words echoed in her mind as she closed her phone. "Be careful."

Chapter 21

Feeling like a little boy showing off a prized possession, Brad scooted his chair closer to the conference table as Frank Brower continued to examine the document and artifact. They were on the verge of something big ... really big. The headlines would reach around the world if they made this discovery. *Brad Davis' amazing discovery verified by the Smithsonian.*

Brad chewed on his nail and then forced his hands into his lap. He didn't want press coverage. But the ancient history of the Peruvian people could take on a whole new level with the bounty of information they might find. His excitement grew with each passing minute.

Frank's bushy white eyebrows rose as he peered over his reading glasses. "I'm still not sure. Would you be willing to allow me to examine this further? Perhaps keep it for the next week? Run it through the lab?"

"I'm sorry, I'm leaving town on Saturday."

Frank sat back in his chair and steepled his fingers. "If the document proves true, it could lead to Atahualpa's gold. We are talking the possibility of billions of dollars in today's market." He paused and removed his glasses. "Who else knows about this?"

"My three main government contacts and one family member. No one else."

"Good. This could be a fascinating discovery."

"All this time, the search has been in the Llanganates mountains. If the markings are correct, the treasure's still in Peru."

"Yes. It's quite amazing. Do you have protection for yourself and sister? If word gets out, you will be a marked man."

Sister? He didn't mention sister. Heart slamming against his chest, Brad forced his hand to stop shaking as he stored the map back in his briefcase. "Uh, yeah, we've taken precautions."

Frank's half-smile didn't reassure.

Tension digging in his shoulders, Brad gave a quick handshake and promised to stay in touch. He had to get back to Chase's, warn Bethany, call his Dad, and notify security. As he exited the building, he grabbed his cell phone and groaned. The battery was dead.

Why had Frank asked him to meet in a conference room and not his office? Had he willingly exposed himself and his family to danger? Why didn't he take Dad's offer for a Peruvian bodyguard? Right now, riding in a tank would be nice.

Brad considered clutching the briefcase to his chest, but that would be too obvious. Every person he passed on the sidewalk now took on the form of an enemy. Footsteps behind him signaled danger.

The station entrance loomed ahead. He glanced at his watch. The next train left in a few minutes. Picking up his pace to what he hoped resembled a casual jog he kept aware of his surroundings and prayed.

Taking two steps at a time he reached the platform for the Metro-rail. He wiped the sweat off his forehead and slipped next to a family with three rambunctious children. An elderly gentleman leaned on his cane and smiled at the kids talking about their Washington adventure.

To his right, a group of teenagers shoved and teased one another. A guy in a business suit reading the Wall Street Journal took his place behind the yellow line. Another man, about mid-thirties with a military haircut, stood away from the crowd. Lights flashed to signal the trains approach. A young couple raced down the escalator just as the doors opened.

Brad hurried inside, side-stepped a Lance Armstrong wannabe with his bicycle, and moved to the end of the car, where he could keep an eye on everyone. He really needed to call Bethany or Dad. The military man glanced his way and took position near him too close for comfort.

Brad swallowed hard and tightened the grip on his briefcase. Between desperate silent prayers, he tried to sort through his morning. Was the man he met really Frank Bowers? Regardless of who he was, how did he know he had a sister?

At the announcement for the next stop, the teenagers jockeyed for position to be the first to exit. Seeing an opening, Brad jumped up and sat close to the door. At least he could make an escape if needed. He should have listened to Bethany and told Dad about the map. What if the break-in at the estate *was* his fault?

The guy in the business suit shook his head at the unruly bunch and plopped next to Brad with a huff. The train slowed to a stop and the wild group pushed their way to the platform followed by the young couple and the elderly man. The military man lowered his gaze and moved toward Brad. His stomach knotted and sweat trickled between his shoulder blades.

The announcement for the door closing came over the speaker.

A strong hand gripped his arm, pulled him to his feet,

and shoved him outside. The man in the business suit had him.

Military lunged toward them, tripped on the bicycle, and fell hard against the floor. His muffled curse words sliced through the air as the train pulled away.

"Come with me." The business suited man vice-gripped Brad's arm.

How could someone be that strong? Scared spit-less, Brad could barely muster enough moisture to formulate words as he stumbled up the escalator. "Who are you? Where are you taking me?"

"Shut up and let's get you out of here."

Brad's heart slammed against his chest as he struggled to keep up with the fast pace. Should he try to fight? The last fight he had been in was at sixteen with his older brother. Chase had won.

When they reached street level, a black Mercedes with tinted windows glided next to them and stopped. The man pushed him inside the back door and slammed it behind him.

Trying to keep his briefcase in hand, half in the floorboard, Brad wrestled in the dim light to get in the seat as the car accelerated at what seemed like supersonic speed.

"You idiot!"

Brad gulped and faced the familiar voice. "Chase?"

"What were you thinking?" His brother helped him get settled. "I can't believe you didn't tell us what you were doing. I knew you needed a nursemaid."

"That guy was one of ours?"

"No, he's mine. Dad called this morning to tell me why you were here."

"Dad knows?"

"Yes. He knew you left the Peace Corps, and he's had someone on your team because *you* are an imbecile when it comes to the ways of the world. You've been in the jungle too long. People will *kill* to get that map of yours. I'm taking you to the airport, and you're going back to the estate."

Chase threw him a plane ticket. "Your suitcase is packed and a security member is waiting to escort you home."

Chapter 22

Friday morning, Bethany waited for the coffee to finish in the break room. Today was the appropriate day for her *I haven't had my coffee yet, don't make me kill you* mug. Very fitting after another night of tossing and turning. Brad's phone call last night made her even more paranoid. How did someone in Washington know he had a sister?

At least Brad was now safe at the estate, except for the trouble from Dad and security. Imagining the tongue lashing he'd been given sent a twang of sympathy for Brad. He'd always been the trusting type. But treasure hunting was not for the timid.

Between worrying about her brother and being angry about Joelle, she needed about a ten-mile run to calm down. On top of that, thinking about Jason made her googly and sappy inside, like a blob of whipped-cream had taken over her brain. Bethany poured coffee, leaving enough room to cool it down with a shot of water. After she drank the whole cup, she poured another. Maybe caffeine would firm up that mushy feeling.

Someone needed to invent a body-building exercise for the heart, make it tough enough to withstand life's wounds.

"Hey, girl." Rhonda came in balancing four mugs. "How are you this morning?"

"Totally confused and conflicted." Bethany took two of the cups from Rhonda. "How are you? And what are you doing

185

with these?"

"Some of the people in the office are just plain slobs." Rhonda placed them in the sink and reached for the dish detergent. "I don't think these have been washed since the dawn of creation." She looked over her shoulder at Bethany. "You going to tell me what's got you all worked up?"

"I don't think I can explain."

Rhonda scrubbed like they were infected with toxic mold. "Are you nervous about tonight?"

"Yes." Bethany poured another cup and plopped into a chair. "It scares the stuffing out of me. Dating is easy. Love is not."

"Love? Girl, just take it one day at a time and enjoy yourself. Don't keep worrying about what's down the road or you're going to miss the fun on the journey."

Jason couldn't wait to see Bethany. Tonight, they'd have their first official date. He'd cleaned his car from top to bottom, pressed his slacks, and made reservations at Carino's Italian restaurant. One of those places with white tablecloths and candlelight but still casual enough for most attire. Several movies at the theater had potential, one a chick-flick and the other a romantic comedy. He'd let her choose.

He whistled his way down the hall and checked Bethany's office. The computer and desk light signaled her presence. Maybe she was in the break room.

His cell phone vibrated against his hip, and he checked the caller ID. How could his brother-in-law be calling? Jason flipped open his cell phone. "Matt? Where are you? Is everything okay?"

"Yeah, buddy. I'm coming home tonight. Kelly doesn't know. I need a favor."

"Anything. What can I do?"

"Could you pick up Kelly and the kids and bring them to our favorite restaurant. I want to surprise them. I'll rent a car and should be there sometime after seven thirty."

Jason smiled imagining the reunion. "The pizza place downtown? You got it. I think I have the perfect plan."

"Thanks, Jason. I owe you."

"You don't owe me anything. You're the hero."

He hung up and turned into the break room. Bethany sat at the table, her expression troubled. Rhonda stood at the sink, elbow-deep in dishwater. Neither of them noticed him. He knocked on the wall to get their attention.

Wide-eyed, Bethany jumped to her feet.

Jason grinned. "Do I look that bad?"

"No, you look *great.*" Red-faced, she sat down and rubbed her forehead.

Rhonda chuckled. "Mmm, mmm, mmm."

"I'm sorry, did I interrupt something?" He poured a cup of coffee and walked to Bethany's table. "May I join you?"

She didn't look at him, just nodded.

Bethany could have crawled under the table. Did Jason hear any of their conversation? And even if he didn't, she had to embarrass herself totally by commenting on his looks. And boy, did he look good.

He sat across from her. "I need to ask you about tonight. Something's come up."

All that worrying, and now he was going to cancel.

Unfortunately, the thought only made her feel worse.

Jason touched her arm. "I just talked to my brother-in-law."

"He's in the military overseas, right?"

"Right. I need a favor." He shifted and leaned forward. "He's coming back early and wants to surprise his family. Would you mind going with me? It's the perfect ruse. I'll tell my sister I want her to meet you, and she'll think we're just taking them to dinner. We'll still have time to do something after."

She gulped. The whole group on their first official date? Then again, what better opportunity to meet someone's family than in the excitement of daddy's homecoming from war? "I'd love to."

His smile sent a tingle to her toes. "I'll pick you up at six thirty. I'll have them in the car with me." He stood. "Thanks. This is great."

When he left, Rhonda sat in his seat. "Girl, you two are perfect for each other."

Perfect for a painful heartbreak. Bethany chugged her lukewarm coffee. What had she gotten herself into? It's just a date. She breathed in and out, in and out. Enjoy the journey. Enjoy the journey.

Valerie skipped into the room, far too bright-eyed for early morning. "Happy Friday. Has anyone seen my coffee cup?"

"I washed it for you." Rhonda pointed to the sink. "You may not recognize it since it's clean."

"Wow." Valerie's nose crinkled as she inspected the mug. "I didn't know the inside was actually white."

Rhonda chuckled. "Better watch yourself drinking out of something germ-free. It could send you into shock."

"No problem. I dropped my donut on the floor." She pulled a chair to the table and smiled at Bethany. "So, tonight you and Jason are going out?"

"Yes. And I'll meet the family."

"Woof. You guys move fast."

"Jason's brother-in-law is coming in from out of town and going to surprise them. I'm part of the distraction."

"Ah, I get it. The old, meet my girlfriend ploy while the soldier returns from out of town. You need to film the reunion and put it on the Internet. After that what are you going to do?" Valerie rubbed her hands together. "Some quiet, alone time?"

Bethany's stomach danced with butterflies. Good grief. It wasn't like she hadn't been alone with a man before. But with Jason the risks were greater. If only they had protective vests for hearts.

She returned to her office and spent the next two hours working, or at least made an attempt. Most of her time was spent stuffing down the bazillion thoughts ping-ponging through her brain. The worries and questions about Brad, Jason, Tom, Joelle, and the break-in at the estate were about to make her crazy. If she'd been smart, she would've brought her exercise clothes and worked out some frustration during lunch.

The ring on her cell phone drew her attention. Scott's caller ID flashed on her screen.

"Any good news?" She kept her tone light.

"I'm in the lobby." He paused. "We need to talk."

His seriousness made her chest tighten. "I'll be right down."

She grabbed her purse and hurried to Rhonda's office. "Scott's waiting in the lobby. Something's up."

Rhonda nodded. "I'll be praying, and I'll let the others know."

The elevator moved at a snail's pace, and to top it off, somebody got on and off on every floor. If she'd been a hair puller, she would've been bald by the time it crept to the lobby.

Bethany hurried to Scott who waited by the front doors. "What's going on?"

"Tom's contact sent him a note." Scott led her to his car. "He's to slash your tires, ransack your apartment, get rid of your dog, and leave another note, with a time-frame to get out by Monday."

Her vision tunneled and heat radiated from every pore. *Get rid of Jedi?* The rest didn't matter, but messing with her baby meant war. She'd tear Tom and whoever was behind this into pieces. "What's the plan?"

He opened her car door. "Jedi's been escorted to the estate until we find out who's behind this." He hesitated. "We found Joelle. She stayed the night with Gavin."

Bethany didn't know whether to scream or laugh. Somehow, it almost seemed appropriate. Gavin and Joelle deserved each other –both two-faced, dishonest, and the last people on earth she'd want to be around. "Did you question them?"

Scott buckled his seatbelt and backed out the car. "We tried, but they were already gone." After merging into traffic he looked her way. "The FBI is watching Gavin. Our surveillance team ran into theirs. We've had to drop back."

Chapter 23

Bethany couldn't help herself. She laughed. Gavin and Joelle together? And now Gavin wanted by the FBI. Truly the ultimate revenge for a wayward ex-husband, and she had absolutely nothing to do with it. What were those sayings? God's ways are not our ways. Vengeance is mine, says the Lord. It was perfect—too perfect.

She had to be losing her mind—thinking of Bible verses in the same thought with Gavin.

"Bethany?" Scott gaped at her reaction. "Are you okay?"

"Yes. I'm great. This is too good."

His confused expression tickled her.

He gave her a stern look. "You may still be in danger."

"I am taking this seriously." She adjusted her expression to match his. "What does the FBI want with Gavin?"

"He's under investigation." Scott parked next to a gray warehouse with no identifying signs. "Did you know about any of his activities?"

"I only know he worked in the mortgage industry. He didn't even let me see the checkbook. He handled all the bills."

"Good. The FBI wants to talk to you. They're waiting inside."

###

Jason checked Bethany's office, the break room, and the conference area. He hoped to catch her for lunch. Her car hadn't moved, but where was she?

He spotted Rhonda and Valerie waiting at the elevator. "Have you seen Bethany?"

Rhonda nodded. "She got a phone call and left with Scott."

"Why?" A flutter of unease tightened his chest. "What's going on?"

"I'm not sure." The elevator doors opened and she stepped inside. "Scott had her meet him in the lobby. You want to join us for lunch?"

Jason followed the two women. "I may need to run an errand."

Valerie hmphed. "If Bethany was with us, you wouldn't hesitate."

"You're right."

They both gawked at him.

He shrugged. "I'm not going to lie."

"That's right." Valerie chuckled. "You shouldn't lie, that's one of those Ten Commandment things. I can ask you anything and you'll have to tell me the truth."

Jason tugged on his collar. Valerie would lead an inquisition, and getting too truthful could be embarrassing. Thankfully, they arrived at the ground floor and the doors opened.

Rhonda took Valerie by the arm. "You know the Ten Commandments are for everyone, not just for Christians."

"Yeah, but I don't have to do them since I'm not one of you. The rules are different."

"Girl, we need to talk." Rhonda nodded toward Jason and winked. "We'll see you later."

Maybe lunch would've been entertaining, even without Bethany. Still, right now, he felt the urge to pray.

Bethany's pulse pounded in her ears as she followed Scott down a gray-carpeted hallway accented by gray walls. Could the place look any more dingy or foreboding? Why did the FBI want to talk to her?

He stopped at the last open door and motioned for her to enter. "They've set up a temporary office. I'll be outside waiting."

She swallowed hard and peeked inside. *Donna?*

Her next door neighbor sat behind a steel desk perusing through a folder. "Hi, Bethany, have a seat."

"You're FBI?" Now more confused than anxious, Bethany eased herself into the offered chair and did a quick check of the office. A tall, gray filing cabinet stood in the corner. Donna's desk neat, except for a stack of folders, a coffee mug, several pens, and a writing pad.

"We appreciate you taking the time to talk with us."

"Not sure I had a choice."

Donna responded with a mild chuckle. "We just need to ask a few questions about Gavin and Joelle."

Bethany rubbed the tension in her neck. At least it wasn't anything she had done. "I have a few questions about them myself."

Donna closed the folder and picked up the pad. Her curious gaze rested on Bethany. "With your permission, I'd like to tape our meeting." At her nod, Donna continued. "Have you been in contact with Gavin since your divorce?"

"No." *Other than fantasies about beating him senseless.*

"No phone calls, letter, e-mails?"

"No." She wrote a long letter and then burned it to a crisp. "I really didn't want anything to do with him."

Donna noted Bethany's every comment. "Would you mind telling me the circumstances surrounding your divorce?"

"I found Gavin in bed with my best friend. I packed my suitcase and left." She took a deep breath, blew it out and tried to shake off the memory.

"Did either of you try to reconcile?"

"No. He was thrilled I finally left."

"Could you clarify?"

"He wanted me to leave. He blackmailed me into keeping quiet."

"Blackmail?" Donna's stare pierced her.

Heat crawled up her back and across her shoulders. "He used to send me to meet his customers at coffee shops, hotel lobbies, or restaurants to pick up envelopes or packages. Before our divorce, he showed pictures of me talking with these men." Bethany hesitated before she plunged further. "Gavin said if I ever gave him a hard time or said anything about his behavior he would show the pictures to my friends and family and tell them I was having affairs."

Donna's expression softened. "Did you have any idea what might be in those packages?"

"As far as I could tell, they were just loan papers or something to do with a mortgage. I didn't ask. I was young, stupid, and naïve."

"How much did Gavin make while you were married?"

The question caught her by surprise. "I don't know. He was tight-fisted with the money and handled the checkbook. I got an allowance for groceries and gas. Funny, there never seemed to be enough to buy any extras for me, but he sure did find it for himself."

"Didn't you work at the time?"

"I didn't make much, and what little I made was deposited directly into our account."

"When you divorced, who was your lawyer?"

"I didn't get one. I just used his. I didn't care about anything. I just wanted to get away."

"How much did you get in your settlement?" Donna flipped to the next page and resumed her note taking.

"Ten thousand dollars, my car, clothes, and a couple of pieces of furniture my parents gave us."

Donna pulled a folder from the bottom of the stack on her desk. "At the time you were married, Gavin made $80,000. Your combined income put you around $100,000. You were entitled to much more than $10,000. Why didn't you take it?"

Bethany's head looped and dived. The way Gavin acted they hadn't made much above poverty level. "I didn't know." She studied the brown stain on the carpet in front of her. Everything with Gavin had been a lie. "And even if I had, I didn't want his money. It was the one thing that he cared for the most."

She could barely remember the next thirty minutes of questions or eating the fast-food taco Scott bought her on the way back to her office. Evidently she wasn't a suspect, but whatever Gavin had gotten himself into stirred up a FBI hornet nest. Because of their investigation, Dad's security team had to pull away from watching Gavin or Joelle, which left a nasty hole in solving her case.

Maybe she should change her name, leave, and start over in some other town. Make it easier for everybody. Everybody but her. Dredging up the past only reopened all the old wounds. Why not just throw her in a blender and turn it on high?

Her stomach still in a tangle of knots, she sat at her office desk and stared blankly at the stack of work.

"I want details." Valerie darted into her office. "What's going on?"

Rhonda came behind Valerie. "Is everything okay?"

Bethany studied her friends. Thankfully, the past was over. "I don't know. I really can't say much because of an ongoing investigation. Life is so weird."

Valerie plopped on her desk. "You telling me. Rhonda just gave me the ten commandos."

Rhonda shook her head. "The Ten Commandments."

"Yeah, right. They sound more like the ten command no's. No this, no that, no fun, no nothing."

"They were written to help us enjoy life by not doing things that would hurt us or others."

Valerie raised an eyebrow and looked at Bethany. "What do you think?"

"Rhonda's right, they are good. If my ex-husband had lived by them, he wouldn't be in trouble with the law."

"I don't know." Valerie chewed on the top of her pen. "These are radical ideas. My folks believed in the totality of the universe not any of this kind of stuff."

Jason almost bowled over Rhonda when he squeezed past the others to get to Bethany. "Is everything okay?"

Bethany's throat tightened at the concerned look on his face. "Yes. Just more weird happenings with security."

"You know you can call me anytime."

Valerie nudged Jason. "I bet there's a command *no* for this."

He turned toward her. "What?"

Bethany placed her hand on his arm. "Don't ask. You

don't want to know."

Chapter 24

Jason wiped his sweaty palms on his slacks as he waited for Kelly and the kids to finish getting ready. Between an actual date with Bethany, and Matt meeting them at the restaurant, he could barely keep his feet on the floor. "We need to go."

Kelly, still putting on her earrings, rushed past him. "Kids! Make sure your hair's combed and your teeth are brushed."

Both kids thumped down the hallway and gave their uncle a hug. He chuckled at the contrast between them— Elizabeth, the picture of the perfectly coiffed female compared to Daniel whose hair looked like it had been licked by the family dog.

"Daniel, what have you done?" Kelly corralled him and combed out the mess. "There. I think we're finally ready." She grinned at Jason. "I'm looking forward to meeting Bethany. She's had you worked up since the first day you met her."

"That's an understatement. Just keep praying I don't make a mess of things."

"You'll do fine." Kelly leaned against him while she put on her shoes. "I'm just proud you're actually dating."

Jason locked the house and chased the kids into the car. "I brought the camera. Would you mind sneaking a picture or two of Bethany and me?"

Kelly grinned. "I'd love to."

Elizabeth buckled her seatbelt. "Uncle Jason, is Bethany pretty?

He smiled as he turned on the car. "Yes, she is."

Daniel giggled. "As pretty as Mommy?"

"Definitely."

Elizabeth squealed. "If you get married, will you have lots of babies so I can help?"

Jason gripped the wheel. What had he gotten himself into?

Bethany busied herself flipping channels on the television. Would Jason's family like her? Would she like them? She gulped down the onslaught of dancing dragonflies in her stomach. What would she and Jason do after dinner?

Everything was in place to keep her safe tonight. Scott would stay close but not too close. She'd have freedom to welcome Jason and then say goodnight. Once he left, Scott would call.

A knock signaled Jason's arrival. She checked the peephole to make sure. He smiled and placed his eye next to the tiny opening. When she opened the door, he nearly fell against her.

Grabbing the doorframe, he grinned. "You look wonderful. Are you ready?"

"Ready as I'll ever be."

Jason, looking great and smelling wonderful, led her to his car with his hand pressed gently against the small of her back. Her heart skipped at the warm touch of his fingers. Jason introduced everyone as Bethany buckled her seatbelt. Kelly, Daniel, and Elizabeth squeezed into the back seat.

"Miss Bethany?" Elizabeth sat behind Jason. Her blonde hair pulled back in a ponytail, hands folded neatly in her lap. "Thank you for letting us come on your date."

"I wore my best sneakers." The little guy in the middle held up his feet clad in bright red tennies.

Elizabeth tapped on the seat to get Bethany's attention. "Uncle Jason told us you were pretty."

Bethany smiled at Jason who stared straight ahead. "He said that?"

"Yes." Elizabeth's ponytail bounced with her nod. "And he's right."

"How sweet. Thank you both."

Kelly grinned. "Since, we're on the subject, has Jason been behaving himself at work?"

The children giggled. Jason's neck reddened.

Bethany couldn't resist. "Well…" She paused until Jason gave her a nervous glance. "He's always been the ultimate gentleman."

Daniel nudged his sister. "What's ultageman?"

"It means he's been good."

"Is she?" He pointed at Bethany.

Elizabeth shook her head. "No, silly. She's a woman."

Daniel's little eyes went wide. "She's *not* good?"

"Miss Bethany is good too. Right, Uncle Jason?"

Jason chuckled. "Yes. Miss Bethany is very good."

Daniel blew out a big breath. "Whew. It wouldn't be good if she wasn't good."

Bethany smiled to herself. The relationship between Jason and his family was absolutely precious. Did she just think *precious*? Oh man, she *was* in big trouble.

When they arrived at the restaurant, the kids took her by the hands and led her inside the historic building. The place hadn't changed since her high school days. The dark wood floors and brick walls brought back fond memories of Friday evenings, talking and laughing with her girlfriends.

The hostess led them to a table in the back, and a waiter took their drink orders while they decided on pizza toppings.

Bethany followed Kelly's gaze to a table nearby where a young man still in desert uniform dined with his family. Bethany choked on the empathy welling up inside her. If only she could tell Kelly everything would be okay.

Kelly's eyes rimmed in tears, with a swallow, she pasted on a smile and handed the children extra napkins. "Bethany, do you have brothers and sisters?"

"I have two older brothers."

"Do they live in the area?"

"My oldest brother lives in DC, and the other is in Peru."

"Peru?" Elizabeth sat up straight. "Isn't that where Machu Picchu is?"

Bethany couldn't hide her surprise at someone so young knowing about the mountain ruins. "That's right."

"I saw it on a TV show. It's really neat."

"I haven't been myself, but my brother says it's incredible."

Elizabeth's mouth dropped open. "Your brother has *been* there?" With a total look of awe, she sat back in her seat. "Wow."

Daniel screwed up his face. "What's achew, pinch you?"

Elizabeth shook her head and let out a big sigh. "Macchu Picchu. And it's the coolest, neatest old city, way up on a mountain, that anyone has ever seen."

A man dressed in uniform carried their drinks to their table. Jason squeezed Bethany's hand. This had to be Matt. He stood behind Kelly and placed her soda beside her.

She thanked him and glanced up. With a scream, she shot out of her chair into his arms and covered him with kisses.

Both children squealed. "Daddy!"

Daniel bounced up and down and grabbed his legs. "My daddy's home, my daddy's home!" Elizabeth let out a wail and clung to his side.

Bethany, smiling through tears, rubbed the goose bumps on her arms as the family cried and laughed together.

Applause broke out in the restaurant as others joined in the celebration.

Jason, tears in his eyes, hugged Matt, then sat next to Bethany. "I'm glad you're here."

She could barely speak. "I wouldn't have missed this for the world."

Dinner passed quickly. Between having Matt home and Bethany by his side, Jason couldn't have asked for a better evening. She fit right in and it was obvious the family loved her. Kelly even gave him a thumbs-up.

Watching Bethany's interaction with his family tightened his resolve to find out as much as possible about her. "Are you ready to go? We'll let them have the rest of the evening together."

She nodded as he stood.

He gave Kelly a hug. "We're going to head out. I'll see you at church on Sunday."

Both kids grabbed him by the legs, thanking him for the "best surprise ever."

Before he got any more emotional, he turned toward Bethany, who was now swamped in hugs from his family.

"Okay, you've spent enough time with her. It's my turn." He waved goodnight, took Bethany by the hand and led her to the door.

Once outside, he kept hold, not wanting to let go. "Are you still up for a movie? We can make the late show, or go for dessert and coffee. "Your choice."

She squeezed his hand. "I vote dessert."

Bethany still couldn't get rid of the tingle from their hand holding. Plus, the scene at the restaurant made her giddy one moment and teary the next. Sharing emotions that strong created a bond. And right now, the thought of bonding with anyone, especially someone she worked with and saw everyday, scared her to death.

He pointed ahead. "The best ice cream in Southburg is on the next block."

They walked without talking, the silence comfortable, until they arrived at a two-story pink building. Customers sat at the small café tables and a line of people filtered outside the door.

Once inside, she studied the menu chock-full of funky flavored homemade ice cream. A cup of decaf and a helping of raspberry chip sounded perfect. Jason ordered a scoop of Dirty Berry. A small table opened in the back, and they squirmed through the crowd.

He held the chair out for her. "How's yours?" He pointed to her cone and gave her one of those smiles that could melt her ice-cream, and her heart, in less than two seconds.

All she could do was pray for help. "It's really good."

"Kelly and the kids love this place."

"You have such a sweet family."

His face beamed. He nodded, swallowed hard. "I think so too. I appreciate you coming tonight."

"I loved it. The only soldier reunions that I've seen were on the news or an Internet video. Being right there and seeing it first hand was amazing. I won't ever forget this night."

His dimple showed with his smile. "I hope not."

Bethany dug into her dessert, hoping a brain freeze would hit before she got mushy.

He finished his cone and leaned back in his chair. "You've seen a slice of my life. I'd love to know more about you and yours. As Valerie said, we keep dancing around some issues."

Danger, danger, danger. "Dancing is good."

"We'll have to try that sometime." He rubbed his chin, his gaze resting on her. "I know the *basics* about you. May I ask something personal?"

Bethany sipped her coffee and charted the path to the front door. "Maybe."

"I'm twenty-seven, I've made major mistakes, but now I'm trying to live right. I'm looking for more than a few dates or a one-night stand. I don't want to waste my time, and I don't want to waste yours. I know this is fast. But are you willing to see where this leads?"

She choked. Totally choked. The coffee sucked down the wrong pipe, and she couldn't get air.

Jason jumped out of his chair and rushed behind her positioned as though to give her the Heimlich maneuver.

If she didn't die from lack of oxygen, she'd die of embarrassment as every one in the shop watched them.

A gargantuan woman pushed through the crowd. "Stand back! I'm a trained EMT."

Gasping for oxygen, Bethany collapsed in Jason's arms before the woman could accost her. Bethany waved at the advancing behemoth. "I'm...." *Breathe, breathe.* "I'm okay." Vision tunneling, on the verge of passing out, she clung to Jason. "Please, get me out of here."

He scooped her into his strong, absolutely wonderful arms, carried her outside, and didn't put her down. She thought about protesting or saying something. But why spoil the fun? He carried her all the way to the car before gently setting her on her feet. "I'm sorry."

"Why? You saved me." She put her hand on his chest—his muscular chest. "You're my hero."

"My question almost killed you." He hung his head.

"Jason, I didn't choke because of what you asked. Okay, maybe it did surprise me a little. I'll be honest, a relationship scares me. You don't know who I am or what I've done. I may not be worth your time."

He touched her chin, focused on her eyes. "I may be wrong, but there's something between us worth exploring. I know you're divorced. I know you've lived a wild life in college. It doesn't matter. I want to know who you are now."

He knew? Did *everyone* know about her? "I'm scared, totally and absolutely scared to death."

He moved his hand behind her neck and pulled her toward him. He kissed her, tender, gentle, slow, the kind of kiss that makes fireworks explode in the air, women weep, and horns honk.

Horns?

She jumped out of the way as a junker car pulled into the space next to them.

A teenage boy opened his creaky door and high-fived Jason. "Way to go, man."

Jason grinned and shook his head. "Maybe we better get going." His gaze locked with hers. "So, are you willing to try?"

Could she take the risk? What Gavin hadn't destroyed, her own irresponsibility had damaged. Plus, she was divorced. And in some people's eyes, that meant she totally screwed up her chance and wasn't worthy of happiness. Maybe deep down she believed that too. "Please don't break my heart."

Jason wrapped Bethany in his arms and held her close. For someone so tough, why was she so afraid? He wanted to do the right thing this time. Be a man of honor. "I promise to pray about our relationship, and I promise to try to never hurt you." He'd fight dragons for her at this moment.

But how would he fare if things didn't work out? Stepping off a cliff might be easier. At least in the end, he wouldn't feel anything.

She wiped her eyes, cleared her throat, straightened her back. "I didn't mean to get emotional."

It took all his strength not to kiss her again. "I guess I better get you home."

They rode in silence back to her apartment. She seemed deep in thought as she stared out her window. He should have waited to talk so openly about his plans. He was an idiot. A total idiot. No matter how right it felt to discuss the future with her, asking her to basically commit to seeing him for a serious relationship was crazy. Did he ruin any chance with her?

When they arrived, he parked and turned toward her. "Bethany, about earlier ... I shouldn't have said anything."

She glanced his way, and a smile curved her lips. "No. You're right. Let's see where this leads."

Bethany tried to ignore the million and one reasons she should avoid dating Jason as he escorted her to the door. What was she thinking? They worked together. How could they see each other almost every day and date?

He shoved his hands in his pockets and rocked on his heels. "I had a great night."

"Me too."

"Can I see you again? Is tomorrow night too soon? We could actually make it to the movies."

She smiled at his sudden nervousness. "Tomorrow night sounds nice."

He pulled her towards him, his forehead touching hers. "Six thirty, okay?"

Movement caught her attention. Scott had to be watching. Right now it didn't matter. If they were going to jump into this thing, why not make a big splash. She planted a kiss on Jason she hoped curled his toes.

He looked dazed when they parted. Not that she fared much better. Wow, the guy could kiss. Before she went after him again, she put her key in the lock. "I'll see you tomorrow."

"You bet." His grin bordered on goofy. "Six thirty. Rain or shine."

Bethany closed the door and leaned back. What a wild night. Scott would give Jason time to drive away before he called or came up to check on her.

She flipped on the light and stared at the barrel of a gun.

Chapter 25

"Hello, Bethany." Joelle, gun in hand, stood by the window in a stance that would make a female lead in a spy movie proud. Her skin-tight black pants and top completed her ridiculous outfit.

"Why are you here?" Bethany dropped her purse on the kitchen counter.

"I could ask you the same question."

You've got to be kidding. "I live here." If the situation wasn't so absurd, she might actually be nervous. Besides that, even if the gun was loaded, Joelle wouldn't pull the trigger, she might break a manicured nail.

Joelle stamped her foot. "I mean why did you come back?"

"Because my family asked me to."

"Likely story." Joelle pursed her botoxed lips. "I know why you're really here. You want Gavin back."

"Gavin is the *last* person on earth I want to be with. *He's* the one who had the affairs."

"I don't believe you. Why else would you stay with all those threats?"

"Why would being here be a problem? Didn't you say he lived in Ohio with his wife?"

Joelle's lined eyebrows moved toward the middle as though for a conference. She tossed her head and let out an exasperated huff of air. "You *shouldn't* have come back."

The phone rang.

Joelle surged toward Bethany. "Don't answer that."

"If I don't, my date will be worried."

"Fine, but make it quick." She jabbed the revolver in Bethany's ribs to make her point. "If you say anything wrong, I'll shoot."

Tingles rushed down her spine. The gun, a LadySmith revolver, *was* loaded. It didn't make sense. In High school, Joelle would get squeamish if someone stepped on a bug. Surely she wouldn't use real bullets, must be blanks.

Bethany picked up the phone, relieved to hear her bodyguard's voice. After she thanked him for dinner and a movie, he replied, "I'll see you very soon." The situation could get interesting.

Joelle motioned for Bethany to sit. "Gavin loves me. We're going to be married next month."

"Good luck on that one." Bethany positioned herself on the couch for a quick move if Scott broke in.

"You're just jealous. Gavin's doing really well in business." Joelle studied a family picture on Bethany's mantle. "I should know. He's sent me on tons of errands to pick up information from his contacts."

Bethany shook her head, almost felt sorry for her. *Almost.* "You have no idea what he's doing. He's setting you up."

"He loves me." Joelle waved the gun like it was a toy and glanced around the apartment. "He always has. Told me he married you just to get at your daddy's money."

That did it. Gun or no gun, next time Joelle looked away, she was going down.

"Now back to the issue at hand." Joelle pointed the weapon level with Bethany's heart. "I want you packed and out of here tomorrow."

"Fine." Bethany focused behind Joelle and watched the door. The knob turned … slowly, silently. Heart thumping in her chest, she tried to act casual as she stood for better mobility. "I'll leave."

"You will? I mean, good." Joelle backed toward the entrance. "Don't make me come back here."

"Don't worry, you won't need to."

The door burst open hitting Joelle in the back.

Gunfire split the air.

Shouts.

The lamp exploded, shards of glass showered around Bethany as she fell. Someone plastered a screaming, cursing Joelle to the floor.

Bethany's vision faded, the breath rushed out of her lungs.

Chapter 26

"Are you okay?" Scott's voice reverberated in her ears.

Bethany forced open her eyes, her head pounding and vision still swimming. "She wanted to kill me?"

He leaned over her. "Are ... you ... okay?" He spoke slow and loud, as though she couldn't hear.

"Yes." Did she faint? How embarrassing. Careful not to get glass on her hands, she pushed up to a sitting position. "She had real bullets."

"Obviously." He glanced at the remains of the lamp before helping her to her feet. "The FBI took her into custody."

"I didn't think she'd do something like this. She was always too busy being a drama queen."

"Well, she went out with a bang."

Bethany stared at Scott. Did he just make a joke?

He cleared his throat, stared at the carpet. "Sorry."

"Thanks for saving me."

He nodded. "Next date, I'm checking the apartment before you come in."

"Won't be necessary. We caught her."

Donna came through the still open door. "Need to ask you a few questions. What did Joelle say?"

"She wanted me out of the way so she could have Gavin. He's got her running his errands. When she finds out that he was using her like he did me, she'd probably wish she had a bazooka to use on him. "

Donna didn't smile but amusement showed in her eyes. "You won't have to worry about Joelle or Gavin for a long time. He was picked up this evening by the other team for mortgage fraud."

Squinting in the morning light, Bethany kept the air-conditioning on high and the music blaring as she drove along the tree-lined road to her parent's home. By the time the FBI completed their investigation, she answered all their questions, cleaned up the mess, reassured her family she was safe, and then had a long, wailing cry, she didn't get into bed until the early-morning hours.

Sleep was more a thought than an action. Her emotions were shot, one minute she felt like a weight had dropped off her shoulders, the next she'd collapse on the floor in tears.

Out of habit, she checked her rearview mirror. Scott followed, and far behind him was a black pickup truck. Even the fact she still needed a bodyguard drove her crazy. She needed a few hours alone in the woods or a run at the park without someone watching.

For now, she had to get herself together. Brad would leave for Peru this afternoon, and Jedi waited at the estate. A few hours to visit with the family, then maybe have time for a quick nap before her date with Jason.

Dating, along with a relationship that actually involved the heart, scared her more than staring down the barrel of a gun. Taking that step, that leap of faith to reveal who you really are put her way beyond her comfort zone.

The usual security personnel waved her through the

front gate. She drove down the winding drive and parked in the driveway at the back of the house. On the lawn, near the patio, Jedi and Brad played fetch with a tennis ball. Knowing her brother, he probably fetched more than the dog.

A gentle breeze made for a nice morning to sit outside. If only coffee shops delivered. She whistled at Jedi, which sent her tail-wagging baby running toward her. Tears stinging her eyes, she scooped him up in her arms and held him close. Boy, to get this sensitive she really needed more sleep.

"You okay?" Brad followed her to the glider.

"Long night."

"Dad told us what was going on at breakfast. I'm sorry your life's been so crazy."

She sat and placed Jedi between them. "I could say the same about you. You still up for a treasure hunt?"

"I don't know." He stared at the ground before he looked her way. "I think Chase was right. I've been in the jungles too long. I forgot that money makes people do crazy things."

"I'm sure Chase made some interesting comments when he found out."

"Yep. Most of them I can't repeat with someone young present." He pointed at Jedi who sat with his mouth open in a puppy grin. "Wouldn't want to taint little ears. So. How's your love life?"

"I met Jason's family." *His adorable family.*

He tilted his head and smiled. "That fast?"

"His brother-in-law came in early from serving overseas. I was the bait to hook the family to come to the restaurant."

"From the look on your face, I'd say you're the one who's hooked."

Bethany stifled her grin and pushed with her feet to get

the glider in motion. "I'll admit to being interested. But all this dating-for-real stuff, is pretty scary."

"Dating for real? So you two already talked about this?"

"He doesn't want to waste his time or mine." She nodded, suddenly embarrassed by how strange this must sound. "How on earth am I going to know if it would work? I screwed up before."

"You didn't know Gavin was a jerk."

"My point exactly. Gavin was kind, loving and attentive until we got married. Then he wanted to crawl into bed with every woman he came in contact with. How can I make sure I don't make another mistake?"

Brad shrugged. "I don't know. You're older and wiser now."

"Gee, thanks for the reminder that I'm older."

"Ah, you're still a pup. Don't worry so much. God will take care of you."

"I trusted Him last time, and it didn't help." *Ouch.* She really needed a nap.

He gave her a puzzled look. "It might not have saved you from the heartache, but you made it through."

"Yeah, and left me with a semi-pulverized mess limping in my chest."

"Do I detect some residual anger?"

Where are all these negative thoughts coming from? "I think I'm just tired and scared to get into a serious relationship."

"You've been stalked, chased, and had a gun held on you, and you're afraid to *date*?"

"Physical scars heal, emotional hurt causes deeper wounds."

He paused and seemed to ponder her reply. "Quite the philosopher this morning, aren't you? I can't tell you what to do, and I can't guarantee you won't get hurt. But if you wall yourself inside a protective cocoon you won't emerge a butterfly."

"Now who's the philosopher?"

"You know what I mean. You just gotta trust."

Bethany mulled over Brad's comments while she spent the morning with her family. That trust issue kept raising its head. She liked a protective cocoon, but then again, spreading butterfly wings sure did sound tempting.

Back at her apartment, she tried to nap but couldn't sleep. Knowing Brad left to return to the jungle and treasure hunting made it even harder to watch him leave. Dad sent a bodyguard to keep him safe on the flight, and another waited in Peru. Since they still didn't know who broke in at the estate, Scott remained her guardian.

Walking Jedi, taking a shower, and three outfit changes made her even antsier. She sat on the couch in her sundress.

Jedi snuggled beside her and fell quickly asleep. Little dog snores gave her a smile. He trusted without worrying. A gentle nudge in her spirit told her she, too, needed to stop worrying and trust.

Her past had been tied up in a neat bow and the truth revealed. She took a deep breath and let that thought take root. Yesterday's sins and heartache erased. With a prayer of thanks, she closed her eyes.

Only a moment later, tension crept across her shoulders. Unfortunately, nothing could clean up her reputation.

Chapter 27

Jason popped a mint into his mouth as he walked to Bethany's apartment. Since arriving early, he'd sat in the car for fifteen minutes. He'd have been here at eight this morning to spend time with her if she hadn't been busy with her family. He wanted to ask her about her hopes and dreams. Hopefully, those same ideas were beginning to take root in her heart as well.

At her door, he knocked and waited. Her little dog's barking announced his arrival. When she answered wearing a sundress his questions fled as his eyes feasted on her beauty.

She smiled, closed the door, and locked up behind her. "Ready?

He forced himself to stop staring. "I have reservations. You like Italian, right?"

"Sounds wonderful."

He directed her to his car and opened her door. "How was your night?"

"Interesting."

"Hang on, I want to hear more." Jason hurried to his side and slid into the driver's seat. "What do you mean interesting?"

She tilted her head, her face pensive, as though sorting her thoughts. "Joelle was waiting with a gun."

"What? Are you okay? Did you get hurt?" He turned to hug her but stopped himself and instead gripped the wheel.

"Bethany, I shouldn't have left you. I should have checked your apartment."

She shrugged. "Maybe. But that probably would've made the situation more difficult. She wanted me out of town so she could have my ex-husband. I would have paid her to take him. The FBI took her away and arrested Gavin." She shook her head, shrugged again and smiled.

She may want him to believe she was okay with everything, but the smile didn't meet her eyes. Something about her past still rocked her world. He fought the urge to wrap her in his arms and hold her close. "We can wait to go out."

"I'm fine." She straightened her shoulders, her smile making a feeble attempt at widening. "Dinner and a movie sounds good right now."

"Will you promise to tell me if you want to go home?"

She turned toward him, her body stiff. "Jason, I was raised with two older brothers and a dad in the military. I was taught when tough things happen you move on. I messed up after my divorce by replaying all the wrong my ex and others did and said. Now, I'm just *really* ready to get on with life."

He studied her for a moment. "You don't always have to be so tough, you know."

Bethany swallowed hard and a rim of moisture appeared in her eyes. "Please don't talk like that."

"It's okay to cry."

Tears spilled and ran down her cheeks. She wiped them away and cleared her throat. "Don't do that. I don't want to cry."

Jason put his hand on her soft cheek, rubbed away a fallen tear with his thumb.

Her bottom lip quivered. "Okay, I'll admit it, I'm a

wimp."

"You're not a wimp. Most people would be curled up in the fetal position if someone held a gun on them."

"Fetal positions are for babies. No one got hurt. My lamp is terminal, but there were no other fatalities."

"Your lamp?"

"Yeah, I still can't believe she actually had a loaded gun."

"You were shot at?" At her nod, he literally saw red as his blood pressure flew through the roof. She could have died. It took several deep breaths to calm down. "I've never hit a woman, but if I'd been there, I'd have—"

"You would have slain the evil dragon lady for me?" She nestled against the seat, her smile meeting her eyes.

He shook his head. He's supposed to be calming her and she's calming him? "Are you taking applications for a white knight?"

Her eyebrows rose for a moment, then she chuckled and rested her hand on his arm. "We've got to see where this thing leads, don't we?"

His heart hammered double-time at her touch and words. He nodded way too fervently, and heat crawled up his neck. Before he said or did anything else to embarrass himself, he merged into traffic.

At the restaurant, Jason pulled out Bethany's chair. Candlelight danced across her face and shoulders as she studied the menu. Between the restaurant aromas and how great Bethany looked, he had to concentrate on not drooling.

The waiter dropped off a hot basket of rolls, sprinkled roasted garlic chips on a plate, covered them in olive oil, and then took their drink orders.

Jason offered her a roll, curious to see if she would dip

her bread. No way, he'd get garlic breath if she didn't. "Have you decided what you'll have? They have some spicy entrees."

"I'm considering the Grilled Chicken Diavolo."

"Great choice. I may join you with that selection." Good grief, he sounded like a waiter. He could ask her more about her night, but she had already side-stepped that issue as quickly as possible. He could ask her about her past, but that would be prying. Maybe he could ask her about the future? Something safer. Then again, what if she'd think he'd be referring to the future with him?

He broke off a piece of his roll and dipped into the garlic and oil. With his lack of communication skills he probably wouldn't need to worry about his breath.

She joined him and let out a heavy sigh. "I love garlic. I'm glad you took the first bite, I didn't want to overwhelm you with garlic breath."

He chuckled. "We're both safe now."

The waiter brought their drinks, took their order, and then left.

Bethany shifted in her seat, her expression troubled. "Jason, I'm not sure how to approach our dating. Working together is going to be awkward. And I'll be honest. I'm not even sure how to act on a date."

He leaned toward her. "You did great last night."

"Watching your family was incredible. From there, I remember choking and almost getting run over by a jalopy."

"I remember some great kisses."

A grin tugged on her lips. "Basing a relationship on kiss-ability is probably not the best way to go."

"It's a good start."

"You're not making this easier."

"There's no rush. I enjoy your company, and I want to

get to know you better."

She lazily swirled her roll through the olive oil and garlic. "You may not like me when you know the rest of my story."

"Trust me. I made a mess of my life. We can't change what happened or what we did."

"You make it sound so easy."

"It's taken me years to understand grace." He held up his hand as though his sister were watching. "Believe me, I'm still learning."

Bethany met his gaze, her face solemn. "I don't want to mess up again. I don't want to wake up with regrets. I want a chance at a new life."

"Same here." His throat tightened at her vulnerability. "Bethany, I like who you are. I like that you're gorgeous, fun, witty, tough, and tender."

Bethany let the waiter finish delivering their entrees. Jason reminded her of her brother—easy-going and easy to talk with. But the feelings she had for Jason were definitely not brotherly.

She took a bite of her food and contemplated the man sitting in front of her. If only based on physical attraction, their relationship didn't have a chance. Gavin had been smooth and said all the right things—while they dated.

Deep down, she knew Jason wasn't the same. The tenderness in his eyes begged her to let herself go and trust him. The dreaded "T" word again. If only she could convince her heart.

"Bethany, will you do me a favor?" His smile reminded

her of a kid about to embark on some adventure. "Let's pretend we're just starting out. No baggage. No adult fears. Just have fun getting to know one another." He placed his open hand near hers. "Will you trust me?"

She reached out to touch him, and warmth spread from head to toe as his fingers intertwined with hers. "You want to play fairy tale?"

"Fair maiden." He brought her hand to his lips and kissed her fingers. "Will you allow me the pleasure of your company on this adventure?"

The joy in his eyes just about made her liquefy into the olive oil. "Dear Sir, I can think of nothing I would like better."

Bethany floated into her bed still amazed at the wonderful evening with Jason. He had been the perfect gentleman, the perfect everything—witty, sweet, kind, gentle, and loving. A true fairy-tale date. They held hands, giggled like teenagers, told silly jokes, shared popcorn at the movie, and kissed on her front porch until her lips were tender.

She closed her eyes, remembering his embrace, the softness of his hair, and the sound of his laughter. He was different from any man she had ever dated, and yet he had qualities she never thought she'd find in one person. She *really* liked him, and what was even more amazing, the thought didn't frighten her. Maybe she had eaten too much ice cream and frozen away her worries. Whatever the reason, she couldn't stop smiling.

And if she didn't get to sleep and cut out these sappy thoughts, she'd be completely useless in the morning. She rolled onto her tummy, snuggled against the soft sheets, and relaxed into blissful dreams.

Bethany's eyes flew open. She blinked at the night's darkness and let her gaze sweep over the bedroom. What had awakened her? The numbers on the nightstand clock glowed: 12:13. Jedi lay next to her, snoring.

Her heart slammed against her chest, every muscle tensed.

She was not alone.

Chapter 28

Bethany sucked in air and froze as fear pulsed through her veins. A sensation of slow, steady, movement crept up her lower back. Clutching the sheets, she willed herself to be still.

Something crawled against her bare skin. Inside her nightgown. The feathery touch of the intruder sent terror pounding through her. It had to be a spider, a *big* spider. Silent screams echoed through her mind laced with prayers for help. If she rolled over, she could crush the thing. But what if it bit her, sunk its venomous fangs into her skin? She'd be trapped with some eight-legged monster against her.

The thing stopped. Bethany concentrated on her breathing and hoped the pounding of her heart didn't alarm the creature. Was it looking for a good place to bite? Panic threatened to send her screaming into the night. *Oh, God. Oh, God, please help!*

The prickle of tiny feet started up again. Another step and another, moving closer to her neck. The gargantuan spider paused as though getting bearings, pondering where to go next. Would it get tangled in her hair? Or was it going straight for the jugular?

Holding her breath, her pulse raced in her ears. She could feel, hear, sense the thing moving from her skin to the pillow. How long before it would be far enough away? Tiny thumps, thump, thump, thump, then silence.

With a scream, she shot out of the covers and sprang for the light. Shuddering, she swept her arms, legs, body, her hair, and tore off her nightgown. Jedi tail down and eyes wide, cowered at her feet.

Where was the spider?

She yanked up her pillow and banged against every inch of her bed, then jerked back the covers.

Nothing.

"Help me find it. Please, oh please, God don't let it get away." Heart-racing, she found the flashlight. She steeled herself, knelt on the floor and shined the light under her bed. Smattering of dust bunnies and a web reflected like silver threads. In the corner, something twitched, jolted.

She moved the bed away from the wall. *Where was a bodyguard when you needed one?* And what do you use against a spider? She grabbed a tennis racket and threw herself across the bed.

Her visitor lay on the floor twitching—a wolf spider, big, hairy, not-deadly, but a bite that could pack a painful punch. Racket held high, she screamed a war cry. "I'll show you!"

Whack!

Ugh. She couldn't help it—she jumped back on the bed.

Jedi barked hysterically.

What was left of the blob on the floor had the audacity to move.

Whack!

Woozy and a touch nauseous, she swayed and tried to catch her breath.

A bang at her front door made her heart somersault. After checking a fresh robe for any unwanted guests, she threw it on and staggered forward.

"Bethany, are you okay?" Scott's voice sounded frantic.

Keys jangled in the lock and the door flew open. He burst in, gun drawn.

Jedi pranced toward him, tail wagging as though every evening they conquered spiders the size of Texas.

She wrapped her robe tighter, pointed Scott to the bedroom, collapsed on the couch, and tried to get rid of the sensation that lingered on her spine.

Weapon raised, he crept to other room.

Back in a flash, he knelt in front of her. "Talk to me. What happened?"

"Big. Hairy." She trembled and swallowed hard to keep her roiling stomach from losing its contents. "Spider."

"Oh." He gave her one of those looks men give women for being women.

She picked up Jedi, led Scott to the bedroom, and pointed.

When he spotted what was left of Tyrannosaurus spider he shook his head. "That *was* a big one." His voice sounded impressed.

Bethany pulled her robe tighter. "It crawled up my back."

He visibly shuddered.

"Would you get him out of here for me?"

His tough façade seemed to waver for a few moments. "Sure." He went to her kitchen, tore off a handful of paper towels, and scooped up the remainder. "Got him. You going to be okay?"

"I'd be better if exterminator's made night calls."

He nodded and shut the door behind him.

After Scott left, Bethany changed the sheets, swept, and checked every nook and cranny to make sure nothing else lurked in her apartment before she could even think about getting back to bed. Pajamas with feet and a high collar sounded good about now. Sleeping on her stomach was out of the question. She still couldn't figure out how anything that big had gotten in. Her windows and doors always stayed closed.

The fireplace flue?

Sure enough it was open. No wonder her electric bill had been high last month. If it wasn't summer, she'd start a fire and burn out anything and everything. Shoot, she'd use a flame thrower or a grenade if something else lived up there.

Something in the back of her mind continued to send danger signals. What if the spider gained entrance some other way? Several more passes around the apartment and she still couldn't shake the uneasy feeling.

Leaving the bathroom light on, she got back into bed. With herculean force, she tucked the covers around her until even a gnat couldn't crawl in, much less breathe. She lay awake, blinking in the semi-darkness, wondering if she could wear a spaghetti strainer as a face-mask.

When her eyes finally got heavy, she pulled the sheet over her face and prayed for protection and sleep.

Chapter 29

Jason came in early for a meeting with management. The team's progress had caught the attention of corporate in Chicago. If all went well, headquarters might fly the group up for a project review, complete with bonus possibilities.

He needed to get a few things done before he visited with Bethany. Her call in the early morning as she vented about the spider, still got to him. Not that he was arachnophobic or anything. Creatures like that belonged outside, killing mosquitoes and flies, not crawling up his girlfriend's back.

Girlfriend. He smiled at the thought. They *were* dating, and Bethany definitely was more than a friend. He tried to think of something appropriate for their ages instead of sixteen-year-old terminology. But that's how he felt with her, like a kid again and also the man he hoped to become.

He grabbed his coffee cup as an excuse to pass her office. The least he could do was say good morning.

Bethany looked deep in thought as she studied a stack of diagrams. He sneaked behind her and feathered his fingers across her shoulder.

She shot straight up, her chair shoving into his gut with enough force to double him over. Definitely not one of his brighter ideas.

"Jason, are you okay?"

Still gasping for breath, he managed a nod.

"Good." She thumped him hard on the back. "Don't try to scare me like that again."

Just what he needed. He straightened as air rushed in refilling his lungs.

Her face paled. "You weren't okay." She stood in front of him, placed her hand on his chest. "I'm sorry. I didn't know you were really hurt."

Jason considered giving her a wounded look to play on her concerned expression. But what he really wanted was take her in his arms.

Valerie barged in. "*What* is going on?" Her eyes sparked with mischief. "Go ahead, kiss. I won't tell anyone." She leaned against the doorway as though in no particular hurry. "Don't let me stop you."

Bethany's hand still rested on Jason's chest. For some reason she couldn't seem to move. She focused on his eyes then his lips. Those sweet, gentle lips that made everything right with the world. She glanced at Valerie. "I'll give you a dollar to make you go away."

"Make it a five, and I'll monitor the hall and won't tell anyone."

"Deal. I'll pay you later."

Valerie snorted a laugh and pranced out the door.

A smiled tugged on Jason's lips as he pulled Bethany toward him. His mouth touched hers and swept her far away from the confines of her cubicle.

"Ouch!" Nicole's irritated voice came from the hall. "You little worm, what the heck are you doing?"

"Sorry, Nicole." Valerie's response dripped with

sarcasm. "I didn't mean to bump into you."

Jason grabbed a file and leaned against the cubicle wall.

Bethany tried to calm her racing heart as she sat in her seat and faced the computer. Paying Valerie would be worth every penny.

"You did that on purpose." Nicole's shrill words grated like fingernails on a chalkboard. "If my coffee had spilled on this outfit, you'd be paying through the nose."

Valerie sniffed several times. "I don't think you'd get much money that way."

"Where is Jason?"

"Jason? Team leader, Jason? Tall, decent-looking guy? Oh, I think he went to get something from Bethany's office."

A guttural snarl oozed Nicole's frustration. "*You* are a pest."

"Yeah, but I'm a well-paid pest."

Nicole stepped into Bethany's office, beet-red and still seething. She stopped in front of Jason. "There you are. I need your help." Her voice took on a seductive tone. "You're not busy are you?" She gave a sideways glance at Bethany.

"No, I was just checking on a few things." He dropped the folder back on the desk. "Thanks, Bethany, we'll discuss this further."

"Anytime. I promise to do my best on this project."

His ears tinged red. "I appreciate that more than you'll know."

Bethany waited until they left before she got her purse and took out a five. Office dating could get very expensive, and with Valerie, extremely entertaining.

###

Jason had little concern for what Nicole was saying. He couldn't take a risk like that again with Bethany. They'd have to maintain a professional front during the week. If dating became a problem, he'd talk to management about a transfer when the project ended. He could work with the group on the other side of the building and still see her for lunch.

Nicole glared at him. "You haven't heard a word I've been saying."

"Sure I have." To her amazement, he repeated word for word what she had just said. He couldn't explain the auto-pilot gift he had inherited from his dad but was thankful when it worked.

"Well." Nicole tapped her pen on his desk a look of impatience on her overly made-up face. "Are you going to talk to the others about this? We need a decision."

He blinked hard as though the words had sucker-punched him in the gut. "I'll put out a memo. It shouldn't impact our schedule."

She gave him a look of disgust and stormed out of his office.

Her earlier words brought back memories of the night when his world imploded. *We need a decision.*

His parents smiling and laughing as they left for the committee meeting at church. Kelly away at college, while he was at home studying for finals. The news of the head-on collision. The agony as he paced in the hospital waiting room, praying, hoping his parents would survive.

The doctor's words echoed in his mind. "We need a decision." Kelly, still bleary-eyed from her all-night drive home, clung to Jason as she signed the papers to turn off life support. His parent's drunk-driver killer had served five years without so much as an apology.

The raw emotions blind-sided him, sent him reeling. Why, after all these years, did those memories resurface? Had they been hiding in some dark recess of his brain, waiting to pounce when his life finally moved in a positive direction?

Ignoring the situation had been successful. Until now.

"Hey." Bethany stood across the desk from him. "It's lunch time. You want to join us?"

He kept his head down, his forehead resting against his hand. "Not today. I've got to get some things done."

"Come on." She skipped her fingers across his hair. "In fairy tales there's always time for play."

"There's no such thing as fairy tales." Jason jerked back and turned away—not wanting her to see him like this. "Close the door when you leave."

Alone, his grief rolled over him, suffocating as though once again he was seventeen. He slid to his knees.

He should have told Bethany the truth. But revealing that side of him, the side that felt pain, the side that still missed his parents, only made him feel weak and less of a man.

Before he did anything, he had to forgive. Saying it was easy. Meaning it was another matter.

More than the door shut as Bethany walked back to her office. The walls rose in force around her heart. Trying to squelch the moisture building in her eyes and the lump swelling in her throat, she grabbed her purse, threw apologies at Rhonda and Valerie and hurried to the elevator.

Chapter 30

Jason didn't leave his office until he sorted through his emotions and prayed. Maybe that was part of the reason he had such a hard time forgiving himself—he hadn't released the burden he'd carried for over a decade. He would always miss his parents, but finally letting go of his anger at the drunk driver, and truly trusting that God would do what was right, made Jason feel lighter.

He finally made peace, but he still needed to apologize to Bethany … if she'd let him. She wasn't in her office, and Rhonda and Valerie hadn't seen her since lunch. He checked the break-room and then the conference area. Bethany wasn't there. He dialed her cell. The call went straight to voicemail.

Standing in the hallway, he tried to think. Maybe she took a long lunch, went for a drive or to her apartment. Either way she'd be safe. Her bodyguard would be with her. Then again, that's what he thought when he dropped her off after their date the other night.

Panic spurred him to the elevator. He punched the button and waited. *Stupid thing's stuck on floor three.*

He shoved through the side door and lunged down the stairwell two steps at a time until he reached the third floor. Some idiot had propped a chair to keep the elevator open while they loaded supplies. He shoved it aside and caught his breath while the elevator moved at a snail's pace.

The ding announced the ground floor. He squeezed through the doors the moment they cracked open. Bethany's bodyguard sat on the couch working on his laptop. Jason blew out a breath of relief. She must still be in the building.

Scott glanced his way. "You okay?"

"Yeah, I just thought Bethany was gone. If you're here, she's here, right?"

Scott stood, surveyed the parking lot, and let out a string of curses.

Bethany's running shoes crunched on the gravel as she made a second loop on the trail. Scott didn't see her leave, and that was fine with her. She'd confess her escape when she returned. The park gave her the opportunity to change into running gear and spend some time alone. The sweet smell of fresh-cut grass scented the air but didn't ease the tightness in her chest.

There's no such thing as fairy tales. Jason's words echoed through her mind. Her sneakers thumped as she crossed the bridge. Throat constricting, she exchanged a nod as she ran past an older couple holding hands. All she wanted was an opportunity to jump into a fantasy and believe that happily-ever-after really did exist.

Sunshine flitted through the trees, the shade bringing a welcome cooling. Why had Jason been so loving one moment and ice-cold the next? Did Nicole say something, or did he find her more attractive? Her stomach knotted. Jason wouldn't be like Gavin, would he?

The rhythmic stride of another jogger came from behind. She moved to the right to let him pass. He threw her a glare.

Obviously she didn't move fast enough for his taste. Maybe that's what she needed to do—move away from Southburg and start over somewhere else.

Sweat trickled down her face, and she wiped it away with the back of her hand. Why should she stay? Nothing worked right anyway. First Gavin, then her own indiscretions at college, the mess with Joelle, and now Jason shoved her away.

How far did she have to run to get away from the past? She picked up the pace. The trees blocked the sunshine and covered her path with dark shadows.

Ouch!

Something sharp poked into her heel. She stopped, pulled off her shoe, and removed a pebble. Amazing how something so tiny could hurt that bad. Life might have irritating moments, but how long would she keep allowing them to mess up her future? She couldn't change what others did and sure couldn't change her mistakes.

Still clutching the rock, she closed her eyes and prayed to release her whole messy life—the things she'd done and the things done to her. She didn't want to carry them anymore, and in her mind's eye, she released them to God.

A light breeze fingered through her hair, enveloping her in peace. She dropped the rock where it melded, became part of the trail, no longer an irritant.

With renewed vigor, she sprinted toward the sunshine.

At the parking lot, she removed her car key she'd tied to her shoe. Hopefully, she could wash off enough in the restroom to not be too odiferous. Her car sat hemmed between a gray SUV and a dirty, black pickup. She squeezed past the truck, leaving a clean swath on the door. While opening the trunk, she hesitated.

Her car listed toward the passenger side. She took a step back and groaned. The rear passenger tire was completely flat. Having Scott nearby would have been nice. Calling him or a car service would take at least thirty minutes, and she was already late. Plus, she didn't want to hear the tirade from security about safety.

She got herself into this. She'd get herself out. Changing a tire wasn't necessarily hard, as long as the lug nuts weren't too tight. Dad had made sure she could check the oil, change a tire, and a few other basics before he ever agreed to her driving her first car alone. She popped open the trunk and reached for the jack.

A cold blunt object jabbed in her back. "Do as I say, and you *might* not get hurt."

Chapter 31

"When did you see her last?" Scott grabbed his laptop and typed in a Web address.

"She came by about lunch time. Around eleven." Jason checked his watch. She could have been gone over two hours. "Didn't you see her leave?"

"I've been here the whole time except to grab a cup of coffee around eleven." Scott shook his head, anger clouding his expression. "Her phone has a GPS, we'll find her." Linking to the tracking site, he zoomed in on her location, and cursed again. "She's near Lakes Park." He flipped open his cell, dialed a number, and reported the situation. "I've called for backup just in case."

"I'm going with you."

Scott hesitated then handed Jason the computer. "I'll drive. You keep an eye on her coordinates."

Jason followed Scott to his car. Why would Bethany be at the park? Maybe she just wanted to be alone for a little while. The sense of foreboding wouldn't stop. His throat closed at the last words he spoke to her. If only he could go back in time. What would happen if he lost her before he even had a chance to spend time with her?

He couldn't lose someone else he loved.

###

Bethany froze, blood whooshing in her ears. Praying silently, she inched her hand forward to reach her cell phone. Just a little more and she had it, the casing hot in her fingertips.

"Stand up nice and slow." The object dug harder into her back. "Don't do anything stupid. Drop it."

The phone thudded on the carpeted trunk.

"Keep your hands by your side." The voice calm, low, seething. "If you do anything to draw attention, I'll shoot you."

Did everybody want her dead? She stood, staring straight ahead, wishing the young couple walking by would notice.

The man stood close to her, so close she could smell his sweat and alcohol breath. "Take a few steps to the driver's side of my truck and slide in."

Heart battering against her chest, her feet rooted to the hot pavement. No way she would go with him. Her chances for survival in another location would drop dramatically. The verse ran in her mind, *I can do all things through Christ who strengthens me.* She still had a life to live. And whether Jason believed in fairy tales or not, she wanted another chance. She wanted to love again.

"I said move." The man's hand clamped on her left arm, squeezing with enough force she had to grit her teeth to not cry out. "Your daddy will pay a nice ransom for his baby girl."

The voice. She knew the voice. The voice that greeted her the first week she moved into the apartment. The creepy guy with the black pickup. "Clint, you don't want to do this."

His grip faltered a moment, then regained in strength. "Sure, I do. If your dad hadn't *fired* me, I wouldn't need the money. You're worth a half mil. Regardless of the condition you're in." He prodded her forward. "Did you like my eight-legged present the other day?"

That did it! Spiders and the thought of her parents receiving a ransom note or her winding up dead made her want to spit fire. She cemented her resolve. No one was going to ruin her chance for happiness—not Gavin, Joelle, spiders, and definitely not creepy Clint.

Praying silently, she took a deep breath. With every ounce of her strength she jabbed her right elbow back against his arm and into his gut.

His breath whooshed out, and the gun skidded across the pavement.

Free from his grasp, she pivoted and followed with a left forearm smash to the bridge of his slimy nose.

Clint staggered back, cursing as blood gushed from both nostrils. Fury rose in his eyes. "You little—"

Bethany's muscles pumped, she positioned herself and threw a roundhouse kick to his ribcage, followed by another quick one to his head.

He groaned and crumpled to the concrete before she could stomp him into the ground.

Jason didn't wait for the car to stop before he threw open the door and took off running. He dodged as a white SUV almost side-swiped him. Throat clogged, he tried to call Bethany's name.

Bethany stood over a man, her shoulders heaving.

Grounding to a halt, Jason reached out and touched her arm.

Pain tore through his head and exploded stars into his vision as her kick connected with his chin. He stumbled back battling to stay upright and blinked through blurry eyes.

Scott and others grabbed and wrestled her cursing assailant.

Bethany stared at Jason through wild eyes, first in shock, then recognition, her breaths fast on top of one another. Pushing away the hair stuck to her sweaty face, she gave him a look that curled his blood. "How dare you try to destroy my fairy tale!"

His jaw unhinged ... almost literally after that kick. "Did you do that on purpose?"

"No, I thought somebody else was attacking. *You* just happened to get in the way. But the next one might be on purpose." Eyes flaming, she jabbed a finger into his chest. "I finally let my guard down to trust you, and you sent me packing."

Scott chuckled as he placed a zip strip on the wrists of Bethany's assailant.

Jason steadied his breathing. She was okay, and she looked downright cute and sexy standing there ready to take on the world. "I'm sorry. It wasn't about you. My parents were killed by a drunk-driver when I was a teenager, I couldn't deal with it this morning."

Her shoulders sagged, and she took a step toward him. "Why didn't you tell me?"

"I don't know. I just needed some time away." He pulled her toward him, studied her face, her eyes, her lips. "I don't know what I would've done if something happened to you. Will you forgive me? Are you sure you're okay?"

She nodded, her gaze resting on his mouth.

He leaned down and kissed her, and a small moan escaped from the back of her throat. As the kiss deepened so did the realization that he loved her enough to spend his life getting to know her, to wake up every morning with her by his side.

"Bethany." Scott stood next to them. "The police need to talk to you."

She clung to Jason, then drew away. "I …" She gulped hard, her fingers traced his face. "Don't leave."

He smiled. "I won't ever leave."

Bethany tilted her head, and tears welled in her eyes. "Is that a promise or a threat?"

Jason pulled her back into his arms. "A promise." He kissed her with every ounce of his strength, wanting, needing her to know and understand the depth of his feelings and love.

Bethany's arms and legs dissolved into wet noodles. She draped herself against Payne Tanner's SUV and could barely concentrate on the questions from police and security. Jason stood in the distance watching, wearing the cutest smile or at least what she could see over his swollen jaw. She was definitely in love with him, and right now, it didn't scare her. His last kiss had sent her heart leaping and dissolved every fear. She could float on air. Who cared about almost getting kidnapped? Did anyone else notice the smell of flowers and the songs of the birds?

Between prayers of gratitude for safety and for Jason, she turned her attention back to the officers. Clint, whose real name was Sam, had been the one sending her family threats and who burglarized the estate.

If he hadn't been handcuffed in the back seat of the police vehicle, she'd smack him again. Probably not a very lady-like or Christian thought, but the man had kept them on edge for months. Then again, she could probably thank him and a cast of others—her return to Southburg had not been boring.

She glanced back at Jason. Dad's security honcho, Payne Tanner, had him in a deep conversation. Judging by Jason's pale expression, Payne was giving him quite the talk. If Payne messed things up for her, she'd smack him too ... if she could get her arms to move.

When the policemen were finished, they took her would-be-kidnapper to jail, and Scott escorted Bethany to her car. Payne and Jason worked together to fix her flat tire. Thankfully, she had purchased a full-size spare when she bought the car.

Jason wiped his forehead, leaving a black streak across his brow. "Are you okay?"

She took a steadying breath to keep from collapsing into his arms. "I think so."

Payne returned the jack to her trunk. "Until we make sure Sam worked alone, Scott will stay on duty. If you're comfortable going back to work, Jason can drive you."

Bethany nodded and thanked Payne and Scott.

Jason gave her a lopsided grin thanks to the bruise forming on his handsome jaw. "You pack quite a kick. Any other secrets I need to know?"

"That's for me to know, and you to find out."

He stepped closer. "Is *that* a promise or a threat?"

"Both." Bethany considered a kiss, but leaving him hanging would be far too much fun, plus if she got any closer to him she'd just melt. "I better get cleaned up and change."

"Right." He straightened, disappointment clouding his expression.

She whispered in his ear. "I'll thank you properly later ... when we're alone."

Jason's face blazed red, and he swallowed hard. "Thank you."

Thank you? Jason inwardly kicked himself.

Suave or debonair would have been nice with a snappy comeback, but instead he sounded like a little kid—drooling and needy. His jaw ached, and his heart hurt. Why didn't he say he loved her? He'd used the words before, except now he really meant them. Bethany was a contradiction—tough yet gentle. He had fallen in love with the woman and the little girl who lived inside.

How on earth could he stay good?

His thoughts dissolved into a mass of prayers for help.

Bethany returned in her work clothes, carrying her running gear and a wet paper towel. She grinned. "You've got a smudge on your forehead."

Jason leaned down, and she gently wiped his forehead.

Her hand lingered on his face. "I'm sorry about your jaw."

"I'm just glad you're okay."

Staring at Jason's expression, Bethany wanted to throw herself into his arms and pledge her love forever. Reality niggled at her brain. Living a fantasy life usually led to a bona-fide painful ending. Did she love him because of all the strong emotions and experiences she'd had the last several months? Or could he be the real thing?

Did she really know him? They needed time together.

Then again, being with him could probably throw her back into some nasty habits. If the attraction was any stronger, they could bottle and sell the stuff on the Internet and make millions.

Scott leaned against the car, staring in the distance as though he wasn't watching behind his dark sunglasses.

She backed away from Jason and popped open her car door. "We better go."

Scott gave her a grateful look. "Mind if I stop off at a fast food to get something to eat since Jason's with you?"

Jason rubbed his jaw. "Who's going to protect *me*?"

Bethany grinned and handed him the keys. "I promise to stay on my side."

On the way back to the office, she knew Jason watched her. She'd pay money to get in his head. "What did Payne talk to you about?"

"He told me he'd personally kill me, slow and painfully, if I hurt you."

"He did not."

"Yes, he did." He shuddered. "I'll leave the details to your imagination. He said you'd been through enough."

Not sure if she was angry or grateful at Payne, she patted Jason's arm. "You poor thing."

Jason gave her a slow smile that made her heart stroke double-time. "After what you've been through I think you could use some therapy after dinner and a movie this weekend." He kept one hand on the wheel and with the other, rubbed her shoulder. "What do you say?"

With his gentle touch, she had to concentrate not to let her every inhibition fly out the window. "Some one-on-one therapy?"

"I'm a good listener. The session starts six thirty Friday and then again Saturday if you need additional time. There's never a charge for my services."

"How come you get to be the therapist?"

"You'd prefer to analyze me?" His smile faltered.

"We could take turns."

"It's a deal." Jason's fingers massaged her neck. "Just one request."

If he kept up with his magic touch, she'd agree to just about anything. "What?"

"We need to pray about our relationship. I want to treat you right."

A million happy emotions bounced inside her heart. Swallowing the lump in her throat, she laid her head on his hand, the warmth swathing her from head to toe.

Back at the office, Bethany finally finished answering everyone's questions and talking to her parents about her interesting afternoon. Security and police concluded Clint, or whatever his name was, had worked alone, which meant the threats were through and her life could go back to normal. She leaned back in her chair and took a deep breath, letting it out slowly.

No bodyguards, no checking over her shoulder or her rearview mirror. She was free. If Nancy had been here she could let loose with a Snoopy dance.

She glanced up in time to see Jason hurry past her office. Now the only thing she needed to worry about was keeping out of trouble.

Valerie strolled into Bethany's office and propped her skinny backside on the desk. "You sure did a number on Jason. Did you knock some sense into him?"

"I honestly didn't mean to. But yes, he seems to be thinking much clearer."

"Good. If I send a few people your way, could you give

them a kick for me?"

"I hope to be out of the business after today. I want a nice, quiet life. I've had all the craziness I can stand."

"*Au contraire*, my little friend." Valerie twirled one of Bethany's pens. "If you and Jason keep dating there won't be anything nice or quiet about your life."

"Why do you say that?"

"Because you two will be spending so much time trying to keep your hands off one another, you'll either get married in a few weeks or have to hire a chaperone."

Bethany chuckled. They would have a tough time. "I'm sure we can take care of matters all by ourselves." *Along with lots of prayers.*

"Yeah, right, and then you'll wind up having to walk on glass or beat yourselves with rods or something because you've been bad." Valerie jabbed the pen at Bethany. "And if you don't, you'll be in bad trouble. Your God will send down a lightning bolt or squash you like a bug."

"He doesn't operate that way."

"He seems pretty tough with those Command No things."

"If God wasn't patient, kind, and loving, I would have been zapped long ago."

Valerie hummed, her arms moving in slow easy circles. "I, for one, believe in the cosmos, the totality of the universe. We are one, and we are free to live within the constraints of our Mother Earth until it's time to become worm food."

"I'd rather know I'll spend eternity in Heaven."

"That infinity thing is too far-fetched for me. Of course, I would like to drive one of those fancy Infinity cars. But I digress. When I die, my life force sinks into the earth to feed the next generation."

Bethany studied her flippant air. "You ever curious?"

Valerie lifted her chin and crossed her arms. "Yes, but if you tell Rhonda, I'll deny it to the end. James found this religion stuff, and we're still seeing each other. He and Rhonda are always trying to revert me."

"You mean, convert?"

"Yeah, whatever, revert, convert, pervert … I don't know. It makes my brain hurt."

"Valerie, your cell is ringing." Rhonda's voice carried from the hallway.

Noticing Valerie's hesitation, Bethany touched her arm. "You want to talk about this later?"

"Yes and no." Valerie pushed off the desk. "I'll let you know when I have a question."

After Valerie left, Bethany glanced upward and sent up a silent prayer of thanks. She rubbed her eyes as tears threatened to escape. In the quiet, an onslaught of emotions rolled over her. The tough part of her wanted to puff up her chest and strut at being a survivor, while the little girl in her wanted to crawl under the desk and sob. And to top off the emotional upheaval, she was thinking about taking the risk of loving someone again.

Running away to a deserted tropical island sounded like a better idea. Problem was, she'd want to take Jason. And with Jason, came the risks of another broken heart.

Chapter 32

Grateful that Friday finally arrived, Jason checked the clock. A few more hours at work and he'd pick up Bethany for their date. Tonight, they'd enjoy a nice relaxing dinner and some time alone. Fortunately, their relationship stayed on a professional level at work—other than the 81,452 times he wanted to kiss her.

George Canton strode into Jason's office. "Good news. Corporate has made arrangements for the team to fly to Chicago."

"All of us?" He sounded like a little kid, even felt like one.

"Yes. I'll update everyone on Monday afternoon, and we'll finalize the reservations." He slapped Jason on the back. "Have a great weekend. I'm proud of you."

After George left, Jason couldn't move. Just sat there grinning. Not only would their team be the first to experience the benefits of a trip to corporate, he himself personally received a statement he longed to hear. *I'm proud of you.* Those words shouldn't matter now that he was a grown man, but they did. He wanted to make someone proud.

###

Bethany couldn't get her hair right. Why tonight the

battle to remain untamed? She combed and brushed, hoping she wouldn't have to use some other hair product. If she walked by an open flame, she'd combust. Plus if she used more, she'd stick to Jason's face if they hugged. And she wouldn't miss a good hug.

Jedi tilted his head as though even he couldn't figure out the hair situation.

"Don't say what you're thinking."

He wagged, and from the look on his puppy face, smiled at her misfortune.

"You are not helping." She gave him a quick pet then checked her watch—ten more minutes to get dressed.

A knock just about unhinged her and her hair.

Barking, Jedi dashed to the other room.

She wrapped her robe around her and peeked through the peep-hole. Jason stood outside with roses in hand. Was her watch slow? She cracked open the door. "Hi."

"I'm sorry I'm early. I've got some great news."

"I'm not properly dressed."

His face tinged red. He stepped back, clutching his gift. "I'll wait out here."

How could one man be so thoughtful and downright cute? With a smile on her face, she finished getting ready in world-record time.

When she reopened the door, Jason handed her the bouquet. "Man, you *really* look good."

His smile sent heat to every inch of her body. "Thank you for the compliment and the flowers."

"You're welcome." He stared at her a moment then cleared his throat. "Guess what? Corporate is sending our team to Chicago."

"Really?" She held the flowers to her nose and sniffed,

then smiled at his enthusiastic nod.

He followed her into the kitchen. "We're the first team to get this privilege. They've never done anything like this before. Chicago has the best museums and restaurants. The winters are tough, but there's always something to do, some neat convention, show, or movie."

"You sound like a travel agent." Relishing the sweet smell, she filled a vase with water and arranged the bouquet.

"Sorry." His smile turned sheepish. "I'm pumped about this trip."

"You should be. You've worked hard." After making sure Jedi had food and water, she locked up her apartment. "So, where are you taking me?"

He offered her his arm. "First stop, dinner. Then you have your choice of three movies. A chick-flick, a drama, or an action movie."

"I'm definitely not in the mood for a drama. I've had enough to last a lifetime. Let's go for some action."

"You like to watch them?" His look conveyed that her status moved to a higher level.

She grinned. "Yes. Remember, I do have brothers."

"You know, that kind of answer leads straight to a man's heart."

"That so? I can top that, I've actually watched action movie marathons."

Jason put a hand over his chest. "I think I love you."

Bethany stared at him. His eyes widened as the repercussions of his statement hung in the air. He looked so helpless, she couldn't resist. "I even watch and enjoy sports. What would you say to that?"

He coughed, sputtered.

She moved closer. Shark circling prey, smelling blood,

sensing his fear. "What else do you love? Salsa? Hiking in the mountains? Spicy food?"

"You *really* want to know?" He put his arms around her, drew her toward him.

She gulped.

He kissed her, slow, easy, and gentle. "Bethany," he whispered. "It's you I love."

Her heart whimpered and dissolved in her chest. An all-out war raged inside her—common sense pounded feelings, past experience screamed and assumed the fetal position, cupid zinged arrows all over the place, and she couldn't think, much less speak.

He kissed her again. "You don't have to say anything. Let's get some dinner." With a smile, he took her hand and led her to the car.

It's you I love. His words played over and over in her mind—so sweet and formal, like a romance novel. Goosebumps formed on her arms and kept her tongue firmly glued to the roof of her mouth. How and why would he love her? After the mess she'd made of her life, she didn't deserve someone like him. Believing God loved her was tough enough.

Jason's smile never waned. He kept the conversation light, talking about work, the upcoming trip to Chicago, and his family. She studied him at the restaurant, his mannerisms and his handsome face. Still she remained confined in a virtual well, watching, listening, but unable to respond.

He slipped his strong hand over hers. "Where are you?"

She laced her fingers with his. "Trapped in the state of confusion."

"Bethany, I don't expect you to return my sentiment unless that's how you feel."

She nodded, her voice still caged by some nasty imp

called fear. *But I do love you.*

At her apartment, Bethany waited for the coffee to brew in the kitchen. Jason played with Jedi in the other room complete with dog toy squeaks and good natured growls from both of them. Even though the movie had been exciting, with plenty of gunshots and explosions, all she could think about was telling Jason she loved him. She should've just said it when he told her.

Now what was she supposed to do? Hand him a mug and say, here's your coffee and oh by the way, I love you too? Would you like sugar and cream and a helping of I love you?

"Hey, what ya thinking?" Jason held a contented wagging Jedi.

Bethany jolted, sending her coffee cup spinning wildly across the counter. She grabbed it before it careened off the edge.

"You okay?"

Her mind whirled trying to think of something to say. "Would you believe I was thinking about the preview for the alien movie?"

"Right." He grinned and shook his head. "You look like the type who believes rocks from Mars spawn strange mutations. Then again, if they had based it on the bottom of my fridge it could be believable."

Ignoring a slight uncomfortable rumbling in her stomach, she filled their mugs. Maybe she shouldn't have eaten leftovers for lunch. *How old was that tuna salad anyway?* "Do you need cream or sugar?" *And me?*

"Nope." Jason set Jedi on the floor. "I take my decaf straight." He puffed his chest. "It's a man thing."

"You'd fit right in with our action hero."

He accepted the offered cup and followed her to the

251

couch. "Well, I didn't want to brag about my past, but in my younger days, I could leap buildings and stop speeding trains with my little finger."

"Really?"

"When I was seven, I had the best train set in the neighborhood."

"You are my hero." *And I love you.* She sat in the center of the couch making sure to leave enough room for him.

"I don't know about that." He plopped in the chair across from her. "I have to confess. I tied Kelly's Barbie doll to the tracks. Fortunately, GI Joe did come to the rescue in the nick of time."

"*You* were mischievous?"

His grin and the glint in his eyes confirmed her suspicion. "I had my moments."

Bethany sipped her coffee before she did something stupid like jump up, attack him with a flurry of kisses, and pledge her love forever.

Jason set his mug on the side table. "It's time to get down to business."

She choked on her coffee. "Excuse me?"

"We talked about this earlier. As your therapist, I need to ask you some questions."

Therapist? The memory of their conversation from the other day came back. "You were serious?" A metallic taste coated her mouth followed by a sudden queasiness. Her lunch had come back to haunt her.

Eyes sparkling, he opened an invisible notepad and poised an imaginary pen as though ready to take notes. "Miss Davis, I'd like to ask you some questions. I want you to answer honestly, don't hold anything back, and remember, I am your therapist. What is your full name?"

"Bethany Ann Davis"

"These next questions will be rapid fire. Please say the first thing that pops in your head." He paused, looked at her like a professor examining a student. "When night falls who picks it up?"

She giggled. "God."

Jason's expression remained studious, but a grin twitched on his lips. "Since there is a speed of light and a speed of sound, is there a speed of smell?"

"Yes, and always intensified by the degree of hunger."

"What makes cheese so confidential that we actually need cheese shredders?"

Her stomach churned and lurched. She stifled a burp. "To protect the lactose intolerant."

"If white wine goes with fish, do white grapes go with sushi?"

"As far as I'm concerned, nothing goes with sushi. Sushi is bait." The thought of raw fish sent her tummy into a major revolt. With a quick apology, she flew out of her chair and rushed to the bathroom.

One eternity later, Bethany wrapped her arms around her middle and heaved again. If she didn't die from embarrassment, there wouldn't be anything left in her body within the next few minutes. Thank goodness for the exhaust fan. Why did she have to get sick when she finally was getting the nerve to tell him that she loved him?

"Bethany? Is there anything I can do, can I get you something?" Jason's worried voice from the other side of the door made her want to cry. If he wanted anything to do with her after hearing the unearthly noises coming from her bathroom, he deserved a medal.

She sprawled on the floor, a towel under her head. "Just

shoot me."

"I'm sorry about dinner."

"No, it wasn't what I ate tonight. It was the leftovers from hell." The memory triggered another round of sickness.

"Do I need to get you to the doctor?"

Riding in the car? She doubled over. "Please, no."

"I'm going to the pharmacy. Can I borrow your keys so I can lock the door?"

"They're in my purse."

"I'll be back in a minute."

Jason calculated he broke the land speed record on his trip to the drug store. He bought everything the pharmacist recommended and included anything that even remotely sounded helpful. Out of the thirty-five dollars of medications, hopefully something would work. He tapped on the bathroom door. "Bethany?"

No answer.

He knocked harder. "Bethany?"

Again, she failed to answer.

Jedi stared at him. His furry eyebrows twitched, and he looked from Jason to the door. If a dog could look worried, he did.

Jason tried the knob, and it turned in his hand. He peeked inside. Bethany lay on the floor, a crumpled towel under her head. Praying fervently, he knelt and touched her face. "Bethany?"

Bloodshot eyes opened, and she swallowed several times. "I think I'm better now."

He tried not to recoil at the green frog coming from her

breath. "I've got something that might help. Can I get you to your room?"

She struggled to sit, her arms shaking as she pushed her body upright.

"Let me help." He picked her up, her head resting on his shoulder as he carried her to her bed and tucked the covers around her. "I'll be right back."

A few minutes later, he sat in a chair, his arsenal of supplies and an empty trash can at his feet, just in case she didn't feel well again. He dabbed her forehead with a cool washcloth. "Do you feel like taking a drink? And I've got some crackers."

She nodded and accepted a small sip and a bite of cracker. "You don't have to stay." A single tear rolled down her face and into her hair. "Oh, Jason, I—"

He held up his hand. "Shhh, it's okay, I'm not leaving. Just get some rest."

Her bottom lip quivered, she bit it back and closed her eyes.

Jason stayed at her side until she slept soundly. Even ill, she remained beautiful. He didn't want to leave, and he couldn't lock the deadbolt without taking her keys. He turned off the lamp beside her bed, opting to leave the one in the bathroom on.

Settling back in his chair next to her bed, he summoned Jedi to his lap. Together they kept watch. Maybe it was wishful thinking, but he refused to let go of the notion that maybe, just maybe, this time he could have it all—a beautiful girl, living the good life, and living right.

Then again, could he trust himself to not fall back into his old ways? And could he really trust another person enough to risk his heart?

He sat Jedi on the floor, stood, and with one more look at Bethany, walked out the door.

Chapter 33

Bethany pried open her matted eyelids and squinted at the morning light streaming through the windows. Besides terribly sore, her stomach felt somewhat better. Fully dressed, she lay in bed, her covers tucked around her. An empty chair stood next to her bed.

When did Jason leave? Then again, how on earth could he stay with all the ungodly noises from her bout of what had to be food poisoning? What a rotten night—trapped in the bathroom instead of telling him she loved him.

She grabbed the glass of water from the nightstand and gulped, half hoping to remove the fuzzy, polluted taste in her mouth. Her teeth and tongue seemed covered in furry socks. She trudged to the bathroom and brushed her teeth, gargled, and brushed again. She caught a whiff of herself. Her breath might be better, but her body reeked.

A quick look in the mirror made her gasp. Every bit of makeup was gone or smeared, her hair looked like it had been attacked by a mixer, and her face drained of color. No wonder Jason left.

He did leave, didn't he?

Bethany double-checked her bedroom, took a few steps, turned the corner, and surveyed the den. Jedi snored on top of pillows and a heaped up afghan on the couch. The front door was bolted tight. Jason must have taken her keys and locked up after himself. Swallowing a lump clogging her throat, she blinked back the moisture swimming in her eyes. She didn't even get to tell him she loved him.

She dragged her fingers through her hair and shuffled to the bathroom. After a shower, she'd give him a call. Maybe he'd come back with her keys, and she could thank him with a kiss and tell him … *Jason, thank you for taking care of me, I love you.*

Surely she could think of something less antiseptic. *Jason, you're handsome, wonderful, and more than I deserve, I love you.* True, but surely she could do better. *Jason, you hunk of a man, I love you madly.* Ugh. Maybe, he'd tell her again, and she could just say I love you too.

When she finished her shower, she fixed her hair and face, and put on clean clothes. Now she was ready. With hope and prayers, she could make a quick phone call, and she could get the words out before it drove her crazy. She turned the corner and screeched to a halt.

The afghan moved.

Jason?

She took a step closer. His head peeked from under the covers. He looked so cute, his hair all mussed to one side. He stayed all night? For her?

"You're much too good for me," she whispered.

His eyes fluttered open, and he squinted at her. "Nope. Your guard dog had me pinned down all night."

Jedi gave her a lazy wag, stretched, and jumped off.

Jason sat up and yawned. "I hope you don't mind me staying. I was worried about you." He patted the couch next to him. "How you feeling?"

Even though she wanted to be close, she moved aside the cover and sat a cushion away. "Much better, thanks to you and your truck full of meds."

He pulled a mint out of his pocket. "Sorry if I have morning breath."

"Don't worry. Mine could've peeled asphalt off a road."

"I hope I didn't soil your reputation spending the night."

"What reputation? After having a bodyguard watching my every move and the FBI crawling all over my apartment, I'm sure the neighbors will keep their distance."

He just sat there staring at her.

Was something stuck to her face? She rubbed her nose. "What?"

"You really are beautiful."

The room temperature cranked up twenty degrees. "Do you always wake up this nice?"

Jason's dimple showed with his grin. "Only with you."

"You're laying it on pretty thick."

"Can't fault me for trying." He stood and straightened his rumpled clothing. "I better get going."

She pushed off the couch. "I could make you some breakfast. I'm actually kind of hungry." *For something extremely bland.*

"I better not. I need a shower or at least brush my teeth."

She considered holding her stomach and groaning to keep him around, but dishonesty at this stage of the dating game was probably not a good idea. "I have a spare toothbrush. I mean, it's not used or anything. I always have a spare from my dentist visits."

He hesitated. "You sure you don't mind?"

"It's the least I can do since you stayed to make sure I was okay." She backed toward the bathroom. "I'll get it for you."

Rubbing his hand across his cheek, he followed. "I'm kind of scruffy."

"I've got an extra razor, if you need one." Oh man, she was sounding way too desperate. She hurried to grab the supplies.

He leaned against the doorframe. "You've got quite the setup. Have extra clothes for me too?"

"No." *Thank goodness.* She handed him a towel, washcloth, razor, and toothbrush still in the package. "Would you believe I was a Girl Scout? Always prepared or something like that."

"I think that's the Boy Scouts."

"No wonder I never got my merit badge."

He blocked her path. "I still love you."

Her heart turned into a tennis ball, bouncing, flinging itself against her chest. She finally had her chance to tell him. "Jason, —"

He put his finger on her lips. "Hold that thought."

Jason stepped around Bethany, shooed her out of the way and closed the door. If he didn't have time alone, his bladder would burst. Someday *maybe* this would be funny. Right now, it was his worst nightmare. Finally gets his nerve up to risk everything on love, and he closes the door on her. Somewhere in the cosmos, angels laughed.

Pots and pans banged in the kitchen as he shaved and brushed his teeth. *Great.* She was mad at him, probably getting ready to tell him to leave, that she didn't love him. Maybe he could send a text message to Kelly and have her call so he could escape with some level of dignity. No. He'd have to explain something to his sister. And what would he say?

Might as well take his punishment like a man. He forced

in a deep breath and reached for the doorknob.

Bethany grabbed the oatmeal and banged the cabinet shut. If she didn't tell Jason soon she would absolutely explode—heart shards would fly all over the apartment. Poor Jedi would be left an orphan, destined to wander the streets alone without love or proper grooming.

Why did she make this so difficult? Why couldn't she have just told him earlier? She measured out coffee for the two of them and added an extra five scoops. Maybe some high-octane caffeine would bolster her nerve. Why brew it? She could take it straight and chase it with a swig of water.

"Hey." Jason stood next to her. "I better go."

She didn't even hear him walk up. How long had he been watching? "Please stay."

He shrugged and stared at the floor. "I'm sure you have plans."

"I do." Bethany wrung her hands and tried to steady her breathing. "I need to tell you something."

Jason nodded. "I understand. I'll go." He took a step toward the door.

"No. I don't want you to go." Bethany clutched his arm and waited for him to look at her. "I want you to stay. I want to be with you." She kissed him. "Jason, I love you."

The next kiss probably set off every fire alarm in the city. If they didn't ignite in flames it would definitely be because of divine protection. *Whoa, baby.* She could feel his kisses all the way to her toes, tugging on her, pulling her foot out from under her. *Tugging?* She glanced down to see Jedi with her pant leg in his mouth.

Bethany kissed Jason again. And again. "Someone needs a walk." She pointed to her furry baby.

"Allow me the honor." Jason picked him up and gave her a look that made her heart sigh and snuggle in her chest.

She poured a cup of coffee and leaned against the counter. Jason loved her, and she loved him. She gulped hard.

Love.

What was she thinking? Jason didn't really know her. Would he think differently if he really knew what she'd done?

All her warm, fuzzy thoughts sloughed off and clunked to the floor in a quivering mass. She gagged on the sludge she'd made earlier and added six cups of water to the pot.

Jedi pranced in with a huge contented puppy smile, followed by the most wonderful, handsome man on the planet. Oh man, she was *so* in trouble. She had to talk to him, couldn't risk him finding out later.

"We need to talk." She focused on the floor as she took the hundred-mile walk to the couch. "I have to get this off my chest. I don't want you to find out later." Moisture built in her eyes, and she blinked repeatedly and wiped it away.

Jason sat next to her. "What's wrong?"

"You know I'm divorced."

He gave her a slow nod.

"It's just not the divorce. I kind of went wild. I guess you could say I was looking for love in all the wrong places."

"Lots of people do."

She sniffed and cleared her throat. "You deserve some pure-as-the-driven-snow girl who hasn't said or done anything wrong."

"Definitely not. I haven't been a hermit." His hand brushed her cheek. "The past is over." He tilted her chin to look at him. "I wish I could change my past, but I can't. We have today and the future. Okay?" He waited.

She responded with a tentative nod.

"Good. Then let's get on with our lives, and let God be God." He smiled with his eyes. "I really love you, Bethany Davis."

"Oh Jason, I really love you too."

He kissed her. A kiss beyond any she'd ever experienced. His strong arms enveloped her, and his lips carried her away, floating—safe and hopelessly in love.

By the time the kissing ended, her lips had to be double their size, plumped up from hours of incredible, amazing, ecstasy. Forget Botox, why didn't someone tell her about pure passion, with emphasis on the pure, years ago? Did anyone else know that something so simple could be this much fun?

Fanning herself, she collapsed into the sofa cushions. "How did you learn to kiss *that* good?"

Jason seemed to take a moment to focus. "I was going to ask you the same thing."

"So, what do we do now?"

He cleared his throat and shook his head. "Hire a chaperone."

Chapter 34

Bethany paced the length of her family room. Jedi followed behind, his tail keeping time with her stride. In five minutes, Jason would arrive to take her to his apartment to cook dinner. Fortunately, they'd managed to make it through work today without getting caught sneaking a few kisses, but now they'd be alone. *Really alone.* In his place. The thought made her stomach do bungee dives.

How on earth could they keep being good? And *why* would they keep being good? They did love each other, and had even talked about a long-term relationship. So how could loving each other physically be wrong? She knew the answer to her selfish question. Scripture made it plain. Sex belonged in marriage.

She stopped and stared at the ceiling. "I could really use some help here. You know I want to do the right things. Okay, you know sometimes I don't want to do the right things. Please help me when I'm having trouble being good."

Returning to her bedroom, she checked her outfit in the full-length mirror. Her new jeans were perfect, but her scoop neck top scooped way too much. She needed something not quite so inviting. With a quick move, she threw it off and grabbed a short-sleeved, button-down shirt. When she finally got it fastened, the gap between the buttons over her chest invited attention.

"Argh!"

Jedi sat on the floor, his head tilting to the side. She patted him. "Maybe you should come with us, and bark if things get out of hand."

Desperate, she pulled out a paisley-print top with a dropped waist. Thankfully, the v-neckline wasn't too plunging, and the flutter sleeves butterflied much like her stomach.

A knock sent Jedi scurrying to the apartment entrance.

Bethany breathed deep, sent up a last minute plea for divine help, and opened the door.

Jason smiled. "Hi, you ready to go?"

"Yes." She gulped at how irresistibly handsome he looked in cargo shorts and a t-shirt. Boy, did she need help. *God, only you can help me be good tonight.*

"I have a surprise." Jason's grin warmed her heart.

From behind him, his nephew and niece popped out. Both spoke in unison. "Hi, Miss Bethany!"

"Hi, Daniel and Elizabeth. What a nice surprise."

Daniel, in his shorts and t-shirt, mirrored Jason, only smaller. Elizabeth wore a pair of pink jeans, pink shirt with a large sequined flower, and pink tennis shoes. They both held out flowers that appeared suspiciously like the ones growing in the field near her house.

Jason looked curious and hopeful. "Matt and Kelly are on a date night. I hope you don't mind."

Saved by the children. "I'm glad they're here. I'm sure we'll have a really *good* evening." She smiled at the pun she knew God would catch and leaned down to accept the flowers. "Thank you. I can't wait to see what your Uncle Jason has planned for us."

The group followed her back inside. Bethany took a vase from under her sink, filled it with water, and arranged the clumps of wildflowers.

Elizabeth stood next to Bethany. "Uncle Jason hired us as chaperones."

Bethany stole a glance at Jason, whose face took on a red hue. "Did he tell you what you were supposed to do as a chaperone?"

"Yes." The little girl's blonde pigtail bobbed with her answer. "We need to make sure you don't get bored or anything."

"Well now, we sure wouldn't want that to happen. Would we?" Bethany nudged Jason.

He responded with a mischievous grin and shrug of the shoulders.

If the guy was any more perfect, her heart would explode in her chest. She wanted to jump into his arms, run her fingers through his hair, kiss him, hold him ... *Whoa!*

She handed the vase to Elizabeth. "Would you mind putting these beauties on my kitchen table so I can enjoy them every day?"

"Yes, ma'am." Walking to the breakfast table, Elizabeth carried the flowers as if they were a fine treasure. Her sneakers squeaked when she stumbled, but she quickly caught herself.

Bethany sidled next to Jason and whispered, "Thank you."

He took his hands in hers. "You really don't mind?"

"No, it's a *perfect* way to spend an evening." They'd still have time together without any worries of their burgeoning passion getting out of hand. However, she'd pay big bucks if Valerie was here to distract the kids. Jason's incredible lips just begged for a good solid kiss.

"Miss Bethany?"

Daniel's voice moved Bethany back a step. "Yes?"

"We helped Uncle Jason make cookies." Daniel sat on the floor, playing with a blissfully happy Jedi, based on the speed of his wagging tail.

Jason grinned. "They were great helpers, even if it did take a while to get the kitchen clean." He wrinkled his nose and leaned close to Bethany. "I'll tell you which cookies to avoid."

Jedi whimpered in delight and flopped on his back, belly up for a good tummy rub.

Daniel obliged with abandon. "What kind of dog is this?"

Elizabeth daintily stood next to him. "It's a Shih-Tzu."

Daniel's face screwed into a look of utter horror. "I'm telling mommy you said a bad word!"

Jason turned his attention to his nephew. "No, it's okay. That's really what he's called. Like a poodle or a German shepherd."

Daniel giggled and muttered *Shih-Tzu* under his breath.

"Okay, kids. Time to go." Jason picked up both kids and carried them out the door like sacks of potatoes. Their laughter echoed down the sidewalk.

Bethany locked her door, glanced heavenward, and smiled. Her prayers had been answered in ways she never would have imagined.

The fifteen-minute drive passed in a blur as she talked with the kids. She couldn't help wondering about Jason's apartment. What would it look like—modern, rustic, bachelor messy, or something surprising?

Jason turned his car into the downtown district and followed the river until he came to an old building now restored as loft apartments. He parked in underground parking and turned toward her. "Home, sweet home."

The kids scrambled out of the car and ran to the elevators, each pushing the button.

Jason hurried around the car and opened Bethany's door. "Welcome to Rossville Manor."

"Ah, kind sir, I'm impressed already." She looped her arm in his as they walked toward the children. "How long have you lived here?"

"Moved in two years ago." He stepped aside to let her enter the elevator.

Daniel, eyes wide, stood at the back, both hands braced against the wall. "I'm ready."

Elizabeth humphed and punched the button. "It's only an elevator."

Daniel grimaced as the doors closed. "But that's what they thought at Willy Wonka's place."

Jason squatted and put his arm around his nephew. "It'll be okay, buddy."

Daniel leaned against Jason and responded with a stoic nod.

A lump the size of Texas formed in Bethany's throat. How could one man be so sweet? She loved Jason, and better yet, he loved her. She'd do a happy dance if Nancy was here.

They arrived safely on Jason's floor without flying through the roof like in the Willy Wonka movie.

Daniel wore a big smile as he trotted off the elevator. "I knew we'd be okay."

Elizabeth caught up to him. "We've been here a billion times, and nothing ever happened."

"Yeah, but you *never* know."

She shook her head and heaved a dramatic sigh.

Jason unlocked the big oak door and waved his hand in a flourish. "Bethany Davis, welcome to my home."

Bethany held her breath as she gazed around his fourth floor apartment overlooking the river. Hardwood floors, a wall of windows, brick walls, exposed beamed ceilings, open kitchen, the fireplace separating the living area from dining/kitchen, and bedroom in the loft above. Did the guy have a decorator? The place was perfect, just like him, and she wouldn't change a thing. She reeled in her thoughts, they were still just dating. But, oh my, she did like his taste.

Jason grinned at her. "From your expression, I'd say you're pleased. Wish I could take credit, but my sister and one of her decorator friends helped me buy everything when I moved here."

"They're good. I love the place."

"I'm glad you do." Wearing a slight smile, he tilted his head as though deep in thought.

She returned his smile. Maybe he was thinking how much he'd like to have her join him at his home. She needed to get a grip. Five minutes inside his place and she'd already decided how well she'd fit in his life.

The kids giggled in the kitchen, and Jason excused himself to check.

Bethany perused the pictures on his fireplace mantel. Neatly arranged were pictures of Jason with the children, Kelly and her family, and two photos with what had to be his mother and father. Jason was the spitting image of his father, Kelly of his mom.

The thought of losing parents as a teenager, made Bethany's heart lurch. What would she have done? And how would she have turned out if she'd been left in the care of her older brothers? She shuddered to think.

"Hey." Jason came up from behind and put his arms around her, his breath against her ear. "What ya thinking?"

She turned and nestled into his embrace. His presence warm and comforting. "I'm sorry about your parents."

His body tensed, then relaxed. "I still miss them."

"They'd be proud of you." She reached up and traced his jawline with her fingertips.

His eyes misted. He blinked and cleared his throat. "I hope so."

"Hey!" Elizabeth, wearing a stern expression, pried them apart. "You're not supposed to get mushy."

Daniel rushed out of the kitchen, a trail of white powder flying behind him. "Are we gonna eat now? I put lots of the fluffy sugar on the cookies."

Jason smiled at Bethany before stepping away. "I think we better get dinner on the table."

While Elizabeth and Jason finished dinner and prepared the table, Bethany helped Daniel clean up his trail. She could only imagine the flourish of activity to cause this much destruction from one little boy.

"I didn't mean to make a mess." Tears lined his lashes as he scrubbed the floor with a paper towel.

The little guy was absolutely precious. She wanted to take him in her arms and give him a big hug. "Oh, sweetie, it's okay. We know you were only trying to help."

He sniffled, wiped his nose with his arm, and gave her his stoic nod.

She couldn't resist. Picking him up, she held him close. His body stiffened, and then eased against her. His hair smelled of kid shampoo with a touch of little boy. She could get used to this, but dare she let herself go there?

Daniel leaned his head back to look at her. "Are you a mommy?"

Bethany's heart went to mush as an intense longing overwhelmed her. "Not yet." Her voice came out a mere whisper.

"Can I play with your boy, when you have one?"

Her throat went raw at the sweet thought. "I would love that."

"Okay, you two." Jason grinned and took Daniel in his arms. "Are you trying to steal my girl?"

Daniel giggled. "Not me. I want her to be a mommy."

Elizabeth's sneakers squeaked as she halted in front of Bethany. "You're going to be a mommy?"

Heat roaring up her neck, Bethany held out her hands. "No, no, no. Not anytime soon. Maybe someday."

"She's going to let me play with her boy." Daniel tossed his head in triumph.

Elizabeth's eyes rounded. "But, I want to play with him too."

Jason knelt in front of them both. "Okay, Miss Bethany isn't going to have a baby. First, she'd need to have a husband, and then maybe she could have a baby."

"But, you can be her husband." Daniel piped up.

A smile crossed Jason's face, he then gulped, cleared his throat, and jumped to his feet. "Dinner is going to get really cold if we don't get moving." He guided the kids to the table.

With Jason's initial reaction, her heart felt as if it would soar out of her chest, but did she really deserve happiness? Especially with a sweet guy like Jason. *Oh, Lord I'm falling so hard for him. Please don't let my heart be broken again.*

Jason pulled out Bethany's chair for her as the kids settled in their seats.

Daniel held up his hand. "Can I say the prayer?"

Jason nodded. "That'd be great."

His nephew folded his hands in front of him and closed his eyes. "Dear God. Thank you for this food. Thank you for Mommy and Daddy. Thank you for Uncle Jason and for Miss Bethany. And thank you for the dog, and for Elizabeth, and for my room, and for my toys, and for cookies, and for not letting the elevator crash through the roof. In Jesus' name, Amen."

"Thank you for the sweet prayer." Bethany patted Daniel's arm and cleared her throat to keep the lump away. Man, she was getting mushy, but being with Jason and his family felt so right. She didn't realize how ready she was to settle down.

"I love bsgetti." Daniel shoveled a mound from the serving bowl to his plate.

"It's spaghetti." Elizabeth gently corrected.

"But that's what I said."

Jason helped Daniel before the rest of the noodles slithered onto the table.

Bethany looked away, fighting tears. Obviously Jason's nephew and niece adored him, and he them. The sweet family dynamics made her want to chunk all her fears, grab Jason's arm, and haul him off to a wedding chapel. Thank goodness they had their little chaperones tonight.

The rest of dinner passed without any major incidents, and she was even brave enough to try one of Daniel's cookies. The kids and adults made quick work of cleaning up the kitchen. When they finished, the kids ran to the entry closet and pulled out bean bag chairs—pink for Elizabeth and blue for Daniel—and moved them in front of the television.

Jason plugged in a DVD and settled next to Bethany on the couch. "I hope you like animated movies."

"Definitely. I haven't had a good excuse to watch them since my nephew and niece came to visit."

"Good." He put his arm around her and pulled her close. "I'm glad you're here."

Surely, life couldn't get any better. She had to swallow hard before she could answer. "Me, too."

He kissed her, and his smile made her heart do a happy dance. "I love you, Bethany Davis."

"I love you too, Jason Ross."

By the time the movie ended, Daniel slept in Bethany's lap, and Elizabeth was asleep nestled between them. The children's presence and Jason's love made for a perfect evening, and one she would love to replay. If fairy tales came true, someday, she'd be sitting on a couch with Jason and their children. She was sooooo in trouble.

Jason lifted Elizabeth in his arms. "I'll take her upstairs, and come back for Daniel." He winked at Bethany.

"I'll bring him." Curious to see the rest of Jason's place, she picked up the little boy and followed Jason to his loft bedroom.

They laid the kids on his bed, and while Jason covered them with a blanket, Bethany stole a quick look around the room. The furniture looked right out of a showroom, wooden, masculine, but not too masculine. On his nightstand sat a well-worn Bible and a picture of his parents, and on the back wall, over his headboard, a picture of mountains in fall.

Warm hands slid over her shoulders and pulled her close. "I love you." His breath tickled her ear and just about melted her on the spot.

Bethany turned into his embrace. "I love you, too." His gaze locked with hers, and the love and passion she saw made her want to do things she shouldn't.

As though reading her thoughts, he took a deep breath and let out a sigh. "We better go downstairs."

She could only nod, and on wobbly legs follow him down the stairs.

Jason prayed with each step he took. Bethany ignited emotions that could turn into a forest fire of regret. Whatever happened with their relationship, he wanted to live right this time, be a man of honor. Bethany's gentle, loving touch with the children, made him love her all the more.

He sat on the couch, and she curled against him, fitting perfectly into his arms. Having her near, everything in his world seemed to fall in place.

Bethany snuggled closer, the faint scent of her perfume made him smile. "What are you thinking?"

"About you. How nice it is to have you here."

His heart stuttered with worry when she didn't immediately comment.

Finally, she adjusted to face him, her gaze searching his. "I love you, Jason." She kissed him, her lips tender, warm, and inviting. She pulled away, her turquoise eyes glinting with moisture. "And, I love watching you with your niece and nephew."

He moved his hand up her neck, his fingers touching her soft hair. "You're great with them too."

"In case you're wondering, I love kids."

He didn't hide his smile. Without a doubt, Bethany Davis was the perfect woman. He hoped his next kiss would keep her around forever and not throw too much gasoline on an already smoldering fire.

Chapter 35

The next evening, Bethany propped her feet on her couch. Did her feet even touch the floor while she was at the office? Every time she thought about Jason and last night, she probably levitated another foot or two. *Whew, can he kiss!* She fanned her face.

They were going out again—this time to dinner and a movie. Instead of wearing jeans and a top, she should be wearing a weighted suit to keep her grounded. God healed her broken places, but no man had ever touched her heart like Jason.

Jedi perched at the front window, keeping watch. His tail wagged with gusto. Jason must be on his way. She grabbed her purse and checked through the peep-hole. Sure enough, he stood out front. His muscular, manly, perfect chest silhouetted against his polo shirt—an ideal compliment to his jeans.

She opened the door before he could knock.

He smiled and held out a bouquet of peach roses. "Hi, beautiful."

Why waste time talking? She pulled him inside, and thanked him with a kiss she hoped would rival his from the night before.

When they finally parted, she could barely stand.

"Wow." Jason's glassy eyes held a look of admiration. "What did I do to deserve that?" He wobbled and studied the flowers. "Note to self, always bring peach roses."

"Those weren't for the roses. That was just for you being you, and baby you ain't seen nothing yet."

He whimpered.

She giggled.

He held out the flowers again, his expression hopeful.

Bethany burst out in laughter. "We better get out of here before we get in trouble."

"Can't fault a guy for trying." He sniffed the roses. "But, don't you need to put these in water?"

"Oh, and thank you for the flowers. They're beautiful. Give me a minute." She bolted to the kitchen to get a vase.

If they spent more alone time, she might regret her next actions. Or maybe she wouldn't regret her actions, which would be an even bigger problem. How was she supposed to handle this situation? Nothing worked before. Gavin had taken her virginity, used and thrown her away. Then, in college, she allowed herself to be used by men to salve her wounds. Both had only left her soul tattered and worn.

She shot a prayer heavenward for help. Falling in love with Jason would definitely be the ultimate challenge. She knew what she was missing, and she missed being in someone's arms. Especially someone she knew actually, *really*, loved her.

Since Daniel and Elizabeth's wildflowers were still on the table, Bethany took a tall glass from her cabinet and filled it with water. Shoot, she ought to splash herself while she was standing there or dive into the freezer for an hour or two to cool off.

Jason's arms slid around her and pulled her close against his chest. His strong, muscular chest. "You smell wonderful." He nuzzled her neck, his lips sending tingles of delight down her spine.

Danger, danger, danger. She grabbed the edge of the sink to avoid losing her balance. She was swooning. *Swooning!*

"I love you, Bethany Davis."

His whispered voice liquidized her hopes to keep out of trouble. She loved him and wanted to show him that love. Surely, she could stop herself before things got too far out of hand.

After placing the flowers on the counter, she turned into his embrace. "I love you, too." She wove her fingers into his hair, and kissed him, slow, gently, easily, then with passion. Part of her wanted to stop. The other part didn't.

Their moans intermingled. Still kissing, he swooped her into his strong arms and carried her down the hall.

Oh, God, I'm so sorry.

Even in the heat of passion, a terrible sinking feeling overcame her.

Really overcame her.

They were falling!

Her arms flailed. They bumped into and careened off the wall and landed on the floor with a crash.

Bethany blinked and stared at the ceiling. *Talk about divine intervention.*

Jason still cradled her. His poor arms must have taken the brunt of the fall.

He groaned, his eyes moist. "Baby, I'm sorry. Are you okay?"

Not knowing whether to laugh or cry, she rubbed her sore bottom. "I'm fine. Are you?"

"Besides being soundly chastised by the heavens, having my pride entirely decimated, and breaking both arms, I should be fine." He glanced over at a wagging Jedi. "Your furry chaperone darted in front of me."

She got on her knees. "You're hurt?"

He grimaced as he moved to sit up, then checked himself. "I don't think they're broken, but I'll have some interesting bruises for a few weeks." His sad gaze locked with hers. "Please forgive me."

"It's not your fault." She shot a glare at Jedi. He responded with a double-time wag.

Jason lifted her chin to look his way. "No, I mean, please forgive me for almost taking advantage of you."

"Taking advantage of *me*?" She scooted to the wall and leaned back. "If you hadn't picked me up, I probably would have attacked you on the kitchen floor and traumatized Jedi for life."

He ran a hand through his hair. "I want to be a better man than this."

"Jason, you *are* a good man. I'm as much to blame as you. Probably more so."

"I don't want you to think I'm just dating you to get you in bed."

"Bummer." She elbowed him until he smiled. "Just kidding, kinda, sorta. Jason, it's hard to be good. Neither of us are naïve. We know what we're missing. You've always been a gentleman. And you still are. Nothing happened."

"Only because your dog tripped me ... or God pushed him under my feet.

He chuckled, cupped her face in his hands, leaned forward and kissed her. "You *are* wonderful."

Jason pulled away before things got out of control again. "We better get in public before we get hit with an earthquake or plague." He helped her to her feet, wrapping her in his arms. She fit against him so perfectly. He let out a groan, hating how he longed for her.

"Are you hurting?" Bethany squirmed to get free. "Do you need anything?"

He wouldn't touch that question. "I'll be okay. But, if I stay with you much longer, I'll run over Jedi and anything else that gets in my way."

Her beautiful eyes sparked with mischief. "Is that a promise or a threat?"

"Both."

She squealed and sprinted toward the front door. "Catch me if you can."

Jason sent up his gazillionth prayer for help. He'd love to chase her and carry her off into the sunset or the next room. He cringed and sent up a silent prayer for forgiveness.

His cell phone vibrated in his pocket. *Odd.* He normally turned it off. The caller-ID showed Warren's number. Figuring this had to be another divine interruption; he flipped open and answered the call. Warren was hurt again, but didn't want to call the ambulance. Jason told him to sit tight, and they'd be there as soon as possible.

"What's wrong?" Bethany stood in front of him, her hand resting on his chest, making his heart beat faster. "Is everything okay?"

"Warren needs help. He may have broken his leg."

"I'll go with you."

"Are you sure? This isn't the evening I had planned."

279

She smiled, her fingers playing with his shirt button. "Me neither, but I'm thinking it's probably *much* safer."

He grabbed for his keys. If he didn't move fast, he'd be in danger and his friend would be on his own.

They were both quiet on the drive to Warren's small brick, fixer-upper near downtown. Jason could kick himself. The last thing he wanted to do was ruin the relationship, or start something they wouldn't stop and then regret later. Why was the attraction between them so strong? Couldn't they just have a nice attraction, and then when they got married, they could have incredible, guilt-free fun?

Married? What was he thinking? They hadn't known each other that long. Then again, how long did you have to know someone?

He parked in front and hurried to the door with Bethany following. Warren's yard looked the same—the hedges still half-mutilated, and grass growing in sporadic patches. The large sweet gum tree in front still needed a dead limb removed. Hopefully, Warren wouldn't try to fix that problem on his own.

Jason stepped behind the hedges. "He told me he has a spare key somewhere back here. Look for an Orange Crush can."

Bethany rummaged next to Jason. She giggled as she held up the key. "Found it. The container was appropriately crushed. The key stuck to the bottom."

He shook his head, blew off the dust, and unlocked the door.

Warren lay sprawled on the family room floor at the bottom of a ladder, a half-hung ceiling fan precariously perched on the top. The box for the fan sat upside down on the couch and parts scattered throughout the room.

Jason knelt next to his friend. "What happened this time?"

"I wouldn't have called you, if I knew you had company. Hey, Bethany."

"Hi, Warren." She stood next to him, worry creasing her forehead. "Are you okay?"

"I don't know. My right ankle's swelling. I tried to stand on it a couple of times but couldn't."

Bethany leaned down to check. Warren's ankle was already puffed up and turning some interesting shades of purple and blue. "I think we need to get you to the doctor."

"I don't want to impose. I can always call someone else to take me. Val doesn't live too far from here."

Jason helped Warren to stand. "You do know with your ceiling height, even with a low profile fan, if you raised your hands, you'd have problems."

"But I wasn't planning on raising my hands."

Amusement played in Jason's eyes as he shook his head. "I think maybe you should get a floor fan instead. Much safer. And don't you have some crutches from a few months back?"

"Oh yeah, they're in the hall closet."

Bethany followed where Warren pointed. The closet door stood half open and filled to the brim with sports equipment interspersed with two sets of crutches, back braces, knee braces, various pads for hockey, soccer, and football. She shuddered at the thought of Warren actually playing a team sport. The poor guy probably kept the orthopedic surgeons in the area living the high life.

Looking at the pile of stuff, she wanted to cry. Did she just mess up a good thing with Jason by coming on so strong? Now he probably believed all the junk about her past. Unfortunately, she couldn't deny it. She'd been a tramp in college as she looked for ways to drown out the sorrow left by Gavin. Why didn't she just turn to God? Nooooo, she had to make an absolute mess of everything.

Hopefully, she'd been given a second chance. She wrestled out a set of crutches and took them to the guys. "Are there any doctors open this late?"

Warren shrugged. "I always just go to Plaza Hospital."

Jason held open the door for Warren and her. "Warren pretty much has a revolving account at the ER."

On the ride to the hospital, Bethany sat in back watching the two men interact. Warren didn't say much at work, but in Jason's company he was actually talkative. Warren reminded her of the loveable tool guy from a television show she used to watch. Sweet, but always getting into trouble trying new things.

Her curiosity finally got the best of her. "How and where did you guys meet?"

Jason glanced over his shoulder, then back to the road. "We met at work. Started on the same day."

Warren chuckled. "I still don't think Alex likes me."

"You did ruin his favorite pair of pants."

"How was I supposed to know he'd walk by when I was changing the ink in the printer?"

"That's why you've been banned from working on *any* equipment in the company."

Jason stopped at the drop-off zone for the ER, then came around and helped Warren.

Bethany hopped out. "I'll take him in while you park."

Warren hobbled next to her. "I'm sorry about ruining your evening."

"No, really it's okay. We weren't doing much of anything." *Except getting into major trouble.*

The electric doors slid open, and they landed in front of the admittance desk. The nurse looked up. "Hi Warren, what do you need today?"

"Hi, Nancy. It's my right ankle this time."

"I'll pull your records and let them know you're here. Have a seat. We'll call you in a few."

Another nurse walked by. "Hi, Warren."

"Hi, Louise."

The waiting room was crowded with families, one rambunctious toddler, a lady with a blanket over her head, and one guy sneezing every few seconds. Bethany cringed and helped Warren into a chair, away from the sickest-looking patients. "Do you know everyone who works here?"

His eyebrows furrowed, and he hesitated for a moment before he answered. "No. Not all of them."

A security guard waved from across the room. "Hey, Warren. Good to see you."

"Hey, John. How's the family?"

"They're great. My wife asked about you last week. She'll be glad to know you stopped by."

Jason plopped in the chair next to Bethany. "Miss me?"

"Always. I was just learning the names of the hospital staff." She leaned closer, but not too close. She couldn't take any more chances. "Just how many times *has* Warren been here?"

"Not sure. But he's probably got the record. One nurse said when he was a kid they had a betting pool to see how many times a month he'd come in."

Her stomach sank at the thought. "His poor parents."

"Yeah, I can't imagine. But the good news is, Warren's mom learned so much, she wound up graduating from nursing school. I think she works for an orthopedic surgeon."

A perky teenage volunteer with auburn hair stopped in front of them with a wheelchair. "Ready to go, Warren?"

"Thanks, Rachel." He maneuvered to the waiting chair and nodded toward Jason and Bethany. "Thanks again. One of the nurses can run me home when we finish."

Jason placed a hand on his friend's shoulder. "We'll see you whenever you get back to work. Call me if you need anything." He put his arm around Bethany's waist and guided her to the door. "I vote we get some dinner, somewhere nice and *very* crowded."

Fifteen minutes later, Bethany sat in the booth across from Jason at the pizza place they had taken Kelly and the kids the night Matt came home. The place was crowded and a touch noisy, with a large group in the corner celebrating someone's birthday. At least here, they'd be safe.

How on earth could she keep herself from acting on the desires that kept her awake at night? The Bible talked about temptation, and that there's always a way of escape. Problem was, could she trust herself enough to want to escape?

He took her hand in his, his thumb rubbing lightly against her skin. "Bethany, about earlier, I'm really sorry. I want to treat you right. I don't want to get us both in trouble." His eyes glistened, his voice thick. "I don't want to lose you."

"No, I'm the one who needs to apologize." Bethany laced her fingers with his. "I should have stopped before things got out of hand."

Regardless of her tainted past, she'd been given a clean start, and looking into Jason's gorgeous green eyes, she knew she had to fight for this man. Fight with herself and her emotions to make the right choices. She need to take action. Tonight she'd search the Internet for a full body chastity suit.

Chapter 36

The next evening, after work, Jason sat in his car outside Bethany's apartment and dialed her number. She picked up on the first ring and said she'd be right out. He felt like a jerk waiting in the car for her, but she'd insisted.

They'd decided the safest thing for them was never to be too alone, and after last night they couldn't take any chances. Even saying goodbye after dinner had led to another fiasco. The attraction between them didn't just cause sparks, they were full-fledged lightning bolts.

He jumped out of the car when he saw her coming. "Hi, you look great." And, boy did she. Her cute top matched her eye-color and her shorts that showed off her incredible legs. He had to concentrate not to drool. Good thing he didn't meet her at the door. They wouldn't have made it two feet.

"You look mighty fine yourself, Mr. Ross." She gave him a kiss that curled his chest hair.

Jason steadied himself, held the car door open and admired her legs as she got inside.

She cleared her throat. "You can close it now."

How long had he stood there? Heat roasted his neck. "Right." Praying for help, he jogged to his side.

Her eyes sparking with mischief, she waited quietly while he buckled in.

He pulled into traffic and glanced her way. "You're killing me. What are you thinking?"

Bethany grinned. "I like your legs too."

"You've seen me in shorts before."

"Yes, sir. Why do you think I suggested a casual evening out?"

He feigned outrage. "I can't believe this. You only see me as an object? I have feelings too, you know." He threw in a sniffle to make it good.

Bethany laid her hand on his arm, her fingers warming his skin. "You poor baby."

"I'll let it go this time." He loved her spunky sense of humor. "But you do know, inside this manly body beats the heart of a human being."

She got quiet, studied him for a moment. "Jason, I *love* your heart. That's what makes you so attractive."

He gripped the wheel, her sweet, soft voice making everything inside him yearn not only for her, but her friendship—a true, deep relationship, beyond the physical attraction. The thought made him sit straighter. He could do this. They could date, have fun, and stay out of trouble. The next intersection, he pulled into a grocery store lot, parked, and turned toward her.

"Bethany, you are wonderful." He hooked his hand around her neck and drew her toward him. Her lips soft, moist and inviting. A small moan escaped her. Lost in the kiss, he cemented his resolve to pray that he would be the man who would always treat her with the love and respect she deserved.

###

Bethany chose the putter with the pink handle and waited as Jason paid for their game. Something had happened to both of them in the car. The attraction was still there, but it was as though they'd taken a deeper move beyond just the physical. The flames still sizzled, but now burned at a more intense and pure level. For the first time, she felt they could truly date and not break any of the Ten Commandments, or Command No's as Valerie called them.

Jason handed her a score card and pencil and puffed his chest. "Ready to be trounced by the master of miniature golf?"

"You wish." Bethany nudged his sneaker with her putter. "I'll have you crying like a baby by the fourth hole."

He smiled and signaled for her to go first.

She lined up her shot, swiveled her hips for effect, took several practice swings, and putted with perfection. The ball banked off the right rail and rolled two inches from the cup. Her second hit knocked it in. "Ha. Beat that. I'm one under par."

Jason surveyed the course, stood with perfect form, and knocked the ball straight into the cup. "I would gloat. But I believe that's called a hole-in-one."

She elbowed him as she walked past. "Show off."

"You're not going to be a sore loser are you?" His voice said he enjoyed the game far too much.

By the sixth hole, Bethany wanted to scream. How did anyone make three hole-in-one shots and consistently come under par in the others?

She stepped aside. "Maybe you should go first and give me a little more time to study the course."

Jason grinned like only guys can grin who are overly proud of their abilities. Obviously, he forgot she had the upper hand. She stood as close as she could get to him without touching. "Good luck, baby," she whispered seductively.

He shuddered and swallowed hard. His next shot missed by a putter's mile. "That was *not* fair."

She almost felt sorry for him when he had to chase the ball into the other section past a group of teenagers. His face turned a lovely shade of chartreuse after it took him an additional four hits to get the ball into the hole.

"Two can play that game you know." Jason's fingers feathered down her arm, popping out goose bumps the size of California.

Bethany gripped her putter and tried to concentrate on her shot. No way she was going to let him win. He nuzzled her neck. *Argh!* She disintegrated on the spot. Not caring who was watching, she wheeled around and planted a kiss on his incredible lips. If she couldn't concentrate on her game, then by George, neither could he!

The sound of applause and hooting from the teenagers broke them apart.

On quivering legs she steadied herself by holding on to Jason's arm. "Sorry about that." His loopy grin made her smile.

He took away her putter. "Maybe we should try something safer. Like the race cars and bumper boats."

Jason sloshed out of the boat and wrung out his t-shirt. Bethany had plowed through the water at breakneck speed, stirring up a wave of epic proportions worthy of a movie screen. Doubled over in laughter, she stood next to him completely dry. First, she ruined his golf score, then she trounced him on the race course, and now she practically drowned him.

Man, he loved this woman. The perfect female—beautiful, sexy, gentle, tough, and kept him on his toes and on his knees.

Drenched, he worked up a glare, but for some reason couldn't get rid of his smile. "Just wait until next time. I won't go easy on you."

"Easy on me? Right. I'm really worried."

"You should be." He stepped closer and held out his sopping arms. "Come on, baby, give me a kiss."

She backed away, her hands out protectively in front of her. "No, thanks. I think I'll wait."

"Not so tough now, are you?"

"I'm not afraid of you."

He lowered his voice. "Maybe you should be."

Her eyebrows rose and for a quick moment fear flickered in her eyes. She almost shrunk as though she had transported to another place and time.

Jason's heart sank. He cupped her face in his hands. "You don't ever have to be afraid of me."

She didn't speak for a moment. "I know." She barely whispered.

"Bethany, I will *never* hurt you." He took her hand, led her to a bench in a quiet place.

Sitting, she swallowed hard, and her shoulders slumped as her gaze stared into the distance.

Even with all she'd been through the past months, something in her past caused this reaction. "Please, tell me what happened."

For a long time she didn't say anything, but her constant shifting and readjusting told of an internal struggle.

"You can trust me."

She turned toward him, her eyes moist. "Gavin...," she swallowed "hit me a few times."

"What?" Jason nearly flew out of his seat. "He *beat* you?" At her cringe, he forced his voice to level. He took her hand in his. "Why didn't you tell me?"

"I never told anyone."

"Oh baby." He pulled her against his chest before he did something stupid like finding the jerk and beating him into a bloody mess. How could anyone hit a woman? Especially Bethany. *His* woman. He had to calm down. She needed him to be strong, not vindictive. "I'm sorry. What can I do?"

"Just hold me."

Not caring who walked by or what was going on around them, he held her close, tight but tender. Wishing he could take away her pain and fears. Praying he could be the man who would be the one to love away her past.

###

Bethany nestled against Jason. She had never wanted anyone to know what happened with Gavin. Hadn't it been her fault anyway? If she had been more loving, or appreciative of all his hard work, he wouldn't have hit her. Deep down she knew that was a lie, and yet tonight the old fear resurfaced. Why now?

Telling Jason had been easier than she ever thought possible. He made her feel safe, loved, and protected. Is that why the memory returned? Now that she was safe?

Tears pooled, then streamed down her cheeks. She didn't stop them, just let them flow. Jason held her close and whispered his love. And in that moment she knew there was no turning back. She wanted to be with Jason Ross forever.

Chapter 37

Bethany zigged and zagged through the busy airport as she hurried to keep up with Jason. Finding safe things to keep them out of trouble had produced some interesting and fun times, along with healing for her past. She looked heavenward and said a prayer of thanks.

The team would leave for Chicago in two hours, and Jason insisted on picking her up early. Not that she minded, but having a conversation would have been nice. Even though they'd spent most of their waking hours together the last week, he now seemed lost in outer orbit, barely saying more than a few sentences on the ride over. Maybe all their discussions and laughter had used up his male word count for the month.

Jason stopped at the self-check kiosk and entered their information.

Knowing what went on his head would be nice. For the last week he'd doted over her, telling her how wonderful she was and how much he loved her. Did this company trip cause him to revert back to his earlier days of not even knowing she existed?

Fine. Two can play this game. She turned her attention to check her surroundings.

Valerie, wearing a purple skirt, gray knee socks, and a black off-the-shoulder shirt, waited behind a more conservatively suit-clad Rhonda. The others in the group were

293

nowhere in sight.

Jason smiled as he handed Bethany her boarding pass. "We're together on row fourteen." His fingers touched hers and lingered during the hand-off. Finally, he seemed aware of her presence.

Valerie nudged her and nodded toward Alex and Nicole who were walking toward them. "Do I still get the same fee in Chicago to keep away prying eyes?"

Jason gave Bethany a curious glance. "What's going on?"

She smiled. "Nothing you need to worry about." She didn't plan to share about the arrangement with Valerie, but at the rate they were going, Bethany might need a small loan. Just last week she'd paid Valerie twenty bucks for stolen office kisses with Jason.

Rhonda addressed Bethany. "I'll take care of this." Rhonda grabbed Valerie by the arm and steered her toward security. "Leave those two alone."

Bethany exchanged glances with Jason as they followed behind.

Valerie playfully smacked at Rhonda's hand. "I'm only trying to be helpful."

"You're extorting money from good people."

"It's not extortion. It's protection." Valerie lifted her chin and smiled. "I'm serving the people."

"Girl, what am I going to do with you?"

"Be amazed, totally amazed, at my fascinating personality." Valerie elbowed Rhonda and nodded toward the TSA agent. "Oh, momma, check out the cute airport security guy."

Valerie took off her shoes and placed them along with her canvas bag in the bin for the x-ray machine, then walked through the metal detector. The alarm beeped.

The agent had her step back through.

Again, the alarm sounded. He motioned for her to step to the side.

Bethany, Jason, and Rhonda made it through without incident.

Valerie signaled to the agent and held up her hands. "You might need to pat me down since I keep setting off the alarm."

He didn't seem amused. "We'll have a female agent check you."

"Oh. Then I guess I don't need this." She reached in her pocket and removed a key ring with a metallic peace symbol.

The agent stared at her stone-faced, handed her a small bucket, and pointed for her to go back through the metal detector.

She batted her eyelashes and tossed her key ring and business card in the bucket. "If you wanted my number, all you had to do was ask."

Without changing his expression, he pocketed her card and waved her through.

At the gate, Bethany flipped a chewable tablet in her mouth to prevent air sickness. Flying wasn't the problem, just the air pocket bumps that could send her stomach into a revolt.

Warren, wearing a walking boot for his sprained ankle, stood by the window sipping a cup of coffee. Next to him, a teenage girl wearing headphones bounced to an unknown tune. Warren's finger tapped along with her movements.

Nicole and Alex sat on the other side of the waiting area immersed in conversation. Knowing those two, they probably plotted something evil.

Alex, wearing a slimy smirk, nodded at Bethany.

She responded with a smile she hoped to be syrupy,

sickeningly sweet.

Jason stared blankly at a magazine, obviously totally unaware of life around him.

Bethany tapped his arm. "You okay?"

"Just thinking."

"You haven't turned a page in ten minutes. What's going on?"

His expression serious, he studied her for a moment. "I talked to George before we left. I'm stepping down as team leader when we get back from Chicago."

Her stomach nose-dived to the floor. He was leaving? "But ... why?"

"I don't want to hide our relationship. There's an opening in another department. We can still see each other, and you won't have to keep paying Valerie." He smiled one of those smiles that brought out his dimples and made her heart moan.

"You knew about Val?"

"I was paying her too."

She shot a glare at their industrious workmate. "That little sneak."

"Yeah, she told me she'd have the Zucchini brothers visit me if I hurt you."

"She said that?"

"Not sure what that means, but I can't look at the vegetable without wondering."

Bethany nudged him. "Yeah, you *better* watch your step."

He pointed to a restaurant advertisement in his magazine that took the full page with mouth-watering steaks and lavish desserts. "I'll take you there someday."

"You don't have to spend money to impress me. I'm already impressed."

"The feeling is mutual."

The world faded as he gazed into her eyes. *Whimper.* Maybe she could just lean forward like she was going to reach for something and they could accidently brush against one another, and accidently kiss.

Valerie snatched the magazine and waved it in front of them. "They're calling for boarding."

Bethany's face heated. Half the waiting area was empty, the rest of the team already in line.

Jason stood and offered his hand. "I guess we better get going."

She ignored the glances from Valerie as they boarded the plane. That girl enjoyed their dilemma far too much. Poor Val would be in for a surprise when she got back and couldn't make any more extortion money.

Bethany buckled into the window seat next to Jason. Rhonda and Valerie sat across the aisle. Since Alex and Nicole were seated four rows in front of them, Bethany and Jason actually had some semblance of privacy.

She shoved Jason's arm off the arm rest, daring him with a look to take it back.

He smiled and lightly ran his finger along her open palm sending chills galloping through every nerve.

She jerked away and rubbed her hands together. "You do *not* play fair."

He leaned toward her, melting her with his look. "Baby, the games have just begun."

Only complete concentration kept her from becoming a blubbering idiot. She gulped hard. "Is that a promise or a threat?" Her words barely squeaked out.

"Both." He propped his elbow on the armrest and laced his fingers with hers. "Whatcha gonna do about it?"

As the plane taxied onto the runway, she leaned against him, her lips against his ear. "If I were you, I'd say your prayers."

###

Jason didn't have the heart to tell Bethany he'd done nothing but pray since the day they'd met. The more time he spent with her, the more he liked who she was on the outside and inside. Being around her would either make him a better man or cause a nervous breakdown. He could write a book on the one thousand ways to be good when you really don't want to be good. How did others date without getting into trouble? No wonder guys in medieval times started wars or became monks. Then again, if he lived back then, he could have ridden on his mighty steed, rescued her from all the pain of her past, and taken her captive forever.

"What are you thinking?" Bethany's smile notched up the temperature.

He cranked up the air control making sure it blew full force on his face. "War and monks."

"Interesting."

"You don't want to know." Jason grabbed a magazine from the seat pocket and pretended to read.

"Ignoring me only ramps up my curiosity."

The plane took off, pressing his body against the seat back. He stared into Bethany's mischievous turquoise eyes. "Prayer is the only thing that keeps our relationship honorable and me from going stark raving mad."

Bethany's chin quivered. "I've never had this much fun being good before."

That made him grin. "Me neither, and I don't ever want

it to end."

She studied him for a moment. A smile played on her incredible, luscious lips. "Really? The fun or being good?"

If he didn't kiss her, he'd ask her to marry him. Not caring who was watching, he planted a kiss on her lips he hoped would pull her into his arms forever.

###

Bethany woke with a jolt. Did that snort come from her? *Argh!* How could she have fallen asleep on Jason's shoulder? Following his dizzying, dazzling, display of lip prowess, she could have flown without an airplane. What happened after?

She searched her foggy brain. After Jason's super-kiss, they'd talked for a few minutes, and then her eyelids had folded down like a shade as she succumbed to a medicated sleep, full of some rather interesting and risqué dreams.

Stupid air-sick medicine knocked her out cold. Humiliation burning from every pore, she wiped off the drool pooling in the corner of her mouth. Drool? *Just shoot me.*

From Jason's expression, he enjoyed her embarrassment far too much.

She straightened and shot him a glare. "You tell anyone, and I'll personally hurt you."

"You're charming when you drool and snore."

Her skin ignited. She fumbled to turn up her air control. "I do *not* snore."

"They're very cute, very sweet snores. And … you talk in your sleep."

"I do not." At least, she hoped she didn't.

He nodded, his green eyes dancing with pleasure. "You promised to marry me, along with a few other unmentionable

299

things." His face reddening, he cleared his throat.

Whew! Sweat trickled down her back. If she *did* mention anything about her dreams, she was in big trouble. Surely, he was just teasing. She smacked his arm. "You are full of bull, Mr. Ross."

"I'm shocked." His eyes widened in mock exasperation. "You didn't mean all you said?"

She lasered him with a glare, then turned to check across the aisle on Rhonda and Valerie. Both ladies smiled in ways that made Bethany panic. *Did* she say something?

His gaze softened, and he squeezed her hand. "Don't worry, you spoke softly. Your secrets are safe with me."

Secrets? Every synapse in her brain fired at once, searching for what she could've said and how to fix the situation. She definitely needed to pray for a dream chaperone.

The address system crackled, and the captain announced the plane would soon be landing.

Bethany picked up her purse and rummaged through, anything to keep her focus off of Jason and her vivid, drool-producing dream.

He laid his hand on hers. "Are you looking for something?"

"Yes. My sanity."

"Based on our therapy sessions, I'd say you're completely sane."

"That just proves we're both stark-raving mad." One thing she knew for sure—she was madly in love with Jason Ross.

Chapter 38

"Wow, I knew the company was doing well. But this is really nice." Bethany stood next to Jason in the corporate conference room on the thirtieth floor. A buffet of Chicago style pizza, hot dogs, and Italian beef, spread across the table in front of the wall of windows with a view of Lake Michigan. To her right, the room overlooked the Chicago River.

He nodded. "The global operation took full advantage of the opportunities with oil-rich nations overseas."

"Jason." A man with salt and pepper hair trimmed military style enthusiastically shook his hand. "Good to see you."

"Thank you, Mr. Smith. Great to be back."

"Just because you've been in the South, you don't have to get formal. Call me by my first name." He put his hand on Jason's shoulder. "I talked to George this morning. After lunch, I'd like to discuss something in private."

"Yes, sir."

Mr. Smith extended his hand to Bethany. "I don't believe we've been formally introduced. I'm Neil Smith." He reminded her of a young Ralph Lauren.

"Nice to meet you. I'm Bethany Davis."

"I've heard good things about you." He studied her for a moment, then turned back to Jason. "Looking forward to visiting." Neil excused himself to talk with the rest of the team.

"So Mr. Big Guy himself wants to talk to you." She nudged Jason. "I knew you were special."

He shrugged, his gaze following Neil as he greeted other team members.

She watched him, trying to read his expression. "Do you regret leaving Chicago?"

"No." Jason leaned toward her and smiled. "I found God, and I found you."

If they weren't surrounded by office mates, she'd kiss him.

Valerie stepped between them. "Instead of standing there looking googly eyed, aren't you going to get something to eat?"

Bethany surveyed Valerie's plate full of food. "Did you leave us anything?"

"Flying always makes me hungry. I think the altitude expands my stomach."

"Good thing you didn't become a pilot."

Jason handed Bethany a plate and directed her toward the buffet. "We better get our share before Valerie goes for seconds."

Bethany took her position in line behind Alex.

Alex put a slice of pizza on his plate and turned his gaze toward Bethany. "You and Jason are rather chummy these days."

She leaned close to whisper. "Are you talking about Jason Ross? Actually we're married and have twin boys, Hoss and Boss, and a little girl named Floss."

Alex's glare could have frozen the Chicago River in summer. "Management would *not* be amused."

Bethany considered shoving a hot dog in his face, but thought better of it. Even a hot dog deserved a better demise.

###

After lunch, Jason sat in the leather wingback chair facing Neil's wood and glass desk. In many ways it only seemed like yesterday that Jason had left Chicago. He still couldn't believe all that transpired in the last two years.

Neil slid a piece of paper face-down across the desk. "Before I turn this over, I want to talk to you about your career plans."

"I feel I've worked hard for the company, and I hope you've been pleased with my progress."

"You've consistently received high marks on your reviews." Neil leaned back in his chair, his dark eyes studying Jason. "You were on your way. Why are you stepping down as team leader?"

Jason shifted in his seat. How could he explain? Neil had been his mentor during his time in Chicago. Moving to another department didn't make sense for a rising career path. "My decision is complex and based on work and my private life."

"Fair enough. Care to clarify?"

"I fell in love with a member of the team. I want to pursue the relationship, and I believe that in the best interest of the company I should remove myself from the situation."

Neil leaned back in his chair. "The woman in question is Bethany?"

"Yes, sir."

"You have good taste. I have something in mind that could alleviate the problem and still move you forward." He flipped over the paper. "This is an offer for you to come back and work directly for me."

Jason's stomach pitched. The job opportunity and salary

were bigger and better than he could imagine. His sister didn't need him anymore, and the only thing holding him back was Bethany. He wanted the job, but he didn't want to lose her. He needed to pray. "I can't thank you enough. But if possible, I'd like some time to think this through."

"Not a problem. I'll give you a week." Neil stood and came toward Jason.

Jason shook his hand and followed him to the door. "I appreciate this more than you'll know."

Bethany trekked down the hallway after a bathroom visit. The fact that Jason stepped down as team leader warmed her heart yet troubled her. As much as she wanted their relationship to continue, she wouldn't cause him problems at work. She could always find another job.

Falling in love with Jason was the best thing that ever happened to her, but still a worry nibbled at her brain. What if she was wrong again?

She checked the hall to make sure no one was nearby, then lifted her head. "Please don't let me make another mistake." She whispered. "If Jason isn't Your choice for me. You'll have to remove him. I can't do it on my own."

Neil Smith's office door was closed. She hesitated, wishing she were a fly on the wall.

Voices moved closer and the knob rattled. She ducked into the next office and plastered herself against the wall just as the door opened. The last thing she needed was to look like she'd been listening.

"Go out with the group tonight and celebrate." Neil's upbeat tone carried. "Coming back here will be a great move for you professionally and personally."

Jason thanked Neil, and his footsteps faded.

Blood whooshed in her ears, then silence as everything within her wilted. Even her eyelashes seemed to go limp. She sagged against the wall. Jason was moving to Chicago? A few hours ago, she was dreaming of marrying him. She whimpered out a prayer of thanks, even though she really wanted to scream. Obviously, God had saved her from making a horrible mistake. She forced herself to stand straight.

There was nothing to say, nothing to do, but get back to the team, lick her wounds, leave Southburg, and move to Siberia.

Chapter 39

Jason waited in the restaurant lobby with the rest of the team. The afternoon meetings went fine, but he still hadn't found a moment to be alone with Bethany. She didn't look like she felt well.

The job offer was the chance of a lifetime. If he turned it down, he would in effect be ending his career with the company. If he said yes, he'd be six hundred miles from the woman he loved.

As if she avoided him, Bethany stayed in conversation with Valarie and Rhonda. Maybe he should've been more talkative this morning at the airport or not told her about switching jobs.

Jason clasped Bethany's elbow. "Could I visit with you privately?"

She shrugged and took a few steps from the group.

Everyone's gaze followed them. Valerie leaned so close she almost fell over.

He couldn't take a chance with not being able to communicate effectively with Bethany. "Would you mind if we went outside for a few minutes?"

Her shoulders slumped, and she walked to the door like heading to a firing squad.

As soon as they were away from prying eyes, he took her in his arms. "Are you okay?"

She gave a tiny nod.

"Did I do something?"

"No." Her voice sounded like a little girl's.

"Whatever I did, I'm sorry. Bethany, I love you. That doesn't change when we're away from Southburg." He took a deep breath, not sure where to begin. "I've been offered a job here in Chicago. I'll be honest. I don't want to take the job if it means losing you. I know we haven't talked long-term plans. But I think we've got a shot at something permanent."

Her head popped up, a curiosity sparking in her eyes. "You haven't accepted the job?"

"No." He traced her soft cheek with his fingers. "Neil thinks I have. But he agreed to give me a week. I can't make a decision that big without talking to you." He took her hands in his. "Bethany, you are the best thing that has happened to me. Whatever comes next, I want you in my life."

She blinked and studied his face. "What are you saying?"

Sweat dampened his neck. What *was* he saying? "Will you …" He stared into her eyes.

Bethany's legs threatened to turn into noodles. Was he going to ask what she thought he was going to ask? And if he did, would she be able to say yes? She'd never known any man as sweet, loving, and perfect as Jason. But was she really ready for the next step?

A high-pitched squeal just about deafened her.

"Jason!" A woman with bleached blond hair and a supermodel body grabbed him from behind, turned him, and planted a kiss on his lips.

His neck and face just about turned purple as he untangled himself from her long hair. "Tiffany?" He wiped his mouth. "What are you doing here?"

Bombshell Blonde planted her hands on her perfectly shaped hips. "The bigger question is ... where have *you* been?"

Jason's eyes went wide, and he gulped like a fish gasping for air on the dock.

"We had a good thing going, and *you* disappeared off the planet." She threw a sideways glare at Bethany and then smirked at Jason. "Didn't our trip to the Florida Keys mean anything to you?"

His face drained of color, and he stepped back. More shuffled back, like a drowning man caught in the clutches of his past. Bethany knew all too well that feeling. She couldn't stand it anymore. The poor guy didn't have a chance.

"I'm sorry, Tiffany." Bethany pushed the floozy out of the way and took Jason's arm. "He's with me." She guided or rather shoved him inside the lobby. Thankfully, Tiff-tart didn't follow, and the team was gone, seated somewhere in the restaurant.

Sweat beaded on the top of his lip, his eyebrows forming an upside-down V. "Bethany, I'm really sorry. I told you I have lots of regrets about my past."

She held up her hand before he could sputter out anything else. "Jason, you have to do what you think is right. If you want to move back to Chicago, it's obvious you'll find plenty of company."

His hurt look made her regret the last statement, but not enough to apologize. Seeing him in the arms of someone like that ... that ... overly made-up Barbie doll made her every insecurity march to the forefront.

Stealth-woman Valerie appeared next to them. "What's

going on? A lover's quarrel?"

Bethany crossed her arms. "It's nothing."

Valerie surveyed them both. "I think we need the Zucchini brothers, or perhaps someone violated a Command No?" She jabbed her finger at Jason.

Jason couldn't respond, his brain totally scrambled. By the time he regained his senses, Bethany had followed Valerie into the restaurant. He clenched his fists instead of running after Bethany, throwing her over his shoulder and carrying her off into the sunset. Maybe that would work in the movies, but after the scene with Tiffany, Bethany might slug him.

He deserved a thorough beating. Two years since he'd seen or talked to Tiffany, and she showed up right when he was about to do something totally idiotic. He fingered the small velvet box in his pocket, making sure it was still there.

Ambience. Bethany and he needed to be somewhere alone in a romantic setting, not a busy sidewalk with old girlfriends and the prying eyes of co-workers. But first, he had to talk to Bethany and make sure she understood that she was the only woman for him.

Taking a deep breath, he marched through the restaurant. A man on a mission. All conversation stopped when he found the team's table. Bethany didn't look at him. She sat sandwiched between Alex and Rhonda. Jason had no choice but to sit at the far end in the only available chair.

"We're just about to order." Warren handed him a menu.

Jason couldn't even think about food. He needed to talk to Bethany.

Valerie pointed at Jason and mouthed, *I'm watching you.*

Rhonda smacked Valerie's finger. The waiter took everyone's orders. Alex and Nicole were already on a second round of drinks.

Jason rubbed his forehead. This was not the evening he'd planned.

Bethany half-listened to Alex's conversation about his latest *daredevil* skydiving adventure. She considered telling him about her college roommate's friend who was seventy-five when she went skydiving. But, right now, Alex was a convenient diversion to avoid Jason.

She hated the paranoid, insecure feeling that crept upon her. The Jason she knew and loved was trustworthy, but she had trusted Gavin too. She stole a glance down the table. Jason was rubbing his forehead, probably weighing the pros and cons of women and work.

"Do you want to talk about it?" Rhonda's quiet voice drew her attention.

"I really need prayer."

"I always pray for you and Jason."

Bethany looked at him. He smiled her way, and her stomach flip-flopped.

Valerie leaned in. "Prayer? What did Jason do?"

"He didn't do anything."

"So, what's the problem?"

Rhonda handed Valerie the bread basket. "Take one of these and leave her alone."

Valerie snatched a roll. "I know *something* happened. On the plane everything was fine, *really* fine from Bethany's hot and vocal dreams."

Heat tinged Bethany's neck and cheeks. She would never, ever, ever, take that air-sick medication again.

"And," Valerie continued, "everything was good before lunch. What happened after that?"

Alex and Nicole's volume increased with their latest rounds of drinks. The waiter delivered the dinner salads, which fortunately distracted Valerie.

Bethany took a few bites and acted like eating had her total attention. Did Jason really say he wanted her in his life on a permanent basis? One more look at his smile made her lightheaded. Forget insecurities, that man was definitely worth fighting for.

Jason finished his meal and signaled for the waiter. From Bethany's glances and smiles, he was back in her good graces. If all went well, they would get some alone time, and tomorrow night, at one of the finest restaurants in the area, he would propose.

Once the bill was paid, the group moved outside to wait for the small bus to transport them to the hotel. A chattering group of women wearing name tags from a romance writer's conference stood nearby.

He made his way to Bethany. "How was your meal?"

Her arm brushed against his, and she gave him one of those smiles that rendered him temporarily insane. "It started off kind of uncertain, but after I chewed on a few things, it ended on a positive note."

"I like positive." If only they were alone. He'd pay Valerie big bucks for a distraction.

"The bus is here!" An older lady, looking like a

linebacker for the Chicago Care Bears, shoved through to the curb. "Come on, girls get over here. Mabel, hurry up!" The writer group gabbed their way to the front, making comments about Alex and his good looks and Nicole's impressive show of cleavage.

Jason did a mental count of the number of people. Getting everyone on the transport would be quite an achievement. He squeezed Bethany's hand. "We may have to take a cab."

"Gee, that would be too bad, wouldn't it?"

Valerie scampered next to Bethany. "I don't think you two should show any public display of affection with that crowd. They'll write you into a novel. Then again, I probably could give them some great ideas." She grabbed Rhonda by the arm and jostled onto the bus.

Warren, Alex, and Nicole went next.

Valerie popped open a window and waved to Bethany and Jason. "There's still room left, come on."

The driver stepped out and waited for them to enter.

Leaving would be way too obvious. Bethany followed Jason onto the crowded, noisy bus that smelled of perfume and stale cigarettes. All the seats were taken except in the middle of the last row, with barely enough room for one person, much less two.

Jason sat and grinned at her. "Looks like you'll have to sit on my lap."

"Well, since there just isn't any room." She snuggled into his strong arms.

Alex stood and shot Jason a glare. "Bethany, you're

welcome to have my seat."

"No, really. I'm fine right here."

"I don't think it's proper for a team leader to be cavorting with a workmate."

All chattering stopped, and everyone's gaze turned in their direction.

Jason kissed Bethany and then looked at Alex. "Actually, I'm no longer team leader. I stepped down this morning."

Alex plopped back in his seat and mumbled a curse word. "You're still working at the same location."

Bethany gave Jason a kiss that sent off a few *woo hoo's* from the crowd. Once she recovered her brain activity, she addressed Alex. "Actually, Jason's no longer working with us, he's relocating to Chicago."

Jason gaped at her. "I don't want to leave you."

"We'll commute on the weekends."

The silver-haired woman on the right of Jason rummaged through her purse, pulled out a pen and paper and took notes.

"Mabel." The blonde to their left almost fell out of her seat as she tried to swat her friend. "Leave them alone. They're in a serious conversation."

"Oh, hush, I'm not doing them any harm. This'll be great for my next book." Mabel patted Jason's leg. "Y'all go right ahead. Just pretend we're not here."

Almost every person in the writer's group held a notebook, laptop, or electronic gadget, and sat on the edge of their seats.

Valerie snorted a laugh. "We're waiting. And, make it good. Mabel writes best-selling romance novels under the pen name, Mirabel Mimosa."

Nicole screamed at the top of her lungs. "Mirabel

Mimosa? I can't believe I'm on the same bus with Mirabel Mimosa! I've read *every* one of your books." She grabbed her purse and pulled out a book with the cover of a bare-chested man standing next to a starry-eyed, busty woman. "Could you autograph this for me? My name is Nicole. N...i...c...o...l...e."

Mabel, aka, Mirabel let out a throaty laugh. "Well sure, honey. This here is Cherry Fields and Candy Goodnight." She pointed to two of the writers. "And by the way, Nicole, you and that man of yours—" Mabel pursed her lips at Alex "—ought to consider doing some modeling. You'd both look great on the cover of my next book."

Valerie turned in her chair to face the author. "I call him Luscious 'Lex."

Alex flashed a huge smile, and puffed his chest full of his over-inflated ego. "Well, I don't want to brag, but I have done a few modeling shots for a scuba company in the Caribbean." He winked and pulled out his business card. "Give me a call anytime."

Nicole squealed when her book returned autographed. "Thank you sooooooo much! I've always wanted to meet you. I've written a manuscript in my spare time."

Mabel passed her business card to Nicole. "Feel free to e-mail me your first few pages, and I'll take a look. Make sure you include your picture so I remember you. You two really would look good on my next novel."

Jason kissed Bethany's neck. "I don't..." he whispered, "want to *just* see you on the weekends."

Bethany adjusted her position so she could look at his handsome face. "You've got to take the job. It's too good an offer."

"No, I mean, I don't want to leave you behind. What do you think of Chicago? You could move with me."

"I'm not moving in with you." Bethany drew in a breath as the bus took on an eerie silence.

Jason gawked at her. "No, I didn't mean *that*."

Mabel tugged on Bethany's shirt. "Honey, do you love him?"

"Yes." She gazed into Jason's gorgeous green eyes. "I do love him."

"Well, then you just need to cannonball into the relationship. Go whole-hearted."

"I'm sorry to interrupt." Seated in front of them, a writer with red hair and porcelain skin tentatively raised her hand. "I wouldn't move unless you are married."

Mabel tapped her pen against the paper. "Oh, *please*, you inspirational writers don't know the real score. These young 'uns are in love, and they want to be together. I say go for it."

A middle-aged, short-haired brunette turned toward Bethany and Jason. "I think these two need to seal their love with marriage vows. There isn't anything finer than true love God's way."

Her blonde friend raised her hands. "Three cheers for guilt-free loving!"

A playful argument broke out among the writers.

Jason dodged a flying paper and massaged his temple like his head was about to explode. "This isn't how I intended."

"What isn't?" Bethany rubbed the back of his tense neck.

"I'm not talking about you moving in with me. I'm talking long term. Permanent." He shifted her off his lap and sat her in his seat. Standing, he steadied himself, then rummaged in his pocket and pulled out a small velvet box.

Heart leaping, she sucked in air, or what was left of the oxygen after the collective gasp by those around them.

"Bethany, you mean more to me than *anyone* or any job."

He dropped to one knee. "I love you, and I want to be with you forever. I promise to treat you right, and with God's help be a man of honor.

"Bethany Davis, will you marry me?"

Epilogue

Bethany closed her book, took off her sunglasses, and wiped away happy tears. *A perfect ending.* She couldn't believe or imagine Nicole would have changed her ways and become an inspirational romance writer. Bethany smiled at the cover with a man bearing a striking resemblance to Alex.

She leaned her head back and smiled heavenward. Her whirlwind romance with Jason still held the same sparks as when they first dated.

"Watch this, Mom!" Ten-year old Josh grabbed hold of the zip line, lifted his legs, and zoomed off the fort platform. His resulting splash into the pond sent waves rippling to the shore dislodging the football that now careened wildly on the water's edge.

Bethany stood and clapped. "Totally epic!"

Thank goodness the water had warmed up after the latest heat wave. Chicago's climate left little time for outside play.

Josh swam to the shore and shook off like a wet dog. "Did I splash as good as the time you and Dad had to get away from that bad guy?"

She threw him a towel. "I think you did much better."

"I wish we had been around back then."

"Josh-man if you guys had been born that first year we all would've been in trouble."

"Will you tell us the story again tonight?"

"For the four zillionth time?"

"Yeah, especially when Dad made that guy scream like a girl."

Bethany laughed and hugged him tight.

"Mom, watch! I can do better than Josh!" Caleb followed his older brother's lead but didn't lift his legs in time. His entry into the pond was feet followed by face.

Her heart bee-lined to her throat until her middle son came up sputtering and laughing.

"Yes!" Caleb pumped his fist into the water. "Epic failure."

Bethany laughed. "Definitely a ten pointer."

"Mommy." Noah stood on the platform next to Jason. The tree-fort always seemed higher when Noah was up there. "It's my turn. Are you watching?"

Bethany smiled at their youngest. "Be careful and make sure you tell Daddy to hang on tight. He can't do it without you."

Noah nodded. "I know. He'd crash."

Jason grinned, leaned down so Noah could grip his neck, then held on to the zip line and pushed off. Their splash sent squeals of laughter from all three boys.

Bethany didn't resist. She flipped off her shoes and ran full speed toward the pond. With a leap, she tucked her legs and cannonballed into the water.

The End

"I have blotted out, like a thick cloud, your transgressions,
and like a cloud, your sins.
Return to Me, for I have redeemed you."
(Isaiah 44:22 NKJV).

Dear Reader

Bethany Davis and my cast of characters are only fiction. However, God's love is real. God waits with open arms to welcome home those who feel they have gone too far from God's grace.

Jesus shared in Luke 15 the beautiful story of The Father waiting and rushing to welcome home his once prodigal son. Regardless of what you have done, or what has been done to you, God's love, redemption, and restoration are available.

God's blessings to you all,
Lisa

About the Author

Lisa Buffaloe is a writer, speaker, radio host for Living Joyfully Free Radio, happily-married wife, and mom. Her past experiences—molestation by a baby-sitter, assault, rape by a doctor, divorce, being stalked, cancer, death of loved ones, multiple surgeries, and eleven years of chronic illness from Lyme Disease—bless her with a backdrop to share God's amazing love. God's love is unending and through the forgiveness and grace of Jesus Christ we find healing, restoration, and renewal.

www.lisabuffaloe.com

Coming Soon!
Nadia's Hope
2010 Women of Faith Writing Contest finalist

**The Nightmares continue. Memories won't heal.
Nadia must make a choice.**

Nadia Minsky fled Israel to escape her past, but she can't outrun her nightmares. The throbbing scars along her hip and stomach are cruel reminders of shattered dreams. Even though surgeons mended her body, her spirit still bleeds. Friends claim only God can heal her. For Nadia, trusting a God who allowed her to suffer is inconceivable.

Can close friends, a wild roommate, and a handsome medical student, help Nadia learn to trust? Or will she chose to allow her past to forever cripple her future?

Nadia's Hope Preview

Chapter 1

Faceless crowds provided a place to blend in. A way to become invisible. Just another ant in the busy throng. Students crowed the college campus as Nadia Minsky made her way to the university bookstore.

A cool breeze rustled in the trees, signaling the promise of fall. At the bottom of the bookstore steps, Nadia stopped, rummaged through her backpack, and found cash to buy the notebook needed for the upcoming literature project.

Young men descended the stairs toward her.

Dread slithered down her spine. She stood straight, stayed close to the rail, and focused on the top step.

"Hey, sexy."

"Give it up." Another voice bantered. "She's way out of your league."

Nadia refused to acknowledge them. She squeezed past. Just a few more steps and she'd be safe inside the building.

A wolf-whistle sent a chill from the past coursing through her veins. She stumbled and grabbed for the rail. Her hand met air. She slammed hard against the granite steps, landing on her bad side. Pain exploded down her leg. She wouldn't cry. No one would see her cry.

A strong hand gripped her arm. "Can I help?"

Shockwaves jolted from his touch. "No." She wrenched away and pulled herself to her feet. Steadying herself, she brushed off her jeans.

"You hit hard. Are you sure you're okay?" His deep voice tinged with concern tempted her to look his way.

She locked her gaze on her feet. "I am fine."

"I don't remember seeing you last semester. I'm David Cohen." His broad-shouldered back to her, he gathered her books and papers, including, much to her embarrassment, the Bible her friend Ruth had given her. At least her knife had stayed secure in the hidden pocket at the bottom of her backpack.

Nadia forced herself to ignore the aching throb in her leg and instead clenched the rail. "Please, may I have things?"

"Your things? Sure." He hesitated. "I can carry this for you." His voice seemed gentle and kind.

"No, not is necessary." Careful to avoid eye contact or touch, Nadia retrieved her belongings.

"I like your accent. Where are you from?"

She groaned inwardly and berated herself for speaking. Her hip throbbing, she hurried toward the door. "I transfer."

David's footsteps followed. "I didn't get your name."

She stopped. An intense longing for someone to know her name, to care, welled up within her, staggering her with intensity. She turned toward him and risked raising her eyes. Sandy-brown hair, athletic physique, and blue eyes met her gaze. His white-toothed perfect smile, struck her as honest and sincere.

"Nadia." She cringed as her name left her mouth. He was a stranger.

"Nadia, nice to meet you." He took a step toward her. "You sure you're okay?" He was perfect. Something she could never be.

"I ... I must not be late for class."

"I'll see you around." He bounded down the stairs, stopped, and looked back.

She couldn't believe she watched him. Worse yet, he caught her watching. His grin warmed her face and rustled embers long thought cold. No, she couldn't take the chance.

Not now. Never again.

Fifteen minutes later, inside the classroom, she sat in her usual spot—in the corner, against the back wall, near the door. As the literature professor's lecture droned on, she jotted down the main points. Why did teachers assign a chapter to read and then feel compelled to read it themselves? On autopilot, she gazed out the window, providing a much-needed distraction from the boredom.

In the last month since she'd arrived, the guy on the steps was the first man she'd given her name. Why him?

She pushed a long strand of her hair behind her ear. Then again, why not? He was nice enough to help. Plus, there was something different about him, tanned but not olive skinned, muscular but gentle, and his smile showed in his deep-blue eyes. Last year, with someone that good looking, she would have leaped into his arms and offered her heart freely.

That was then.

Now she could only limp.

###

After class, Nadia tucked her hair inside her helmet and climbed onto the scooter her friends, the Yamins, had given her.

4

The back of her neck heated and tingled as though someone were watching. She hesitated, her darting eyes surveying the parking lot. Slowly, she glanced over her shoulder. Fiddling with the helmet, she scanned the crowd.

Everyone seemed oblivious to her presence and nothing seemed out of the ordinary. She had to stop being so paranoid. Probably just her imagination. Her past was thousands of miles away.

Heavy campus traffic crawled, causing the familiar drive down tree-lined streets to take ten minutes instead of the normal five. She parked in front of the two-story gray house with a wrap-around porch.

Tension eased from her shoulders as she walked along the stone pathway leading to the Yamin's front door. She couldn't explain her bond with Ruth and Isaac. They'd met in Israel and welcomed her into their lives like a daughter—even moving with her to the university. Their generosity and love overwhelmed her, enveloping her in feelings she couldn't understand yet craved.

The wooden porch swing swayed in the gentle breeze, casting a playful shadow on the white trim. She knocked and called through the screen door. "Ruth?"

"In the kitchen." Ruth's voice almost carried a tune.

Nadia set her backpack on the floor next to the mahogany entry table covered with pictures of Ruth, Isaac, their daughter Hannah, and Nadia. The photos were arranged almost as though she were part of their family.

Isaac met Nadia in the hallway and enveloped her in a hug. "Lunch is on the table, and Ruth is hungry." His deep voice reverberated against her ear.

She caught a whiff of the cologne she had given him for his fifty-fifth birthday. "I should drive faster."

Releasing her, he gave her a stern but playful look. "Did you speed?"

"On a scooter?"

"That's my girl."

Her heart squeezed at the sweet words. If only he were her real father. With Ruth and Isaac, she could breathe—the void inside temporarily filled.

She peeked around the corner into the kitchen. Ruth wore dark blue Capri pants and a button down cotton shirt, her silver hair drawn back in a blue ribbon. The outfit looked good on her, but then again, every outfit complimented her tall, slender frame.

"Hi, Sweet Girl." Ruth hugged Nadia, squeezing her tight like a loving mother, making everything seem right with the world. "I heard that tacky remark about needing to drive faster. Are you two ever going to let me forget that one incident?"

"*One* incident?" Nadia grinned and grabbed napkins off the granite countertop. "You are always grumpy when you not eat."

"Okay, I'll admit it, openly and without shame. I'm a bear when my blood sugar drops."

Isaac kissed Ruth on her forehead. "You are the most elegant bear I have ever seen. I still have to fight men away, even after thirty years. But we know better than to make you wait for food."

"I'll growl at you both if you don't get to the table for lunch." Ruth pushed them toward the kitchen table.

Once everyone took their seats, Isaac offered the blessing.

6

Nadia did her usual—bowed her head, stared at her plate, and tried to disregarded the words. Why pray to someone who didn't exist? And even if he did, he didn't listen.

Isaac finished and passed her the salad dressing. "I had an interesting morning. We removed the cast of a motorcycle accident patient, and inside we found a toothbrush and part of a coat hanger."

"Why?" Ignoring her growling stomach, Nadia sprinkled a small amount of dressing on her salad.

"Casts help protect the bone, but the covered body parts do get itchy."

"What else do you find in casts?" Nadia took a tiny bite but kept her gaze on Isaac.

"Rulers, knitting needles, pencils, twigs, table knives, forks, spoons, even sunflower seeds."

Ruth nudged Isaac. "Perhaps your patients should remember to *cast* their cares on the Lord."

Nadia groaned.

"Ah, yes," Isaac tilted his head back for a moment, and then looked back at Ruth. "But where there is no revelation, the people *cast* off restraint."

"Okay, let me think." Ruth tapped her fingers on the table. She grinned, her eyes dancing with mischief. "So then, banish anxiety from your heart and *cast* off the troubles of your body."

Nadia cleared her throat to speak in her most dramatic voice. "And none but fools doth wear it, *cast* it off."

Both Isaac and Ruth gave her a puzzled expression.

"Romeo and Juliet, Scene II, Capulet's orchard."

Giggling, Ruth put her hand over her mouth before her last bite escaped. "I love it."

7

Isaac sat back in his chair. "Nadia, you are a treasure."

Focusing on her plate, Nadia grinned. Like a warm salve over fresh wounds, she craved every hug, every word of encouragement, but she'd never completely belong. There would always be a piece missing.

After lunch, Nadia helped Ruth clean off the table.

Ruth frowned as she scraped leftovers from Nadia's plate. "You didn't eat much."

"I am not very hungry." Nadia busied herself cleaning the kitchen. She didn't need another lecture on healthy eating.

"Did you eat a good breakfast?"

"Sure." An apple and coffee got her through yesterday and the same would get her through today.

Trying to ignore Ruth's concern, Nadia rinsed the plates and loaded the dishwasher. "Can you show me other exercise? The stretches from last week hurt. I hate this physical therapy."

"I know it isn't comfortable, but it does help. Do you still need your pain pills?"

"Sometimes, yes. Is very sore. Plus today I fell on steps."

Ruth's mouth opened as she glanced at Nadia's side. "Oh sweetie, are you okay?"

"Yes, some cute guy helped me."

"You noticed a cute guy?" A grin replaced Ruth's concerned expression. "Good for you."

Heat flashed up Nadia's neck. "How could I not?"

"Don't get defensive. I'm just glad someone was there to help you." Ruth closed the dishwasher and leaned against the counter. "Stop by the office tomorrow after class. I want you to meet one of my patients who had her knee replaced after skydiving. She's seventy-five."

"Seventy-five and skydiving?"

"I've never met anyone who enjoys life as much as this lady does."

"She must have very good life."

"I think she's had an interesting one. You'll have to get to know her. You might be surprised at what makes her tick."

Nadia eased a stray strand of hair over her ears. "Tick?"

"I mean what makes her who she is." Ruth removed a tray of homemade cookie dough from the refrigerator. "Did you make it to counseling?"

"Yes." Nadia folded and refolded the dishtowel. "What is use for talking to complete stranger? Why must I talk to her? Why can I not talk to you?"

"I'm always here for you. I love you like a daughter, but I'm not a trained counselor."

"You give good advice."

"I pray that I do. But counselors have special tools to help. They're trained, and I'm not. Please try to stick it out beyond a couple of visits this time."

Nadia shrugged. No point arguing. "Okay, but only for you I do this."

"Do this for yourself. I promise it will help." Ruth pushed her toward the back door. "I want to show you my latest planting bed. Maybe someday I'll have a yard like your aunt's."

"No one has a garden like Elisabeth." Nadia stepped onto the back deck and surveyed Ruth's latest creation. Fall mums were now planted along with Hostas and Daylilies. The yard, as always, peaceful, orderly, and safe. Nadia sighed. Once again, she was secure in the beauty of nature, the sweet memories of running and playing in Elisabeth's garden.

"I can't compete with your Aunt. Her garden should have been featured in a magazine."

"Very true." Nadia gave Ruth a smug smile. "Probably because I helped many times." If digging in the dirt counted when she was a little girl.

"You stinker. If you didn't have class, I'd put you to work."

"Yes, such a shame." She glanced at her watch. "A student must not be late."

"Alright, missy, but next time you have a free day, I'm handing you a garden trowel and a hoe."

Nadia grinned as she turned and walked away. "Hi ho, hi ho, to class I must go."

David attempted to focus on his clinic duty and away from thoughts of the beautiful girl he'd found on the steps this morning. He'd been honest when he told her he hadn't seen her during the summer session, but he'd noticed her plenty of times the last few weeks. He'd even taken the long way to his clinic duty, hoping to see her. Knowing her name and that she carried a Bible piqued his interest.

From a distance, she was beautiful. Up close, the entire package was stunning—figure slender but curvy in the right places, big dark eyes, eyelashes so long they almost touched her perfectly arched brows, long brown hair, and full lips. Not that he noticed.

Her jet-black eyes captivated him. *Mysterious.* Did he read pain or fear? Why?

And he'd practically chased her up the steps. Probably scared her to death. Of course, he was only being helpful. Wasn't he?

In the emergency room, in front of the closed curtains of the waiting area, he read through the chart of his next patient. *Bicycle accident.*

With a professional smile, he opened the curtain. Four-year-old Michael Adams sat with his head in his mother's lap. The boy held his arm against his small body. Tears pooled in his coffee-colored eyes as his mother stroked his hair.

"Mrs. Adams, I'm Dr. David Cohen." He squatted eye-level with his patient. "What happened, Michael?"

The boy bit his quivering lip and sniffled. "I hurt my arm. And the paint scratched off."

"The paint?"

"Uh-huh." He held up his scratched and bloody arm. The scratches white against his dark skin.

"Don't worry. The paint will come back when you heal." He gently probed his wounds. "You must have been going pretty fast."

The boy rubbed his nose and wiped his hand on his monster truck T-shirt. "I'm faster than Thomas."

"Thomas?"

"He's Michael's best friend," Mrs. Adams added.

"You're one tough guy. It's not every day we get a young man who races so fast he scratches off the paint. I think we need a picture for our files. We have a really cool machine called an x-ray. Mom will come with us."

Michael glanced up at his mother and back to David. "Okay."

Mrs. Adams helped her son off the table.

11

David turned to her. "We need to check for a break. I'll have the nurse give him a mild sedative to help with the pain. If his arm is broken near the growth plate, I'll call Dr. Yamin. He's one of the finest orthopedic surgeons in the area."

Michael gave David a brave nod. His face held a look of determination. "I go to x-ray and orfopedic with you."

David knelt in front of him. "For big guys like you, we give the special treatment."

Michael's eyes widened. "Really?"

"You bet. The x-ray machine is like a camera, only super big, and monster truck cool."

"Wow! Can I see it?"

Mrs. Adams' eyes rimmed with tears. "Thank you for being so sweet to Michael. You must have children."

"No." David closed the chart, wishing he could close off the nagging reminder of his own father. "But hope to someday." And when he did, he'd make sure he'd be there for his own son.

Classes over for the day, her roommate gone as usual, Nadia settled into her bedroom chair to check e-mails. The apartment was way too quiet. She closed the desk drawer and played with the inch worm Beanie Baby she used for a wrist rest.

Two messages appeared. Her brother Gideon asked her to come home to visit. Something had taken place in his life. She shook her head. The *things* in Gideon's life usually meant trouble. She closed his message. He didn't need to know a friend had already sent a plane ticket. Her plans had nothing to do with Gideon. However, his invitation did give an excuse to explain her trip to Isaac and Ruth—if she told them.

The cursor blinked rhythmically as she stared at the second message, a notification from her friend in Israel. She fought her climbing pulse as she clicked it open.

The message was short. *Nothing new to report. No changes today.*

Nadia blew out a breath and hit delete. What happened now didn't matter. Nothing could change the past. Nothing.

Leaving the light on, she crawled into bed and jerked the covers over her head. They were still out there.

Visit Lisa Buffaloe at …

www.lisabuffaloe.com
www.livingjoyfullyfree.com
www.fliterary.com (Fun for the Literary)
www.facebook.com/lisabuffaloe
www.facebook.com/lisabuffaloeauthor
www.twitter.com/lisabuffaloe